Prais

MAJOR JAKE FONTINA

"What an exhilarating read! Imagine something worse than Covid-19—a weaponized version where only one country may have a vaccine that works. *This is terrorism.* Author Rick Steinke's US Army Major Jake Fontina, based in Paris, teams with experts from the FBI and their French and Italian counterparts, as one united team to disrupt this plan to kill millions. Steinke nails this global thriller with accuracy and plausibility."

—Lauren Anderson
Former FBI Executive and Global Women's Advocate

"Rick Steinke has written a must-read page turner that I found to be very relevant to the threats we see today, full of intrigue and mystery. I enjoyed it immensely. Major Jake Fortina is an archetypal leader that represents many real-world warriors who have answered our nation's call."

—Lieutenant General Kenneth W. Hunzeker (US Army, Ret)
Distinguished Graduate, USMA, West Point; Former Commander, V Corps, and 1st Infantry Division

"Loved this book! Through Jake Fortina, Colonel Steinke sets the stage perfectly with as accurate a depiction of a US Army infantry officer as I have ever read. His portrayal of the noncommissioned officer corps' professionalism was spot on, and the struggles of military families and the sacrifices of military spouses were perfectly framed. A very engaging read, I highly recommend it to fellow veterans and look forward to Colonel Steinke's next one. Geronimo!"

—Staff Sergeant Samuel E. Askins (US Army, Ret)
Combat Veteran, Iraq; Director, PTSD Foundation of America

"Steinke's addictive thriller raises the adrenaline level with each terse, dramatic, and gripping chapter. His protagonist, Jake Fortina, faces a mountain of challenges, some professional and deadly, others deeply personal. Foreign embassies, relentless terrorists, and in-your-face realism combine to make this novel by a military and international security practitioner one book you won't be able to put down."

—John J. Le Beau
CIA Senior Operations Officer (Ret.), Author of *Collision of Centuries*

"Colonel (Ret) Rick Steinke tells a riveting story only he can accurately portray! As a distinguished Army officer, foreign area officer, defense attaché, and respected scholar, Rick draws upon his own personal and professional background to weave a thrilling account of Jake Fortina that could easily be mistaken for a nonfictional narrative. Rick also fills a critical gap in understanding the lives of our soldier-diplomats who selflessly serve on the front lines and in many foreign and hostile locations. This should be required reading for anyone who wants to further understand—beyond the headlines—how our Department of Defense and other federal agencies contribute to our national security."

—Colonel (Ret) John E. Chere Jr.
Assistant Professor, Defense Security Cooperation and Joint Special Operations Universities; Former Defense Attaché and Senior Defense Official to Algeria, Israel, Morocco, and Tunisia

"Jake Fortina could just as well be called 'Rick Fortina' or 'an American in Paris' as Rick Steinke is so accurate with portraying the French way of life! I am delighted to testify what a suspenseful and thrilling ride this is. Read it and reread it. *Vous allez prendre du bon temps!*"

—Lieutenant Colonel Olivier Lardans (French Army, Ret)
Former Aide-De-Camp to the Chief of Staff, French Army

"Rick Steinke has written a rip-roaring, page-turning story of a race across Europe. Leveraging his stint in Paris as the US defense attaché and his many other professional and personal experiences in Europe, he provides a drone's-eye view of the challenges and rewards of US and international law enforcement and intelligence cooperation. Far more importantly, he has created characters that you care about. You are in their personal joys and sorrows, and their professional challenges and successes. His vibrant dialogue keeps you actively routing for them as they fight the bad guys and the labyrinth of legal constraints and ethical challenges of their international mission. Rick's work is the perfect read for a long flight—perhaps to Europe!"

> —**James Q. Roberts**, Colonel (US Army, Ret)
> Senior Executive (Ret), Office of the Secretary of Defense

"Rick Steinke, a master storyteller, does it again! His Major Jake Fortina, a colorful, resilient, and unassuming foot soldier, teams up with an array of military, law enforcement, intelligence, and diplomatic characters to deal with a major US and allied national security threat. Drawing on his deep experience in the field, Steinke takes us behind the curtain of international security cooperation to produce a fast-paced and realistic Clancyesque tale."

> —**Michael Schmitt**
> Strauss Center Distinguished Scholar and Visiting Professor of Law, University of Texas; G. Norman Lieber Distinguished Scholar, US Military Academy at West Point

"An exciting and suspenseful look at terrorism today. Steinke's extensive international experience and expertise provide a realistic look at how nations work together to protect their citizens from the scourge of terrorism in the twenty-first century."

> —**James Howcroft**, Colonel, USMC (Ret)
> Career Intelligence Officer, Former Military Attaché and International Counter Terrorism Program Director

"Rick Steinke's newest book connects the sights, smells, and sounds of a whirling world potentially out of control, full of intrigue while facing both regional terror and the possibility of international genocide. Your senses literally tell you that you are there, traveling across the globe amid his characters and their story. It's as if the reader is seeing tomorrow's online media leads coming at us in a blend of broad history, intimate personal stories, and deadly global possibilities. A sensational read! I can't wait for the film adaptation of this book!"

—Dennis Mansfield
Author, Business Coach and Podcaster (DennisMansfield.com)

"Rick Steinke is not only an outstanding author but not-so-incidentally also happens to be a counterterrorism expert—and it shows in this gripping thriller. Drawing from a wealth of personal experience, he combines a both fast-paced and complex storyline with detailed and accurate depictions of places, persons, and processes. Through Major Jake Fortina—no unrealistic superhero but a highly capable professional, well aware of the necessity of joint and international cooperation – he highlights the need for immaculate analysis as well as bold action in this enthralling novel. In short, an awesome book!"

—Daniel H. Heinke
Former Chief, Bureau of Operations, Bremen Police Department; and Adjunct Professor for Terrorism Studies, HfÖV (Police College) Bremen, Germany

"As a former senior Army intelligence and European-based foreign area officer, the reader can be assured that Major Jake Fortina is a believable character in a very realistic and rapidly paced current plot thriller that only Rick Steinke's personal military background, experience, and expertise could create. How soon can I see Fortina's next adventure?"

—Colonel Alex "Alpo" Portelli, (US Army, Ret)
Former US Defense Attaché to Norway and Director, European Directorate, US European Command

"Colonel Rick Steinke has scored another direct hit with this page-racing novel that captures the role of the 'simple soldier' in tackling global security threats. Drawing from his experience as a commander and troop leader in multiple international assignments, Steinke weaves an exciting tale describing the dangers troops face when handed seemingly impossible missions. The entire package of life's challenges and emotions that go with the territory are also brilliantly presented. An exciting read that I couldn't put down."

—**Dave Stewart**, Sergeant Major (US Army, Ret)

"In this compelling read, Rick Steinke, a well-informed and experienced former practitioner in the world of US–international security cooperation, takes the reader on a fast-moving and realistic 'what-if' threat scenario. Covid-19 has unfortunately killed and sickened millions around the world, but in terms of lethality, it was by far *not* the worst virus to terrorize and kill humans on our planet. What if an enemy was synthetically developing a virus ten times more lethal than Covid-19, with the intent of deploying it against the US and Israel, just when the world thought the Covid-19 virus was being conquered?"

—**Major General Luigi Francavilla** (Italian Army, Ret)
Former Commander of Italian Army Aviation Forces and Italian Defense Attaché to North Macedonia

Major Jake Fortina and the Tier One Threat

By Ralph R. "Rick" Steinke

© Copyright 2022 Ralph R. "Rick" Steinke

ISBN 978-1-64663-733-1

Published by

◤ köehlerbooks™

3705 Shore Drive
Virginia Beach, VA 23455
800–435–4811
www.koehlerbooks.com

MAJOR JAKE FORTINA
AND THE TIER ONE THREAT

RALPH R. "RICK" STEINKE

VIRGINIA BEACH
CAPE CHARLES

AUTHOR'S NOTE

While there are references to historical facts and events in this book, this is a work of *fiction*. Except those prominent individuals obviously referenced in history, all the characters—even though some names may be the same as or approximate living individuals—are otherwise *completely fictitious*, as are some commercial businesses, such as hotels and restaurants.

For one year after this book's publication date, all the author's revenues from the hardcopy, softcopy and e-book/Kindle versions will be donated by the author, evenly divided between the Wounded Warrior Project (https://www.woundedwarriorproject.org/) and the FBI Agents Association (https://fbiaa.org/).

DEDICATION

GONZALO "GONZALITO" MATEO FLETHES-STEINKE, the newest family member of Team Steinwald. May your life's journey be eternally and richly blessed, and may you be a blessing to others.

General (US Army, deceased) Raymond T. Odierno, who as a lieutenant general on official business with French military leaders and US embassy officials in Paris had only one thing he wanted to do during his very limited free time—to pay his respects to the fallen soldiers interred at the American World War I cemetery in the Paris suburb of Suresnes. It was during that visit that the author learned something about many of those brave Americans who were interred in that cemetery.

Staff Sergeant (US Army, deceased) Michael Dennis Kelly, son of loving parents Lester and Joan Kelly, brother to Brian Kelly and Colin Kelly, and friend to many. On August 6, 1969, while serving in South Vietnam, Staff Sergeant Mike Kelly made the ultimate sacrifice for freedom-loving Americans and people everywhere.

Sergeant (US Army, deceased) Adam Ray, son of loving parents Jim and Donna Ray, brother to Betsy Grace Ray, Amanda Ray, Zach Ray, and Seth Ray, and friend to many. On February 9, 2010, while serving in Afghanistan, Sergeant Adam Ray made the ultimate sacrifice for freedom-loving Americans and people everywhere.

Colonel (US Army, Retired) James H. Coffman, Jr., who, because of his gallantry in action while assigned as the senior advisor to the 1st Iraqi Special Police Commando Brigade during a lengthy battle on November 14, 2004, in Mosul, Iraq, was awarded the United States of America's second highest military award, the Distinguish Service Cross. Colonel Coffman's entire citation may be read here: https://valor.militarytimes.com/hero/3674

All US and allied military, diplomatic, law enforcement, intelligence, and other national security professionals who quietly serve in the shadows to selflessly protect American citizens and our international allies around the world.

1.
THE AMERICAN CEMETERY, PARIS

THE TWO MEN STRAINED to see through the American World War I cemetery fence. Aided by a distant streetlight, they could barely make out the perfectly aligned white marble headstones standing watch in the Paris midnight rain.

Hezbollah in Lebanon, the Shiite Muslim militant political party declared a terrorist organization by the United States and many countries around the world, had provided the two terrorists plenty of experience for their mission.

"The rain is a blessing from Allah," said Arman Darbandi.

"Exactly as planned," replied Farhad Gilani.

For weeks, Darbandi and Gilani had surveilled the cemetery, located in the leafy Paris suburb of Suresnes. A three-feet-high hedge, located next to the fence's corner pillar, provided nearby cover in the event of an approaching vehicle.

With the assistance of a rope, a small stepladder, and moderate physical effort, the two men easily scaled the stone pillar anchoring the corner of the cemetery's iron fence, their only hurdle for gaining access to the cemetery.

Standing inside the cemetery, Darbandi and Gilani picked up their rucksacks. "The first grave is in this direction." Darbandi gestured. The two men began walking into the dark field of white crosses and Stars of David.

They walked several yards across the rain-soaked grass and

then stopped. Darbandi shined his yellow-filtered flashlight on a headstone.

"*This* is the first one," he whispered, nodding to the headstone marked by the Star of David.

The name *Daniel Gelb* was engraved into the pristine white marble.

Removing their portable shovels from their rucksacks, the two Hezbollah operatives went to work. First cutting out chunks of sod that measured roughly two feet by one foot, with each slab of dirt about three inches thick. Once all the sod had been removed to the side, they replaced the sod chunks to their original locations.

"How does it look?" asked Darbandi.

"It looks like someone dug up this grave," replied Gilani.

Satisfied with their intended ruse, Darbandi removed a small towel and a red Sharpie Magnum pen from his backpack. He took the towel and wiped the rainwater off the surface of the sacred marble. Beginning at the bottom of the headstone, he wrote in an upwards, diagonal direction in vivid red letters, *Death to the Jews.* This first grave, located not far from the cemetery's main entrance and easily discovered by early-morning workers, would serve as an initial diversion for any investigators.

"This should buy us time before they discover the next grave," said Darbandi.

The less experienced and younger Gilani nodded.

Satisfied with their work, they left the Gelb grave and moved on to their main target, a second grave located at the opposite end of the cemetery gate. They were far enough from the road to avoid detection by Parisians out walking their dogs or driving by.

Of the 1,565 World War I American fallen in the cemetery, 22 were marked with the Star of David. Most of those memorialized at the cemetery, however, did not die from the gruesome combat of World War I. Instead, they had succumbed to the highly lethal influenza that had swept through the trenches, camps, and hospitals towards the war's end in late 1918. The horrific killer virus— commonly mislabeled the "Spanish flu" as there was no proof that it originated in Spain—did not run its worldwide course until 1920.

The virus eventually infected more than five hundred million people around the globe—roughly one-third of the world's population in 1919—and killed upwards of one hundred million by some scientific estimates. The Spanish flu of 1918 to 1920 was among the deadliest influenza pandemics in human history. It's death toll eclipsed the Covid-19 virus of 2020 to early-2022 in its global lethality—even in an early twenty-first century world connected by air travel—by more than tenfold.

Shining his flashlight on the second headstone, Darbandi confirmed what the two men were looking for.

"This is the one, the grave of Ackerman. It is now 1:12. We must finish in two and a half hours."

The two men removed chunks of sod precisely as they had for the first grave. This time, however, they would continue digging to the coffin. After over an hour and a half of almost constant digging, the sounds of which were muffled by the steady rainfall, Gilani was drenched in sweat and mud.

"I struck the top of the coffin. We have to find the hinges," he announced.

The French, British, and American authorities had been worried about disease being spread by hundreds of thousands of decomposing remains, particularly those brought back home to the United Kingdom, the United States and Canada. In December 1918, they insisted that those charged with the remains' final dispositions— either shipping them back to North America or, in accordance with next-of-kin desires, burying them in European soil—must change the coffins from the common pine box variant to one of steel, which would provide a better container for locking in potential diseases and viruses.

With the metal hinges broken and the coffin open, the two men stared at the remains. Using rubber gloves, they carefully removed the left femur and hip from US Army nurse Ruth Ackerman's remains. They placed each of the bones in separate ziplock plastic bags and then into their rucksacks.

Reclosing the hatch, refilling the dirt, and replacing the top layers of sod, Arman wrote, *Death to the Americans* on Ruth Ackerman's headstone.

"We have completed the first phase," said Darbandi. "We will be favored by Allah for avenging the decades of humiliation by the Americans and their Israeli lackeys."

2.
THE GAME: FIFTEEN YEARS BEFORE PARIS

ON A CRISP NOVEMBER Saturday afternoon in Alabama, US Army second lieutenant Jake Fortina was looking forward to the game. Jake's US Army Infantry Officer Basic Course classmate and friend, Second Lieutenant Chet Parker, had invited him to the major college football rivalry between the University of Alabama and Auburn University. The Auburn campus was an easy, roughly one-hour drive from Fort Benning, the Army's "Home of the Infantry," located just across the Alabama-Georgia state line near Columbus, Georgia.

Jake thought about how different this rivalry—the Iron Bowl—was going to be than the one he was most familiar with—the Army-Navy game.

I love the Army-Navy game. It's always a heckuva game, maybe even the greatest in college football. But a bit too much marching and military protocol for me, ha-ha, said his free-spirited, non-conformist soul. *This game ought to be a riot! No heavy uniforms, no spit and polish, and no marching. I'm just gonna be Joe College in the crowd, carousing and having fun with everyone else.*

Parker guided his pickup onto the pristinely maintained Auburn campus, a place he knew like his backyard.

"So, Chet, how did you end up in this beautiful place with all these gorgeous ladies? And why the Army?"

"Ha-ha. Dang good questions, my brother. The pretty ladies

ought to be self-explanatory," he chuckled. "As to the rest, it's kinda complicated. Might bore you to tears."

"I doubt it," answered Jake. "Go for it, amigo."

"Well, I originally came here from Huntsville—it's upstate from here if you don't know—on a baseball scholarship, as a pitcher," began Parker. "That was my *main* motivation for coming to Auburn. Always wanted to play ball at the collegiate level, and this was the only place I wanted to play. In this state, you gotta choose between rooting for Auburn or 'Bama. My dad was a big-time Auburn fan, so that settled that. I grew up watching and hearing about Bo Jackson and Frank Thomas. Also heard stories from my dad about Pat Sullivan, who, like Jackson, won a Heisman Trophy once upon a time."

"Yep, I've heard of Thomas, and I've definitely heard of Bo Jackson," replied Jake. "I remember seeing a video of him breaking a baseball bat over his thigh after striking out. What a badass."

"I recall that, too. He also broke one over his *head*. At least he had a helmet on," Parker chuckled. "No question, a tremendous athlete, maybe one of the greatest ever."

"So, baseball, eh?" prompted Jake. "You must have been *busy*, dude, playing ball while trying to keep up with your schoolwork here."

"Never quite got there, Jake. Fortunately, my high school grades were pretty good, so I was able to get academically accepted here," continued Parker, leaving out that he graduated in the top 5 percent of his high school class. "But in the fall of my freshman year, I played in a stupid, beer-fueled touch football game, which had gotten pretty rough. It became more like tackle football. I wasn't drinking but just about everyone else was. Should have quit but didn't. Thought it would be a knock on my manhood if I walked off the field."

"I wouldn't have walked off that field either," Jake said. "But I probably would have helped myself to that beer."

"Well, there was plenty of it, that's for sure. As the game went on . . . I ended up breaking my pitching shoulder."

"Aw, crap. Sorry to hear that."

"Yah, it was not good. By the next spring my shoulder healed up okay, but not well enough to throw a ninety-three-mile-per-hour fastball anymore," continued Parker.

"Dang, Chet, a ninety-three-mile-per-hour fastball? That's some serious heat! Especially coming out of high school."

"Guess so, Jake. But that speed was not coming back. My baseball dream was over before it got started. Wasn't sure what to do. Then I thought about my dad. He had been a Marine gunnery sergeant who retired right after Desert Storm. And my grandfather was a Vietnam War vet and Green Beret, back in the very early years of the war. My grandfather knew Barry Sadler, the Green Beret sergeant who wrote and sang the song 'The Ballad of the Green Berets.'"

"I know that song, Chet. That's pretty cool."

"Anyway," continued Parker, "my dad and grandfather never once tried to influence me, but I—and my family—really respected them for their military service. So, I decided to check out the Army ROTC (Reserve Officers Training Corps) program here. I'll be danged if I didn't end up liking it—the camaraderie, the teamwork, the physical challenges, the opportunity for leadership. And I know it might sound kinda corny, but the opportunity to serve my country, too. You know the deal, Jake."

"Yep, I get it."

"And because I got hurt messing around outside of baseball, Auburn pulled my baseball scholarship. But then Army ROTC came through with a scholarship for my last three years. I really appreciated that ROTC gave me a goal and the prospect of a fulltime leadership position upon graduation. I was thrilled to get selected for active-duty service, so here I am.

"How about you, Jake? What about West Point? That could not have been a picnic," Parker smiled.

"*Some* of it wasn't," Jake grinned. "Like you I had some relatives who had served. My great-uncle fought across Europe in World War II, with the Army's 2nd Infantry Division. My dad, Jim, God rest his soul, enlisted when he was nineteen and fought in Vietnam in the '60s with the 1st Cav Division. He was blessed to have a great first sergeant and company commander, so he made it home as a new buck sergeant from 'Nam with barely a scratch. Had a *First Team* license plate on the front of his truck until the day he died. But just like you, my dad never pushed me, or even talked about joining the military. It was my mom who really surprised me one day. Her father was a French Army officer who had served with the French Foreign Legion, and her mother was originally from Lebanon."

"How'd she surprise you?" asked Parker.

"While we were doing the dishes together one night and chatting about what I might do with my life, she says, 'Jake, I think it would be pretty cool to be an Army officer.' First time I'd ever heard that from my mom. I think my jaw dropped. Yep, she flat out surprised me with that one.

"It didn't sink in at that moment and she never mentioned it again. But I later thought about it. I had decent grades and played three sports in high school, but didn't have a wicked fastball, that's for sure," chuckled Jake. "I thought, *What the hell, I'll give it a shot. Nothing to lose.* So, I applied for an academy congressional nomination from Big Rapids, Michigan, and applied to Michigan State for a four-year ROTC scholarship. Somebody must have had a crazy sense of humor, Chet, as I got accepted to both."

"No kiddin?"

"Yep. Just like my mom's comment, getting accepted to both surprised me *too*. Then I wasn't sure what to do. Wasn't sure if I wanted that socially broader—and I think a lot more fun—college experience at Michigan State or the 24-7 military environment at West Point. And then I talked with my football coach."

"And?"

"My coach said, 'Jake, I applied to West Point and didn't get in. Went to another school that wasn't my first choice. Why don't you go to West Point for a year, for your dad?' he asked. 'Give it your best. See what happens. You can always leave with your head high after a year or two if you don't like it. After all, West Point is not for everybody.'

"Going to West Point for someone other than yourself normally doesn't work out too well," Jake added. "But seeing as how I respected my coach and was on the fence about where to go, I decided to follow his advice. Like I said, my dad didn't push me. He never even mentioned the words *Army* or *military*. Shoot, when I first mentioned West Point at the dinner table, he about fell off his chair. Son of a gun if I didn't end up graduating from there. It was all I could do to keep my rebel spirit in check and not rack up hundreds of demerits," said Jake, laughing.

"I hear ya on that rebel thing," chuckled Parker as he began to steer the truck into the big stadium parking lot. "When did you go to Ranger School?" he asked, knowing Jake wore the RANGER patch on the left shoulder sleeve of his Army uniforms.

"Went as a cadet," replied Jake. "Volunteered for it. Again, surprise, surprise, got selected to go in the summer."

Jake had left out that his having accrued more than his fair share of demerits, as flagged by an officer on the Ranger School selection committee, almost derailed his goal of attending the Army's sixty-one-day, exhausting, sleep-depriving, all-weather, and all-terrain small unit leadership crucible.

"How was it?" asked Parker, knowing he was headed for the winter Ranger course in January, after the Infantry Officers Basic Course.

"Ain't gonna lie, Chet. It pretty much *sucked.* The chiggers alone tormented the hell out of me," he said, laughing, "but I'd do it again in a heartbeat. Pushed me to mental and physical places I'd never been before. There were times I was hallucinating my ass off from fatigue, imagining all kinds of crazy shit coming out of trees and bushes, especially at night. But on graduation day my dad pinned my tab on me. Pretty cool moment, especially since he was gone before my junior year at West Point was over."

"Sorry to hear that, brother," replied Parker.

"Thanks, man."

Although a rebel at heart, Jake was grateful to have been afforded the opportunity to attend West Point. He reveled in its tactical Army field training, particularly the comradery and teamwork he felt during small-unit field challenges, as well as individual challenges such as land navigation, weapons qualification and physical training tests. For Jake, he considered this training to be the highest form of an individual team sport. He also appreciated West Point's emphasis on character and leadership development. As to its almost weekly military parades in the fall and spring, he could've done with much less of those.

Jake loved military history. His favorite leaders were Ulysses S. Grant, George Patton, and Norman Schwarzkopf. The first two were not exactly model West Point cadets, and although they had their personal character shortcomings, Jake thought of them as fearless and unyielding brawlers—and winners—on the battlefield, as was Schwarzkopf.

Pulling into a stadium parking space, Parker parked the truck and looked directly at Jake.

"Okay, buddy. This is the most important thing I'm going to tell you all weekend, so listen up! When in doubt today, just yell 'War Eagle!' and they'll love ya, man," said Parker. "You copy?"

"Roger that! I think I can do that," laughed Jake. "War Eagle!"

The two walked towards Auburn's massive Jordan-Hare Stadium, navigating through all the pregame tailgate party tents, lawn chairs, smoking grills and *War Eagle* and *Roll Tide* banners.

Parker continued, "And by the way, besides my girlfriend, Cindy, who I already mentioned to you, we'll be meetin' up with a few other folks, too."

"That's cool with me," replied Jake. Looking up: "Wow, that is one big-ass stadium!"

Parker nodded. "Yep. Tenth largest in the country."

"*Almost* as big as Michigan's Big House," chided Jake, referring to the University of Michigan's largest-in-America, 107,000-plus capacity football stadium, while slapping Parker on the back.

"Yeah, whatever," chuckled Parker. "But do you think Michigan is ever going to beat an SEC team any time soon, in that *Big House*?"

"Dang, I had that one comin', didn't I?"

Parker grinned. "Yep, you did, buddy."

Walking several more paces, they approached a milling group of seven twenty-something college students. One giddy girl broke from the crowd and ran towards Parker.

"Chet!" she yelled as she approached. The two quickly kissed and hugged.

"Hey, darlin', I want you to meet Jake Fortina," said Parker.

"Hi, Jake, I'm Cindy. Welcome to Auburn!"

"Thank you, Cindy. It's great to be here. War Eagle!"

"Chet, you got him trained already!" Cindy laughed.

"Of course!" said Parker.

Cindy introduced Jake to the group and the two soldiers were warmly greeted. One taller brunette girl, Faith Novak, caught Jake's eye. In fact, she did more than *catch* his eye. The two locked eyes for a few seconds, which did not go unnoticed by a couple of other students. Jake thought she was attractive and thought he felt something. What Jake did not know was that Cindy had informed Faith the previous evening about Jake's arrival, and Faith had been anticipating it. Jake was as promised and Faith really liked what she saw in the athletic five-feet-eleven-inch-tall young man with perpetually tanned skin, black hair, and dark eyes. Faith had sensed from Jake's steady look at her that his initial impression might be mutual.

The talkative assemblage headed for one of the stadium's entrance gates. One of the guys walked up beside Jake and nudged him in the arm. He held up a well-worn, silver and leather-coated flask, just a bit larger than the palm of his hand.

"Want a shot? It's moonshine. It comes from my granpappy's still near the Chattahoochee River in Tennessee."

Not wanting to offend the enthusiastic guy with the flask containing God only knew what, or perhaps fail a veiled test by the group, Jake grabbed it without hesitation and took a big swig. The group got quiet. Jake was pleasantly surprised that it did not burn a hole in his throat.

"That's some good stuff. Your grandpappy must be a very talented dude," said Jake.

"He *is*, but what makes you say that?" asked the guy, as Jake handed him the flask back.

"That moonshine tastes exactly like Jack Daniels," responded Jake.

Parker smirked. "Funny how that moonshine takes exactly like Gentleman Jack, isn't it?"

Inside the buzzing stadium, the two Army lieutenants and the group of amped-up college students, like ducks in a row, were led by Cindy to their mid-level row of seats looking down on the ten-yard line. Jake followed right behind Parker, with Cindy leading the way. Parker stopped at his designated seat, Jake stopped, too. Standing beside him was a beaming, easy-on-the-eyes Faith Novak. She had followed right behind Jake, whose heart skipped a beat. Sitting down next to Faith, Jake again felt an electrical spark. Faith was sensing the same warmth on the cool, Alabama fall afternoon.

Ten minutes into the game, Jake liked what he'd heard from the bright-eyed young lady sitting next to him shoulder to shoulder on the aluminum bleacher seats. When Auburn decided to punt the football after a fourth down and one yard to go situation at midfield, Faith turned to Jake and said, "They should have gone for it on fourth down. Auburn has a very strong offensive line."

Faith was not just a pretty face. She knew something about

football, too, and by halftime, Jake knew the talkative gal also had a sense of humor.

During the second half, Faith and Cindy left for a bathroom break.

"One thing is for sure," Faith said to Cindy as they weaved their way through the crowded concession stands, "he's different, and I do *like* Mr. Different!"

3.
LEAVING THE SCENE

THE TWO HEZBOLLAH operatives arrived at their rented Peugeot sedan and parked on Rue de Fecheray in the Suresnes suburb of Paris. They were thankful the intermittently lit, early morning Paris suburb streets were clear of traffic. Exactly per their plan, the middle-of-the-night rain had provided acoustic and visual cover during their late spring cemetery operation.

"What are you *doing*?" exclaimed Darbandi as Gilani began to turn on the car's GPS. "Don't you know the way?"

"Sorry, I just wanted to be sure," replied Gilani.

"It's not needed. I *know* the way!" said Darbandi.

As the men pulled out of their parking spot, they were tense, though content that the first part of their mission was complete.

Someday, when he knows what I did, my uncle Sayyid will be proud of me, thought Darbandi.

Uncle Sayyid, a former Iranian Revolutionary Guard member and close friend of Darbandi's father, had been killed in the Iran-Iraq War of the 1980s when Darbandi was six years old.

Within five blocks of driving, the two Hezbollah terrorists came upon a French National Police vehicle, parked curbside with its parking lights on. With its misty windows, Darbandi and Gilani could not discern if anyone was inside the patrol car. Their hearts pounded as they realized they had made the stupid mistake of storing the freshly wet and dirty clothes in their rucksacks, which were now in the back seat. The discovery of the freshly soiled clothes by a law enforcement officer would likely prompt many questions.

Darbandi took a deep breath.

"Just drive normal and do not make eye contact with anyone in that car. And remember our story if we are stopped," he said.

Without turning his head, Darbandi kept a steady gaze out of the corner of his right eye as they approached the police car. As they eased by, Darbandi saw two dark figures seated in the front seats.

Driving on, Gilani's hair rose on the on the back of his neck. Seven long seconds passed by as Darbandi kept his eye on the outside rearview mirror. He then calmly said to Gilani, "Farhad, we are okay. Nobody is behind us."

It would take several more minutes, with light traffic on the Paris roads at four in the morning, for Farhad Gilani's beating heart to calm.

The men drove on to Darbandi's apartment in the Saint-Denis *banlieu*, a suburb in northern Paris heavily populated by residents originating from North Africa and the Middle East. Cruising steadily while most of Paris slumbered, it was a mercifully quicker ride than the normal forty to fifty minutes required in busy Paris traffic.

4.
VICENZA, ITALY:
ELEVEN YEARS BEFORE PARIS

"FAITH, ARE YOU SURE it's okay if I ask the Army to try out for the Army Special Forces?" US Army captain Jake Fortina asked his vivacious blue-eyed, brunette wife, now in her late twenties.

"Darlin', if you want to go Special Forces, go for it," Faith responded. "I'm behind you one hundred percent. We already decided I'll be leaving the Air Force soon. I'm sure we can make this work."

Stationed with Jake in Vicenza, Italy, Faith was about to complete her four-year, post-ROTC Air Force scholarship service commitment, serving as a liaison officer for the US Aviano Air Base to Vicenza's Caserma Ederle US Army base. Located in northeast Italy, the two bases were about ninety miles apart.

Faith had enjoyed serving in the Air Force and the adventure of living in Italy and Europe. She had done well enough to know that an Air Force career was a real possibility. But her heart was not in a long-term commitment to the military. She liked being a mother, and increasingly her dream was to get a degree in business administration and strike out on her own professionally, perhaps eventually working for her father's oil and gas company in Texas. She knew she had it in her to be a very successful business leader. But she also knew that being a mother, and a wife to an Army infantry officer during two wars, was not a piece of cake.

"Being a supportive wife to a man who might come home maimed or whose funeral I might have to attend, while raising a daughter, is the toughest job I could ever have," she told her family in confidence while back in Texas.

On the other hand, Jake was not yet sure that he wanted to stay in the Army for the long haul. He had just completed a three-year tour with the Army's highly deployable and elite 173d Airborne Brigade Combat Team located in Vicenza. Jake thought it was an excellent, high-speed unit with which to begin his Army service. Jake was also thankful that he and Faith were able to live in modest family stairwell quarters (apartments) in Vicenza, even though almost half of his time was spent far away in a combat zone.

Jake had fulfilled his dream of leading American soldiers in combat, and he discovered he was made for it. He deeply respected and loved his soldiers, and they willingly followed, and more importantly, trusted his complete competence, dedication, and willingness to share all hardships with them. Initially a platoon leader of over thirty riflemen and later a company executive officer, second-in-command of about 160 Army paratroopers, then-Lieutenant Fortina would never have his soldiers do anything he would not do himself, and his soldiers knew it.

Jake also appreciated that the Army was a meritocracy. No matter your economic status, gender, race or academic pedigree, you had to merit every promotion and you had to earn the respect and *trust* of your soldiers, peers and leaders. Rank mattered, but personal respect and trust mattered a lot more.

Not totally confident in his wife's we-can-make-this-work answer, Jake pushed her for confirmation.

"Are you sure it's okay? I mean, with the Special Forces, it's gonna be more time away. With Kimberly two years old now, I just want to be sure."

"Jake, you know this is what you want to do," Faith replied. "So yeah, I'm sure."

"Thank you, sweetie," said Jake. "I needed to hear that. It's more like something I feel I need to do. I'm grateful to West Point and the Army for the leadership opportunities they have provided me."

"I think you've already done plenty, *more* than plenty," replied Faith, a bit frustrated. "But I understand where your heart is."

Becoming an Army Green Beret was something Jake had aspired to for a couple of years. After two deployments with the 173d Airborne Brigade—one to Iraq and the other to Afghanistan—he found he truly loved soldiering. It was the honor and privilege to serve with America's best that deeply appealed to him. A gifted linguist, he received a high score on the Army's language aptitude battery test, which measured the aptitude of a soldier to learn a foreign language. A newly minted captain, Jake already spoke excellent French and very good Italian, which he thought might someday also be value-added to the globally deployed US Army Green Berets.

5.

KUNAR PROVINCE, AFGHANISTAN: NINE YEARS BEFORE PARIS

CAPTAIN JAKE FORTINA never thought he'd again see the hell on earth that was the Korangal Valley. He had operated here with the 173d Airborne Brigade Combat Team as a first lieutenant, in charge of thirty airborne infantrymen nicknamed *sky soldiers*. His paratroopers had come from twenty-three states in America, as well as two from Puerto Rico. Now he was back, leading a twelve-person Army Special Operations A-Team. He had passed the US Army Green Beret Qualification Course, the so-called "Q-Course," near the top of his class.

While he was officially in charge of the team, Jake was under no illusion that he was its most important soldier. He understood that although he was responsible for *everything* his team did or did not do, it was the highly professional and experienced non-commissioned officers—the sergeants, his *teammates*—who would ultimately determine the success or failure of the team. Jake understood that it was *his* job to apply his education, training and judgment in striving to live up to the high standards and the honor and the privilege of being the player-coach of this his twelve-man warrior brotherhood. With his deceased father being a former Army sergeant, Jake woke up every morning and put his head down every night wanting to be the best leader for them that he could possibly be.

Lying in thick vegetation with a clear downslope view of the mountain and valley below, Captain Fortina had heard enough. He grabbed the manpack radio handset from his senior weapons sergeant, Brian "Bratwurst" Beske, who had been persistently trying to call in immediate artillery support but was visibly frustrated.

Speaking in a low but forceful tone into the radio handset, Jake said, "This is Tango Zero Six. Listen to me, goddammit. We are facing a serious Taliban force. Got maybe sixty, seventy or so downslope from us. I need the entire battalion to put every fucking round exactly where Sergeant Beske told you to. And I need it *now*, over."

It was uncharacteristic for the normally calm Jake to show emotion or agitation—or to openly use profanity. He believed that in life-threatening situations it was critical to always maintain a calm and confident demeanor. This was especially true on the radio, where his words could be heard by more than one individual on the team. But this was not normal. His A-Team was about to reap the potentially deadly violence of some shoddy higher headquarters intelligence work. The team had stumbled upon on an estimated sixty to seventy Taliban located on the mountain slope below them. And now his weapons sergeant was getting the runaround from their supporting artillery unit.

In the northern part of the Korangal Valley, on a reconnaissance mission against a wayward but powerful former Afghan warlord and two of his Taliban lieutenants, Jake had been misled by inaccurate intelligence reports saying he should encounter only "a few Taliban stragglers, making their way to somewhere else in Afghanistan."

Originating just over the border in Pakistan, the Korangal Valley, the "Valley of Death," as it was called by soldiers and Marines who had fought there, stood astride a longstanding Taliban thoroughfare into Afghanistan. In the past several weeks, however, the northern half of the valley was assessed by intelligence analysts to have gone relatively quiet. The A-Team's insertion by helicopter some eighteen hours prior must have been reported to the local Taliban warlords.

Jake's radio transmission was met with an uncharacteristic delay of almost three minutes.

"Tango Zero Six, this is Zulu Niner-Four. We are unable to complete fire mission at this time. Will get back with you ASAP when we can put steel on target, over."

Unable? What? What the hell? Jake thought. The plan was to have ready the supporting artillery battalion, and at least one artillery battery consisting of eight artillery howitzers, able to fire lethal artillery rounds, six inches in diameter.

Jake was stunned to hear the response that his designated artillery support was unable to provide his team with immediate artillery fires. This was a highly unusual violation of standard warfighting tactics and procedures. Jake was about to get someone else on the radio but then realized he had no time to waste. In any given moment, the Taliban could launch an assault on his team. With other fire support assets possibly available, the only response was "Roger, out."

Team Yankee, the nickname given to the A-Team by their operations Master Sergeant John "Hitman" Heather, a former New York Yankees prospect and New York high school all-state outfielder, needed fire support *immediately.* Their twelve-man team of special operators could hold off an enemy force of thirty or forty, or maybe even fifty or so enemy fighters. But seventy or more? Jake Fortina was not about to take that chance without some heavy outside fire support.

"Brat," he said, using the more familiar team moniker for Sergeant Beske, "we need Spectre, Little Birds, Apaches, fast movers, or whatever you can get . . . now!" Spectre was a robust Air Force plane with multiple major weapons systems onboard, including an artillery howitzer, and "fast movers" were fighter jets. That pretty much covered the range of external fire support that Jake expected to be available to support his team, soon to be in dire straits.

Beske knew that the highly agile Army Special Ops "Little Bird" attack helicopters of the 160th Special Operations Aviation Regiment (SOAR), whose brave and technically and tactically competent pilots had etched their military lore in places like Somalia and Panama, were on alert to support this mission. But he was also aware that the nearby Combat Aviation Brigade from the 101st Airborne Division (Air Assault), with its powerful Apache helicopter gunships, was on standby.

As Beske radioed the aviation brigade, Jake heard a single shot, and then observed some downslope enemy movement. It was coming from his lower left flank and a thicket of big rocks and brush. He knew Team Yankee had to keep its power dry, at least for now. A return shot at this point by anyone on the team would only further expose Team Yankee's position. But it was clear the Taliban were probing Team Yankee. The entire team was on full alert. Team members continued to observe their assigned fire and observation sectors and improve their individual positions of cover and concealment with as much stealth as possible. As best they could, the team assured near 360-degree protection from their semi-oval-shaped perimeter.

For now, the terrain favored Team Yankee. They were upslope and in thick brush, with boulders and smaller rocks giving them good cover and concealment from the searching Taliban eyes below them. The Taliban would have to come across about seventy yards of mostly upslope and open terrain, which Jake knew at some point soon they would try, and then try again.

While some Taliban had been recruited locally in Afghanistan and Pakistan, seventeen and eighteen-year-old "foreign fighters" had come to western Pakistan from places like Amman, Ankara, Berlin, Dushanbe, Marseilles, Moscow, Riyadh, Sarajevo, Tashkent, and Tunis, mostly recruited online through social media by extremist-Islamic recruiters sitting in front of their safe and warm computer terminals in places like Kandahar, Lahore, Islamabad, Istanbul, and Jeddah. The mostly younger recruits were more than willing to sacrifice their lives for Allah and the seventy-two *houris*—the beautiful virgins of paradise—that were promised awaited the sexually repressed young men upon their earthly deaths. While some Taliban were trained in Afghanistan, most were trained in the badlands that constituted western Pakistan, territory that was ruled by powerful local warlords and their networks. They included the infamous Haqqani network, which called North Waziristan, Pakistan, its home.

With time, Team Yankee knew they could get outflanked, or get attacked from above and behind, which could end up being disastrous, even for a dozen extremely skilled and highly trained US special operators. As Jake observed some rustling among the Taliban below him, he knew the Taliban were not going to be static forever. Jake also knew he had to take away their initiative before things got out of hand.

Then Beske told his captain what he needed to hear.

"Got four Apaches inbound. They'll be on station in twelve mikes!"

Twelve minutes sounded like an hour to Jake for the attack helicopters to arrive.

Just two minutes later, Jake heard the words that would stay with him for the rest of his life.

"Johnson's been hit!" yelled Chief Warrant Officer Carsten "Sully" Sullivan.

Sergeant First Class Raymond "Rover" Johnson had been shot through the neck. Blood was spurting through a golf ball–sized exit hole.

Grabbing a gauze pad, which had been taped to Johnson's personal web gear, Chief Sully immediately applied pressure to the bright-red hole. In spite of the best training in the world, he could not stem the blood flow as it rapidly pulsated out all sides of the gauze. Johnson's carotid artery had been obliterated by the 7.62-millimeter Kalashnikov-delivered bullet. By the time Sergeant Manuel "Doc" Alverez, an El Paso-born Latino and one of the two team medics, arrived, Johnson was dead. The rapid shock, blood loss, and the bullet's proximity to his upper spinal cord had rendered their grim result. Nothing in the medic's power or training could have saved Johnson.

"*Jefe*," Medic Alvarez said, addressing Jake in Spanish. "He's gone."

Jake, maintaining his calm while keeping his eyes fixed to his front—every man had to be a ready rifleman now—ordered his teammates to "tighten it up while keeping an eye to the right and rear, in case they try to come in the back door." It was clear to Jake and the senior members of the team that the Taliban were probing Team Yankee, trying to get them to take the bait and expose their positions with return fire.

"And Brat, we need those Apaches ASAP," added Jake.

Master Sergeant Heather calmly followed up with "Ranger, secure Johnson's water, ammo, first aid pouch, and weapon."

With no verbal response, Sergeant Renoir "Ranger" Steine, a nearby teammate, immediately complied with Heather's order. The Minnesota-raised buck sergeant, who could track and harvest an elk with a bow by the time he was twelve, low-crawled to gather the precious gear no longer needed by his fallen battle buddy. As with other Team Yankee members who had completed the US Army's Ranger School, Steine had also served for three years in a Ranger battalion before re-enlisting for Army Special Forces, swapping his tan beret for a green one. That earned him the rarely used "Ranger" moniker among his Army Green Beret teammates.

"Sir, Apaches on station!" Beske broke in to say.

In the next instant, about to hurl a smoke canister to mark their positions, Beske thought better of it. Given the wind direction, he feared that the Taliban would use the smoke for their own concealment, masking their movements as they tried to move closer to—and potentially launched an assault against—Team Yankee.

Instead, Beske transmitted the locations of nearby terrain features to the Apache pilots. The mountain peaks, rock formations, clearings, tree lines, massive boulders could be used as easily identifiable reference points by the pilots in the air to direct their lethal and terrifying .30 mm chain guns and .70 mm Hydra rockets on as many Taliban as they could see. Everybody on the team knew the Apaches would be a gamechanger.

About one minute before the first two Apaches began burping out their fear-inducing and flesh-obliterating munitions, someone called out, "King's been hit." The team engineer and new guy, Sergeant Dennis M. "Mad Dog" King, had a bullet simultaneously hit his rifle stock and glance off his right hand with such force that his weapon was knocked seven feet behind him. The bullet had also stripped King's two smallest fingers of their brown skin, leaving two white, bloody, skeletal sticks. Somehow, someway, King managed to low crawl back, retrieve his rifle, self-apply a bandage, and stay in the fight with a mangled right hand but sufficiently useful trigger finger.

"Compared to Chesterfield Square, this *ain't shit*," muttered King, a Black American who had opted for an Army enlistment as his ticket to escape the oppressive streets of his crime-ridden Los Angeles neighborhood.

King was the team comic. Normally that kind of "This ain't shit" response would have elicited a chuckle from his teammates, and certainly from his battle buddy, Sergeant Jim "Buzzy" Onitrof, a communications sergeant whose standard response was "No shit." He had dropped out of Princeton, scratching a serious itch to join the Army's Special Forces. But with Johnson dead, the mood was now deadly serious. And Team Yankee was pissed.

The four AH-64 Apache helicopter gunships finally went to work, rotating through their airborne firing positions. They unleashed near continuous fires over the exposed Taliban, many of whom were barely teenagers. The Green Berets were grateful as a bolt of adrenaline and hope pulsed through their spirits. Team Yankee was elated to have the Apaches, with their deadly .30 mm automatic cannons, .70 mm hydra rockets and if needed, Hellfire missiles on their side. It was as if four sky-borne archangels had joined Team Yankee in their fight.

Horrific destruction rained on Team Yankee's enemies. Some on the team did not relish that the young men and boys now screaming out in various languages were being massacred. But Team Yankee had lost a brother and had another one wounded, so by God there was no way the Taliban were going to get away with a couple of lucky shots. During a brief lull in the firing, two Taliban desperately tried to run out of the kill zone but were cut down by King and Steine. After seven intense minutes of almost unceasing Apache fire, the silence was deafening. No more than a dozen or so Taliban survived, somehow slinking away to God only knew where.

Surviving Team Yankee members were deeply and forever grateful for the crucial gunship support. But they were devastated to have lost a teammate. Sergeant First Class Johnson had been a key leader on the team. Some teammates loved the experienced Johnson like a brother and others, like a favorite uncle. He had selflessly deployed four times to hot combat zones and had previously been wounded. This time, fate had rendered its final verdict for the combat veteran. He left behind his high school sweetheart and two daughters, aged four and seven.

In the brutal rock-and-scrub-choked terrain that was the unforgiving Korengal Valley, Team Yankee would have to undertake the arduous task of carrying their fallen angel, his weapon and all his gear several hundred yards down the mountain slope to a prearranged helicopter evacuation site. The team, with its focus divided between carrying Johnson's body and gear down a treacherous mountain slope and watching for surviving Taliban, would be very vulnerable. Despite the risk, there was never a doubt that they were going to take their beloved fallen angel with them. Several men felt deeply that Johnson's spirit was still among them.

Straggling Taliban could still be a threat, so Jake decided to wait for twenty minutes to avoid a chance encounter with the retreating enemy. Once he, Chief Sully, and Master Sergeant Heather assessed that their path down the mountain to a suitable helicopter landing zone should be free of straggling Taliban, Jake requested to have two of the helicopter gunships remain on station, just for extra insurance.

Meanwhile, Alvarez, Heather, King, and Steine, led by Jake, moved down the mountain slope to quickly and efficiently inspect the dead Taliban below. While Jake could have called for another unit to be helicoptered in to complete the task, he didn't want to risk more soldiers having another encounter with the Taliban. Team Yankee already knew the terrain and they would complete the vital task.

Jake and his men understood that what they might discover in the possession of the dead Taliban could provide the US chain of command and some of the international allied forces operating in Afghanistan with tremendous intelligence value. Perhaps, scraps of paper, even sketches, or if they really hit the jackpot, a cellphone some Taliban kid managed to sneak by his leaders.

There were numerous intelligence questions to be answered: Where were these Taliban recruited from? Were some brought in locally or farther afield from Afghanistan? What were the age ranges of these fighters? Were their weapons clean, indicating a more disciplined force, or dirty? Were they carrying rations? Water? That might suggest how far away their base of operations was, or if they were supported by the locals. The questions went on, all needing answers to help intelligence analysts and field commanders fight the enemy in the future.

As Steine moved towards the edge of the gruesome collection of blood-stained, disemboweled, and dismembered corpses covering an area about one-quarter the size of a football field, he heard a whimper. As his eyes widened and he took a few more steps, there on the ground was a kid whose life had inexplicably been spared from the 30 mm rounds and rocket shrapnel shards.

Steine guessed the kid to be sixteen years old, tops. He was on his right side, holding up his trembling and bloodied left arm towards Steine, as most people do when they try to shield their eyes from the sun. Except this kid was shielding his face from being shot by Steine.

Keeping his distance, Steine took a couple of more steps for a better look. The kid's left hand and forearm just above it had been blown off, leaving a bloody stump below the elbow. It was a miracle the kid had not bled out, perhaps because of the cauterizing effect of the hot shrapnel ripping through his wrist and veins.

Not wanting to take a chance that the kid was booby-trapped or had a suicide belt on, Steine kept his distance of about fifteen yards and crouched low. Then he kneeled on one knee. Steine knew he was still too close, but he had a job to do. He motioned the kid to roll over. After three attempts at sign gestures by Steine, the terrified teenager finally got what Steine was trying to tell him. The kid rolled over on his stomach, with his arms outstretched above his head and flat on the ground. The kid was moaning in pain as he lay facedown in the dirt, certain the American soldier was going to deliver a bullet to the back of his head, or worse, sexually abuse him and then kill him. After all, that's what his Taliban leaders had told him would happen if he surrendered to the Americans.

Steine cautiously moved in, got down on one knee, and patted the scared kid down. All the while, Alvarez, also about fifteen yards away, aimed right at the kid's temple. If the kid tried to move one of his hands in an attempt to detonate a possible suicide belt, Alvarez would take care of business.

Steine confirmed that the kid was not armed and signaled for the medic. Alvarez moved in, bandaged him up and shot the kid with some pain meds, enough to take the edge off his arm pain but not so much as to knock the kid out. He also gave the surprised kid a drink of water. Steine and Alvarez were thrilled that they could get the kid to stand. The Taliban's youthful resilience gave him an advantage over other fighters who might have been twice his age. The fact that he was ambulatory was huge, making the group's movements back up the slope and eventually to the helicopter far easier.

The kid spoke some Pashto, indicating he might very well be local, either from Afghanistan or Pakistan. Ultimately, he was going to be of major intelligence value, so Team Yankee would be extra careful to get him back to base camp in one piece—minus his left hand. Once on the chopper, Alvarez, with Steine's help, would give the kid a standard intravenous (IV) drip to keep him hydrated.

Jake had now moved over to Alvarez, as Steine put a field expedient blindfold on the kid so that he wouldn't get a look at the rest of the team members, or see the inside of the American Blackhawk he was about to ride on, or see the base camp or a damn thing until turned over to a trained interrogator.

Steine taped the kid's mouth shut so that he couldn't yell out to his buddies in the event they encountered some in their movements back up the slope and to the helicopter. He considered using a zip tie on the kid's arms, but that would only have caused the kid excruciating pain, so he decided to forgo it. Jake directed the group to move up the slope to their designated helicopter rendezvous location.

As the two choppers landed, Team Yankee boarded the primary Blackhawk. Jake, the last to board, had a pit in his stomach. As a platoon leader he'd had three soldiers wounded on his first deployment to Afghanistan. That was tough, *real* tough. Johnson, however, was the first soldier under his leadership KIA. The entire team was deeply affected by it. Seated on their webbed cargo seats around the black body bag on the chopper's floor, it was hard to process that the bag contained the remains of a great American who just over an hour before was a living, breathing and beloved fellow warrior. No one uttered a word during the entire thirty-five-minute ride back to the base camp, where the kid would be taken directly to the combat support hospital and treated by some of the finest US surgeons, all who had volunteered after the 9/11 attacks.

Jake couldn't help but ask himself, *If we had received that artillery fire support immediately as requested, would Johnson still be with us?*

Jake did not realize it then, but that question would eat at him for weeks, months, even years. It would often wake him in the middle of the night or enter his consciousness out of the blue on a long road trip. When his thinking and his emotions began to grow dark and heavy, Jake was blessed in knowing that he could always reach out to his old buddy, Chet Parker, from his Fort Benning days. Talking to Parker, also a combat veteran, always helped Jake keep the post-traumatic stress disorder (PTSD) demons of the Korengal Valley at bay. So did prayer, lots of prayer.

Sitting on the Blackhawk and looking down on the rough, rocky, and mountainous terrain below, Jake's thoughts came back to Team Yankee. They had to find a way to fight on, together. Jake would make sure they did.

6.
CLARKSVILLE, TENNESSEE:
NINE YEARS BEFORE PARIS

SEVEN-YEAR-OLD Amanda Johnson stood in her mother's bedroom door. It was midnight.

"Mommy, I can't sleep. Can I *please* sleep in your bed?"

Julie Johnson had tried hard to get Amanda to sleep in her own bed whenever possible. She knew that within three weeks, her husband, US Army sergeant first class Raymond Johnson, would return to their Clarksville, Tennessee home. It was located about thirteen miles across the Kentucky-Tennessee state line and from the front gate of Fort Campbell, Kentucky. On-base housing at Fort Campbell had taken too long to obtain, and Johnson was financially ready to make a down payment, so he bought his first home, a small ranch style, without garage, in a modest neighborhood of Clarksville.

While his three previous deployments had varied in time, this deployment was scheduled to last roughly seven months, seven months that Julie's best friend and lover was again absent, and seven months that Ray, the father to Amanda and Cindy, was gone from their lives. Every time he came home, the family was ecstatic to have Ray home. But adjustments also had to be made to again accommodate Dad being home, including Dad sleeping in his own bed with Mom. Julie worked hard at compassionately and lovingly getting Amanda to understand that there would be a change, and that change would be easier if Amanda and her sister slept in their own beds.

But on this night, Julie said exactly what little Amanda wanted to hear. "Sure, sweetie, c'mon in and snuggle up."

Amanda practically bounded to her mom's bed, instantly feeling the motherly warmth, and secure. It didn't take more than three minutes for Amanda to fall asleep. But on this night, for some reason, sleep would come hard for Julie.

The next morning, Julie woke the kids up as usual and took them through their normal routine of getting ready for school. Amanda would get picked up with a yellow school bus in front of the house, and then Julie would drive Cindy to the nearby preschool, about three miles away. After about an hour to herself at home, Julie would head off for her part-time job at the local Target store. The job helped with the family finances while also helping the time go by while Ray served overseas. When she finished work, each day she would pick up Cindy from pre-school and wait outside for Amanda's arrival on the bus.

When she got home from dropping off Cindy on this day, she made her usual cup of black coffee before settling in for some time on social media and watching TV talk shows. She liked her routine even better when Ray was sitting with her. Just as she was thinking about Ray, Cindy looked out her living room bay window and saw a gray sedan pullup. At first, she thought it might be an Uber driver who had made a mistake. Then she saw a man emerge from the passenger side with an Army blues uniform. From the other side of the vehicle, she saw another man emerge wearing the same uniform. As she saw no stripes—no chevrons, no rockers, the correct terms for *stripes* she had learned from Ray— she knew they were officers.

What happened next occurred in slow motion for Julie. As she noticed the two men walking up sidewalk, she did not want to get up and out of her loveseat, but she knew she had to.

Dear God, let this be a mistake, she prayed.

She became lightheaded while slowly rising to her feet. Both legs felt heavy, but she was somehow able to make it to the front door. In a flash, an irrational thought—more like another prayer, a hope—occurred to her. *Perhaps they are coming to tell me my father has passed.*

In some ways, given how long her dad had been ill, that would have been a blessing.

As she looked through the door's glass portal before opening it, she saw brass crossed rifles on one of the officer's lapels. She had been around the Army long enough to know he was an infantry officer. On the other officer's two lapels were brass crosses, indicating a chaplain.

Upon opening the door, one of the officer's said, "Ma'am, I am Captain Colin Kelly from the First Brigade, 101st Airborne Division of Fort Campbell, and this is Chaplain Don Williams, who is also with our First Brigade. Are you Mrs. Julie Johnson? The wife of Sergeant First Class Raymond Johnson?"

Julie wanted to answer anything but that which she knew she had to say as this nightmare was slowly beginning its opening scene.

"Yes, I am," she responded.

The thirty-year-old captain had practiced his lines and prayed for Mrs. Johnson before meeting her.

"Mrs. Johnson, I have an important message to deliver from the secretary of the Army. May I come in?"

"Sure," replied Julie as her eyes began to well up and her breathing became more labored.

"May we sit down?" asked Kelly, hoping that Julie would seat herself as well, which she did, sitting back in the love seat. Both officers sat in nearby chairs.

"Mrs. Johnson, the secretary of the Army has asked me to express his deep regret that your husband, Sergeant First Class Raymond Johnson—"

With the captain's words, Julie, as much as she knew that this was a possibility for much of the past seven years, began to wail as only those who have suffered such an unspeakable tragedy can.

As she cried, Captain Kelly completed the message he was duty-bound to deliver, doing so with as much empathy as his soul could muster.

"Mam," he continued, "your husband was killed in combat in Kunar Province, in Afghanistan. The secretary extends his *deepest* sympathy to you and your family in your tragic loss."

As the captain said "family," Julie immediately thought of Amanda and Cindy in school, further increasing her tearful anguish as she struggled to understand the cosmic shockwave that had just hit her.

Chaplain Williams asked her if there was anybody she would like to call or that the chaplain could call for her.

"Yes," Julie answered. "I'd like to call my parents and my brother. You don't need to call anybody."

As Julie called her mother, the chaplain stepped aside and called the head of the Army Wives Support Group of the 5th Special Forces Group at Fort Campbell. The 5th Group commander's wife was also immediately notified, and within twenty minutes the support group had found three wives of US Army Special Forces soldiers who volunteered to be on their way to console and be with Julie through this terrible ordeal. They would also organize meals, help Julie meet Amanda at the bus stop, and with the school's advance permission, pick up Cindy at the preschool. Julie's best friend within the group would also stay with her for two nights until Julie's brother and mom traveled to Clarksville to be with her.

For Julie, Amanda, and Cindy, their earthly journeys would continue, but without the man who, at least when he was home, would read them bedtime stories, take them to the Dairy Queen, play soccer in the backyard and take the family for Christmas trips to Grandma and Grandpa's house in New Hampshire.

Back in Afghanistan, arrangements were being made to ship Sergeant First Class Johnson's remains back to his home in Nashua, New Hampshire, before eventual interment at the New Hampshire State Veteran's Cemetery in Boscawen. Although he could have chosen Arlington National Cemetery as his final resting place, Johnson's final will and testament said he wanted to be buried in Boscawen, "in the state where I met my beautiful bride Julie, and near the New Hampshire lakes I fished in the summers with my dad and brother."

Master Sergeant John Heather volunteered to escort the body of one of his best friends from Afghanistan all the way to Nashua (by a chartered flight), where a dignified transfer would take place with an honor guard from the 5th Special Forces Group. Johnson's remains would then be escorted by ground transportation to Johnson's final resting place in Boscawen. It was there that Heather would say his final goodbye to his fallen battle buddy and friend.

While it was Captain Fortina's solemn duty to compose for Julie Johnson the most difficult letter he ever had to write about the loss of her magnificent husband, Jake felt he needed to do more. He had met Mrs. Johnson at a couple of social gatherings his team and his battalion had before deploying to Afghanistan. He considered Julie and the two girls to be part of Team Yankee's bigger family. And truth be told, Jake loved and respected Ray Johnson like a brother.

While the Army required only one escort to travel with Sergeant First Class Johnson's remains, Jake would buck Army tradition and appeal to his battalion commander to accompany Master Sergeant Heather and Johnson's remains to and through Johnson's funeral in Boscawen. He wanted to personally look Julie, Amanda, and Cindy in the eye and tell them what a wonderful man their husband and father was.

Because of strict Army regulations, Jake was told that his request had been denied. Not taking "no" for an answer, Jake appealed, offering to take personal leave days to do what he felt deeply in his soul that he must do. Jake's request for leave was approved.

7.
TEHRAN:
SIX MONTHS BEFORE PARIS

IT WAS THE FIRST MEETING of the two senior Iranian officials since the covert operation in Paris had been secretly approved by Iran's supreme leader and Shiite cleric, Ali Sasami. Sworn to keep their secret protected from the knowledge of other Iranian government officials, two men were charged with responsibility for the operation by Iran's ruthless vice prime minister Ardishir Dabiri. Much like Ali Sasami, Dabiri was *not* in agreement with those in Iran's government and many of its citizens who believed that Iran should make a nuclear deal with the United States. In fact, Dabiri did not believe Iran should agree to anything with the United States that would limit Iran's ability to inflict serious harm on the US or its main Middle East ally, Israel. Dabiri's twin purposes in life were to cause serious pain and destruction to the US and "to drive Israel into the sea, forever."

Dabiri had chosen the ambitious minister of intelligence, Omar Daghestani, a Shiite extremist, to plan and direct daily operations, as well as coordination with Hezbollah in Lebanon. Daghestani's partner in planning and directing the operation was Mohammed Khorasani, Iran's deputy defense minister.

"We cannot afford to take the chance of the two Hezbollah operators bringing the bones back to our embassy in Paris," Daghestani began. "The French DGSI and local police have our embassy under constant surveillance. We cannot—*will not*—be compromised like the ignorant Saudis were in Turkey when they dismembered that American.

"Sending the bones through the French postal system is also not wise," he continued. "The French postal system is too suspicious of Arabs sending anything through the international mail. Furthermore, with all the Arab freedom fighter operations against France dating back to the 1960s, the French have become very good at screening and X-raying mail. That is another risk we cannot take. Our redundant means of two Hezbollah operators personally bringing the bones out of France is something the French will not expect. It is bold and it is risky, but it is our best option for bringing at least one of the bones back to Iran."

"I agree," replied Khorasani. "And the Hezbollah affiliation of Darbandi and Gilani will give our government plausible deniability if they are caught. We will claim that it was a rogue operation, launched by Hezbollah in Lebanon, and that it was done so without the knowledge of the Iranian government.

"For several years Hezbollah has been expanding its networks, raising money, and conducting money-laundering operations throughout Western and Central Europe. All of the European intelligence agencies know this. Germany has outlawed all Hezbollah members on their territory, recently raiding mosques, educational centers, and associations. While the United Kingdom has not conducted raids, it has done very much the same. It has outlawed not only Hezbollah's military wing but its political wing as well.

"Our own Ministry of Intelligence and Security members would not provide the distance from our government that we would need if they were caught, or worse, were caught and confessed," continued Iran's intelligence minister. "The two veteran Hezbollah operatives are perfect for this mission."

"After the unforgivable murder of General Shirvani by the Americans, our supreme leader was right," said Khorasani, Iran's defense minister. "Something has to be done. To hell with the Americans. They must pay. They are becoming ever bolder, inciting our young people to riot while the fucking US Navy sails around our gulf!"

"Yes, brother," responded the intelligence minister. "And the road of America's and Israel's abuses, often supported by their European allies, is a long one. The cyberattack and destruction of the foundation of our nuclear material–making capability—again, likely by the Americans and most assuredly with the help of the Israelis—was an international crime of great proportions.

"My grandfather's family was tortured in the 1950s by the secret police of that despicable man, that so-called *Shah*. The Americans supported him and were fully aware of his brutal and murderous secret police. And then the American government later gave the Shah and his family refuge in America."

"We cannot fail our supreme leader and our people," replied the defense minister.

As he said it, Khorasani knew full well that a great proportion of Iranians under the age of forty wanted peace, especially with the United States. But Khorasani considered these younger Iranian generations to be delusional. This was another reason that this operation had to be conducted with utmost secrecy.

These young Iranians do not understand the evil perpetrated by the United States and their lackey, the so-called state of Israel, thought Khoresani.

"We must ensure the virus we develop will kill the Jews first, and then we will bring America to its knees," Khorasani continued.

"Yes, by the will of Allah and his prophet Muhammad," responded Daghestani. "But first, our people must be made immune to the virus."

"Ackerman's bones will unlock the final DNA answers we need," replied the deputy defense minister. "Our target in Paris is perfect. We traced Ackerman's Jewish roots back to the Middle Ages. Actually, American, Belgian, and Israeli scientists did that for the world six years ago," he chuckled.

"The advances that have been made in paleovirology and genomics have been extraordinary, especially in the past two years," Khorasani added.

"Ackerman was an Ashkenazi Jew, as about eighty percent of all Jews are," Daghestani said. "You have heard of Albert Einstein. He was an Ashkenazi Jew. Their genome originates from the Middle East, and they are genetically isolated, so our task will be made easier.

"We will develop a virus far more deadly than the Spanish flu of

1918. And after more than two years with the COVID virus, many of the Americans are tired of wearing masks. This will be to our great advantage. The virus will kill—Allah willing—millions upon millions of Americans and Jews. But we must first develop a vaccine to make our people immune to our weaponized version of the Spanish flu. Ms. Ackerman's bones will provide us the last bits of knowledge we need to make sure the virus is sufficiently powerful to overcome any DNA anomalies.

"We will convince our people that the vaccine is for the common flu." He paused. "Of course, it will be *much* more than that.

"We will soon unlock the virus-resistant DNA code possessed by Ackerman. That will allow us to overcome any natural defenses she, the Ashkenazi jews, or certain Americans might have. From there, we will develop virus variants to target specific races and ethnicities, and we will have the Americans and Jew chasing their sick and dying tails. Once the virus is simultaneously released at major sporting events and airports, it will be like shooting goats in a ditch. Our made-in-Iran virus will be more like the Black Plague than COVID-19!

"Thanks be to Allah, who will bring justice against the Jews, their illegal occupation of Palestine, and the Americans who caused years of embarrassment and misery for Iran. Persia will be reestablished to its former glory!" concluded Deputy Minister Khoresani.

8.
FBI HEADQUARTERS, WASHINGTON, DC

"YOU KNOW WHY this has reached my level, right, Jack?" asked FBI deputy director Dennis Meredith.

"I do," answered FBI special agent John "Captain Jack" Morrison, a former Army officer and All East defensive lineman for the Army football team. "It's got our folks in the Bureau and over at the Agency with their radars up. This has serious implications, which could add up to a potential tier one national security threat."

"That's right, Jack. For Pete's sake, how much *more* evidence do we need to arrest this woman . . . this Avalie Zirani?" asked Meredith.

"Sir, we've ascertained the Iranian-American's communications with her Iranian handler, who is living in New Haven, Connecticut," replied Morrison. "But we haven't caught her in the act. We know that Ms. Zirani has been prominent in working with Parker Pharmaceutical in Boston and in developing the COVID-19 vaccine. She has been with the company for six years. She checked out as an excellent and very reliable employee who earned her American citizenship about seven years ago. She lived in the US for another twelve years prior to that. But that's part of our concern. She's been *too* excellent."

"What? *Too* excellent?" asked Meredith.

"Yes, too excellent. A couple of her coworkers observed that she's been spending excessive time after normal work hours in the lab. Of course, everyone had been burning the oil on finding a vaccine and booster for the COVID-19 virus, so there was a lot of overtime work being done, but it always seems like Zirani wanted to hang around long after everyone else had gone home."

"When do you think we'll be able to apprehend her?"

"We need better evidence. We've got some anecdotal information that she's after some antivirus trade secrets. No doubt, being originally from Iran makes her of concern," said Morrison. "We're eventually going to have to set up a sting or find another way to catch her with the goods. And in the process, you know better than I do, we can't tip her off beforehand. If we do, she may flat-out stop whatever nefarious work that she might be involved in, or she might expedite getting information to the Iranians. We're getting close to having enough probable cause to put handcuffs on her, but we're just not legally there yet."

"Well, we need to legally *get* there, Jack. Obviously, don't do anything rash. But the clock is ticking."

9.
NOT NORMAL

IT STARTED OUT as just another morning for Juliette Charpentier. The Suresnes cemetery superintendent's assistant was proud to work for the American Battle Monuments Commission. The ABMC managed not only the Suresnes cemetery but also many US cemeteries and monuments throughout France, Europe, and around the world. Originally from Normandy, Charpentier was forever grateful to the Americans and their allies who liberated her grandparents from the Nazi occupation in the summer of 1944.

Opening the cemetery gates, Charpentier walked up the gentle incline towards the main cemetery sanctuary building. Having covered roughly half the distance to the sanctuary, her eye caught something. It was a headstone among many other pristine white marble headstones, which, after countless steps up this pathway before, did not seem normal.

Not seeing clearly through the steadily falling rain, she squinted. Did a visitor leave some kind of a red adornment on that headstone? She walked on towards the headstone, trying to sharpen her focus.

It was not unusual for a cemetery visitor to leave a US or French flag in front of a headstone, or occasionally—as had become the tradition at Arlington National Cemetery in Washington, DC—a military challenge coin or similar small token on top of a headstone.

Charpentier knelt slowly in the wet grass, disregarding the grass and dirt stains that were sure to result on her blue pants suit.

Tilting her head slowly sideways, she read, *Death to the Jews*.

Stepping back from the headstone, she stared at the words.

Am I in a bad dream? she asked herself.

With her hands beginning to tremble, she fumbled for the cellphone in her purse.

"Mr. Roberts, this is Juliette," she began.

"Good morning, Juliette. I'm on my way. Should be there in less than fifteen minutes," the Suresnes cemetery superintendent replied. "Everything okay?"

"Monsieur, I am staring at something I cannot believe. Someone has written *Death to the Jews* on one of our Star of David headstones."

"What? *What?* Where? *On a headstone?* In English or French?" George Roberts couldn't believe what he was hearing.

"It's in English. It's on the Daniel Gelb headstone, about halfway between the gate and sanctuary," she replied.

"That's terrible. I'll be there very soon," replied the portly fifty-year-old superintendent.

Departing his Suresnes apartment and walking several paces, Roberts briefly thought to go back and get his car out of the nearby parking garage. Reconsidering, he thought that a brisk walk might actually be faster than the local Paris suburb traffic. Now he walked the fastest he'd walked in years, maybe ever.

Roberts and his assistant stared at the headstone.

"I can't believe this," were the first words from the trembling cemetery superintendent's mouth. "I've heard that anti-Semitism is present in France, and that several buildings and monuments around Paris have been desecrated over the years. But never in my lifetime did I expect that this hate would touch our American cemetery, or *any* American military cemetery in Europe, for that matter."

Charpentier stood silent, not knowing how to respond.

Looking down, Roberts noticed something unusual.

"My God. Has the grave been disturbed too?" he asked. "We have to call our cemetery headquarters and the French police, *now*."

Heading to his office with Charpentier walking beside him, Roberts was anxious.

"Juliette, please lock the main gate and put a sign on it that says *Temporarily Closed*."

Arriving at his warm and dry office, Roberts made his first phone call.

"Mr. Cairns," he began, addressing the director of all US military cemeteries in Europe and North Africa, whose office was in nearby Garches, also a Paris suburb, "this is George. We had a terrible thing happen. One of my headstones has been desecrated. It must have happened overnight."

"Desecrated? What? How?" answered the man responsible for thirty-nine US cemeteries and monuments throughout Europe and North Africa.

"The words *Death to the Jews* are written on one of our Star of David headstones. Judging by how the ground looks, the grave was likely molested as well. Oddly, however, all the sod seems to have been put back in place."

"George, I have to ask. Have you ever heard of such a thing happening to one of our US cemeteries, anywhere?" asked Cairns.

"No, sir, I have not."

"I will call the US ambassador here in Paris and the ABMC global headquarters in Washington," said Cairns, "and George, I need to you to call the French police. They will have jurisdiction in this case."

"Will do," replied Roberts.

Roberts did not yet realize that this was not the only headstone in the cemetery that had been defaced. Any thought of another headstone potentially being disturbed had been rendered too remote by the shock.

10.
SAFE HOUSE

ARMAN DARBANDI WAS HAPPY to be in his humble third-floor Paris apartment. With Hezbollah-provided cash, he had been renting it for almost three months. Farhad Gilani joined him six weeks prior from Rotterdam. The timing provided the two Hezbollah operators ample opportunity to survey the cemetery, the best routes to it and associated Paris traffic patterns. It also allowed them time to become familiar with their overall neighborhood surroundings. Darbandi's apartment was one of thousands of similar design, mostly mass produced in the 1960s and 1970s in the Saint-Denis suburb of Paris.

Each with a small kitchen, modest living room, bedroom, and single bathroom, the apartments were mainly home to North African, Middle Eastern, and South Asian immigrants, many having made their way to France as part of a mass migration in 2015 and 2016. Others had come to France as early as the 1960s.

In 2020 Paris had the largest Muslim population, roughly two million inhabitants, of any city in Europe. France was estimated to have roughly six million Muslims. The overwhelming majority were completely law-abiding and hardworking citizens, trying to raise families and make their way in prosperous Western Europe. But a small number, roughly a couple of hundred in the entire country of sixty-six million inhabitants, kept French intelligence and law enforcement officials up at night. And the Paris suburb of Saint Denis, home to hundreds of thousands of Arabs, Persians and North

Africans, provided the best place in Paris for the two Hezbollah operators to blend in.

As Darbandi and Gilani sat on the apartment floor and drank tea, Darbandi thought how different he was from Gilani. As young men they had both fought the Israelis during the war in the early 2000s. But that is where their similarities ended. Arman Darbandi had come to Lebanon in the late 1990s as a nineteen-year-old, physically fit young man and recruit with the Iranian Quds Forces. An element of the Quds Forces was in Lebanon to train small units of Hezbollah operators in terrorist tactics. After his term in the Iranian Army, Darbandi left Iran and joined Hezbollah in Lebanon.

The diminutive Gilani, on the other hand, had Iranian heritage but had been born in the Bekaa valley, a Palestinian stronghold in Lebanon. He had embraced the anti-Western and anti-Israeli cause of Hezbollah, but he was not a warrior at heart. In the war with Israel in 2006, Gilani had never harmed—let alone killed—a single Israeli. He was there for his communications expertise.

Darbandi, unlike Gilani, had received the nom de guerre, given by his fellow Hezbollah operatives, of "Jew killer." An expert in bomb making, improvised explosive devises (IED) and booby traps, Darbandi was always in the thick of the action, having somehow escaped death more than once. Later, at the behest of the Venezuelan and Iranian governments, he and Gilani became involved in criminal money-raising operations in Latin America.

Due to their common anti-American interests, President Chavez of Venezuela and President Ahedminejad of Iran had hit it off. Later, the specter of Hezbollah members entering the United States would keep border patrol and customs agents there up at night defending the country's southern borders from infiltrating terrorists.

"I am proud of our mission last night, my brother," Darbandi said to Gilani. "I know we must still deliver our cargo to Tehran, but this first part of our mission was a success. I am proud to be on a mission to avenge a century of neglect and mistreatment of our people by the Americans. American support of the continuing illegal Jewish occupation in Palestine has been criminal.

"My great-grandfather died in the Persian famine of 1917 to 1919, when the British and Russians occupied our country and left it in shambles," continued Darbandi. "In Khuzestan, the provincial birthplace of Persia, the British occupiers created such mayhem that food distribution completely broke down. In the northeast, in Khorasan, the Russians blocked our roads and stole our food supplies too."

"That must have been a nightmare," replied Gilani.

Darbandi, having spent plenty of time researching the mistreatment of his people, and with the intellect to store the information, continued.

"In 1918, we asked the Americans for two million dollars to help feed our starving children. The Americans refused. More than *two million* Persians died in that famine. Many died from the Spanish Flu, but thousands upon thousands died from starvation."

"And now, the Americans and the Jews will get what they deserve!" replied the fawning Gilani. "And if they ask for the vaccine, we will refuse, even if they offer to pay two *trillion* dollars!" exclaimed the Hezbollah operative. "Death to America and death to Israel!"

11.
RARE PHONE CALL

"JEAN-PAUL," said French National Police captain Laurent Lefevre to his colleague, Lieutenant Jean-Paul Schlumberger, "I just got the most unusual phone call. Our local American military cemetery reported that one of their headstones has been defaced. Have you ever heard of such a thing?"

"Concerning an *American* cemetery? No, I have not, sir," replied Schlumberger. "I know we have had incidents, many involving anti-Semitic hate crimes. They have occurred in French cemeteries and on monuments throughout Paris and France. But I never thought we'd hear from our local American friends about such a thing. I thought maybe we'd someday be asked to assist in a medical emergency for one of the elderly American visitors to the cemetery, but not this."

"Jean-Paul, I will leave straightaway for the cemetery. In the meantime, call our Paris headquarters and let them know the basics. If there is anything to this, they will want to know. Since this involves the Americans, our Suresnes headquarters will want to inform the general directorate for internal security," said Captain Lefevre, referring to the law enforcement branch of the National Police, commonly called the DGSI.

The DGSI, Direction Générale de la Sécurité Intérieure, newly named and reorganized in 2018, fell directly under France's ministry of the interior. The DGSI was responsible for France's domestic or "interior" security, law enforcement and intelligence operations and was considered to be France's rough equivalent to the US Federal Bureau of Investigation (FBI).

Lefevre knew it was not typically his place to be a first responder to the report of a crime in his district. That was normally left to a lower-ranking police official. However, this involved the Americans and their cemetery, which the people of the Paris suburb of Suresnes had been proud to host for a century. LeFevre would take this on himself.

The French police captain had attended several ceremonies at the American cemetery, and he knew something about the cemetery's history. It was the first location—of what would eventually be twenty-one such cemeteries—for a US military cemetery in Europe. The Suresnes site had personally been reconnoitered on foot by Army general John J. "Blackjack" Pershing, US commander of all Allied Expeditionary Forces on the Western Front in World War I. He would go on to establish the foundation for the American Battle Monuments Commission.

As he departed his massive stone-block police station with a driver and police sergeant accompanying him, Captain Lefevre thought what many in France still did, and what French children in Normandy learned in their schools.

We are America's oldest ally. We should never forget the American sacrifices for France's freedom in two world wars.

Captain Lefevre and his accompanying police sergeant, Sergeant Pascal Giroux, approached the American cemetery gate. They could not help but discuss the dismal the weather was on this late Paris morning.

"Five straight days of this *merde*, sir," said Giroux to his boss. "And three more days are expected."

"Yes, it's been lousy, Pascal, even for Paris weather standards." Lefevre chuckled. "I'm already looking forward to Bastille Day," he added, referring to the July 14 national holiday and parade that marked the beginning of France's main summer vacation period.

After walking through the pristine cemetery gate, the two police officers could see three individuals on the main walkway just up the hill. The trio was obviously anticipating their arrival.

Raising his voice due to the incessant rain, cemetery superintendent George Roberts addressed the approaching French police officers.

"*Bonjour*, gentlemen," he began, quickly recognizing Captain Lefevre.

"This is Mr. David Cairns our AMBC director from Garches," announced Roberts.

"My pleasure to meet you, sir," said Captain Lefevre to the AMBC director.

"Likewise," responded Cairns.

"And this is Sergeant Giroux." The threesome nodded.

"May I see the headstone?" asked Lefevre.

"I'll lead the way," replied Superintendent Roberts.

As the group approached the headstone, Lefevre could already see the lumpy ground over the grave. Next, his attention focused on the red writing.

After a moment of observing and pondering, he asked Charpentier the first question.

"Is this exactly how you found things?"

"It is," responded Charpentier. Looking at her boss, she added, "We have done nothing except place a sign on the gate, stating that the cemetery is closed."

"That's good," responded Lefevre. "We'll need to keep it that way, indefinitely."

"Indefinitely? How long might that mean?" asked Cairns.

"I can't say for sure, but it will need to be there for at least a week, maybe two," he added, knowing the latter part of his response was far more likely. "The investigators from the DGSI normally like to be very thorough."

"Well, that's quite a long time," responded Cairns. "Isn't there a way we might modify that?"

"Maybe," responded Lefevre, seeking to mollify Cairns. "But right now, it's too early to say. In the meantime, there are some things I need you to do to safeguard this site.

"Number one: make sure the cemetery stays closed to the public until further notice. Number two: to protect the affected area— this crime scene—from view from the street, or from any form of trespassing, even by cemetery workers here, please erect a two-meter-high wall—simple plywood will do, or even a tent—around this entire gravesite. The walls should encompass the headstone and the entire grave area. Number three: please leave enough room, at least two meters, around the grave and the headstone for investigators to do whatever work they'll need to do. Any questions?"

"None from me," responded Roberts, looking directly at his boss for confirmation.

Cairns shook his head from side to side.

"If you do have any in the future," added Lefevre, "please refer them to Sergeant Giroux or me directly. He will know exactly what is needed."

The two police officers then headed down the cemetery's paved path to the gate.

"We'll have to dig into that grave to see what else might have happened. But I'll turn this over to the DGSI now," stated Lefevre to his police sergeant as they exited the cemetery.

When he reached their police car, Lefevre remembered that he had wanted to ask Superintendent Roberts if the entire cemetery had been checked by the cemetery staff. After all, similar transgressions might be present elsewhere on the cemetery grounds. He made a mental note to follow up later. He knew that when the French Ministry of the Interior got word of this, that there would be very high French government interest in this incident that had occurred on the American cemetery in Paris.

12.
KEEP IT THAT WAY

"MADAME," THE HIGH-RANKING French government official began, "there is something I'd like you to take a look at. It involves the Americans."

Deputy Minister of the Interior Thierry Fleuet handed the one-paragraph summary of the Suresnes cemetery report to his boss. She read it slowly.

Within two hours of the incident report arriving at the National Police headquarters in Paris, it had reached the French minister of the interior herself. The rough equivalent of the US attorney general, France's top domestic law enforcement and intelligence officer, Minister Claudette Laplace had risen quickly through the French government executive ranks. She had graduated from the Sorbonne Law School in Paris. At the Sorbonne, she had met many international students, including Americans.

Her professional reputation that of a tenacious, dedicated, and competent professional, who had served in both law enforcement and intelligence roles within France's government, was made mainly through France's decades-long struggle with international terrorism.

"I know that although this incident *might* prove to not be much more than a petty crime—or a hate crime at the very worst, which is bad enough—this involves the *Americans*," she told her deputy.

Minister Laplace had not personally met her US counterpart,

but she was fully aware that the French and the US had maintained an excellent working relationship for several years, if not decades.

Locally in Paris, Minister Laplace—and more importantly, her leadership team—had developed an excellent relationship with the US embassy, and more specifically, the US legal attaché to the French government, who represented the US FBI to France.

Minister Laplace had only met and spoken with the US legal attaché twice, but Minister Laplace's team had assured the minister that Ms. Sanders was "a serious, top-tier individual and representative of the FBI and the United States."

"Thierry," she continued, addressing her deputy minister, "you were right to bring this to my attention. We must respond promptly and with the best of intentions. Make sure the DGSI send their best people to examine this case. It *may not* turn out to be a big thing, but my gut tells me it just might. It's too unusual—not for *us*, unfortunately, but for the Americans. I've never heard of an American military grave being defaced in France. Our relations with the Americans are excellent, and I'd like to keep it that way."

"Absolutely, madame," responded Fleuet.

"And make sure that DGSI director Lardans informs the US legal attaché at the US embassy that we will do our utmost to follow up on this," continued Laplace. "Hopefully, it's just some punks who did something very stupid, but my initial impression says otherwise."

As her deputy was exiting the room, the French minister added, "And I will personally call US Ambassador Hunter as well, to assure her of our support."

"Yes, madame, understood," came the deputy's parting words.

"And, Thierry, one final thing."

"What's that?"

"Just like after 9/11, when we assigned curbside officers to protect the exterior of the US embassy and to support the Marines there, I want to assign at least two security officers to be on duty at all times at each US military cemetery in France. We will do that at least for the next six months. If it needs to be longer, we'll re-evaluate, and I'll make the appropriate decision when required."

13.
THE ENTIRE CEMETERY?

FRENCH NATIONAL POLICE captain Anton Perrier was excited and proud. He had just been told by his boss that he was being sent to investigate the incident reported by the local French police in Suresnes. Perrier spoke fluent English and had consistently performed well in his career. He had a reputation as a dedicated, competent, and wise-beyond-his-years leader who relentlessly pursued all cases in his path. Now, he was serving in the lofty headquarters of the DGSI.

In his late thirties, he thought that it might be a bit over the top—not for someone of his rank but from where he was working in the DGSI headquarters—to be sent on this reconnaissance mission. It was likely going to be a mission that would reveal nothing more than some wayward teenager doing something very stupid, if hateful. Nonetheless, he felt good about being handpicked to be the first on the scene from the DGSI headquarters.

Arriving early in the morning and entering the cemetery gate, the police captain headed directly for the small welcoming party. They were standing on the main walkway, perhaps thirty to forty yards from the grave of everyone's concern.

"Good morning, everyone," the captain addressed the assembled small group of five. "Mind if I have a look?" He gestured to the defaced Star of David headstone.

"Certainly," responded Roberts, the cemetery superintendent.

"As you might know, my assistant, Juliette Charpentier, discovered it yesterday morning. As soon as you finish surveying this spot, we will construct a plywood wall around it to shield it from outside view, but with sufficient room on the inside for any investigation work."

"That is an excellent idea," stated Perrier. "Did you come up with it?"

"No, I did not. Those were the instructions we received yesterday from Captain Lefevre, our local Suresnes police captain," Roberts said.

Captain Perrier smiled as he pulled his glasses from his shirt pocket and surveyed the ground around the headstone.

"I happen to know Laurent Lefevre," he said. "We were promoted about the same time. He's a good officer, and you have done right by doing exactly what he told you."

Perrier removed his glasses and asked the group a general question.

"Were any other similar such markings found?" he asked, nodding to the headstone.

"Uh, in the cemetery?" responded Superintendent Roberts, immediately wishing he could pull back that dull response.

Before Roberts could add another word, the police captain responded.

"Yes, here. This cemetery. Have the entire grounds been checked?"

"Well, no, they haven't. But we haven't observed anything else like this since yesterday morning," Roberts said.

"You should thoroughly check the entire cemetery. It would be a good precaution," said Perrier.

Perrier didn't have a hunch that they would find anything else in the cemetery. He did think, however, that checking the entire cemetery would represent thorough police work. France had experienced anti-Semitism through the years, though rarely as neat and clean as reflected by the writing on the headstone. Normally, the tools used to express anti-Semitism and to deface cemeteries or monuments, included a hammer or hatchet or sledgehammer, or some other blunt instrument, often accompanied by loosely but generously applied spray paint.

"Okay, we will do that," answered Roberts.

As Captain Perrier departed the Suresnes cemetery, he wrote two items in his cellphone notes app: *1. Get grapho-analyst to the cemetery soonest. 2. Have the Daniel Gelb grave fully checked out.*

14.
THE INTERNET CAFÉ

TWENTY-FOUR HOURS since the first phase of their mission at the American cemetery had been completed, Arman Darbandi knew he had another twenty-four hours before he had to report to his Athens-based handler. To minimize the chance of telephonic interception by the French, Americans, or other European intelligence agencies, the ground rules included reporting only once every forty-eight hours, using a "burner" cellphone, and then only if in absolute distress, using anonymous email addresses.

After each report, the next reporting would be reset to forty-eight hours. No report within a forty-eight-hour period meant that one or both of the Hezbollah operatives was in extreme danger or had been compromised. If this were to happen, the Athens-based handler was required to notify his contact in Istanbul, Turkey, who had a direct link through the Iranian embassy in Ankara, Tukey, into the Iranian Ministry of Intelligence. This final link was critical for keeping a handful of rogue officials in the Iranian government informed of the operation's progress.

Given the near ubiquitous availability of cellphones as well as internet and email access, Parisian internet cafes had become difficult to find. But a few had somehow survived. They mostly catered to the recently arrived immigrants in the Saint-Denis suburb who wanted to stay in touch with their families and friends outside of France.

Many could not afford either an iPhone or a laptop, let alone the telephone or a reliable connection service.

As Arman entered the internet café just four blocks from his Saint-Denis suburb apartment, he was happy that two computer terminals were available. He had visited here a few times over the previous three months to do some rather uninteresting internet searches, as well as to send a handful of emails to friends in France. But the place made him uncomfortable. He surmised that it could be under French police surveillance. But this was still the best way to communicate to Navid, his Hezbollah intermediary located in Athens, Greece.

Beginning in late 2012 and into 2013, when Greece's economic crisis began to severely affect the average Greek citizen, Hezbollah members went to work in Greece using tactics they had honed in Lebanon. They focused on providing social services and basic needs such as food, medicine, and zero-interest loans to distraught Greek elderly and families ; it was the best means of gaining the public confidence of destitute Greek citizens. Many Greeks came to believe Navid's purpose was purely charitable, not knowing that Hezbollah social and monetary gains translated to funds for terrorist activities. As a result, it was easy for Navid to move around Athens under the guise of being a social angel.

Using their prearranged email addresses and language codes, Arman typed in his email message into terminal six of the internet café.

> Navid,
> The nân bread one can find here in Saint-Denis is pretty good, and if you look hard enough you can even find sangak. Surprisingly, it is just as good here as it is back home.
> The weather in Paris, however, has not been good. Too much rain and too cold for my blood.
> You should pay me a visit someday. Except for the cooler weather, I really think you'd like it here. After all, it's Paris!
> Be well, my brother.
> Arman

Within two hours, Navid called his contact at the Iranian embassy in Ankara, who relayed the positive news to Tehran's Ministry of Intelligence. Phase I of the operation was complete.

Navid's simple email response to Arman, which Arman received at his next day's visit to the internet café, read,

> My Brother Arman,
> You are right, Paris is too cool for me now. I much prefer the warmer Athens climate!
> In the name of Allah, be well and do not catch a cold!
> Navid

Arman felt good knowing the first coded report of the operation had been received, understood, and acknowledged.

15.
MONTEREY, CALIFORNIA
SEVEN YEARS BEFORE PARIS

CAPTAIN JAKE FORTINA was anxious to see his wife, Faith. With seven hours each day in the classroom and at least two hours of homework at night, studying Farsi at the US Defense Language Institute (DLI) in Monterey, California, had been intense. Faith, on the other hand, had decided to stay with Kimberly and Jake, Jr., at her parents' large home just north of Houston.

Jake's extended time away from home—as well as Faith's understandable career desires—did not make for the easiest of marriages. As an Army couple, it was a challenge to reconcile the pressures of deployments and moves while rearing two children. It was often understood that one of the parents, if he or she had professional or personal aspirations, must give up something to make the marriage work in a military environment, and especially when assigned overseas.

Their relationship had taken a major turn for the better when both decided that no matter their circumstances and challenges, they still loved each other and were going to make it work, no matter what. Faith could have moved out to Monterey with the kids, but decided against it.

"I don't want to have to move the kids *again* after only nine months in one place. The instability is not good for the kids," Faith told her parents.

The thought of becoming a foreign area officer (FAO) had been in the back of Jake's mind for a couple of years. He couldn't quite put his finger on the exact reason why he wanted to work with international military allies. Maybe it was his grandfather's service in the French Foreign Legion? Maybe it was his interest in and aptitude for learning foreign languages?

Heck, maybe it goes all the way back to West Point? he pondered.

Because of his grandfather's service with France, Jake was fascinated by the European military officers who came to the American colonies to pledge their allegiance to George Washington and his poorly trained and equipped Continental Army. They included Colonel Gilbert du Motier (the Marquis de Lafayette, later promoted to Major General by Washington and the Continental Congress); French General Jean-Baptiste Donatien de Vimeur, comte de Rochambeau; Admiral François Joseph Paul de Grasse, comte de Grasse, also of France; Baron Friedrich Wilhelm von Steuben of Prussia; and Colonel Thaddeus Kosciusko of Poland (later promoted to brigadier general by the Continental Congress). Jake knew of all their stories and how they risked all to serve the American revolutionary cause against the then-greatest military force on the planet.

Jake and Faith also thought that maybe this new service route, which Faith enthusiastically approved of, even though it would present different challenges to their marriage as two-thirds of the available assignments were overseas, would allow more stability for his growing family. In his first ten years in the Army, he had been deployed to combat zones four times, for a total of three and a half years away from Faith and the kids.

Jake clearly met all the Army's requirements for becoming a FAO, in essence a strategic scout for US Army and Department of Defense leaders. He had a strong track record as a junior officer, a high aptitude for learning foreign languages, and the academic potential to complete a master's degree in international affairs at a reputable university.

The international working environment appealed to Jake, too. He loved leading soldiers, and his heart ached at the thought that he'd never again have the opportunity to be as close to his magnificent soldiers as he once was as the player-coach of a twelve-man A-Team, or as platoon leader or company commander. But he knew that the longer he stayed in the Army, the farther he would get from direct contact with them, particularly the sergeants, who he highly respected and loved serving with. Most of his time during his second decade in the Army would be spent as a staff officer, with senior command opportunities being few and far between, and then typically only for two years at a time. He decided he needed to make a clean break.

Learning Farsi, his third foreign language after French and Italian, Jake realized he had been gifted with an excellent ear for learning and speaking foreign languages. His time in Army Special Forces had solidified his interest in working in the international realm. Now, with the opportunity for US embassy duty or service on a major US overseas command such as US European Command or US Central Command, Captain Fortina thought this new Army career field would be an interesting, challenging, and useful way to continue to serve.

As Jake looked out of his condo on a typically cool and foggy Pacific Coast evening, he was excited about the upcoming long weekend with Faith. She was leaving the kids with her parents, and this weekend would be just for the two of them on the idyllic Monterey, California, coast. Faith was finishing up her MBA degree at Rice University and didn't want to be away from the kids too long. In less than eighteen hours she'd be with Jake in Monterey.

Sitting on his living room couch, Jake thought of the Chart House restaurant as his first choice for a romantic dinner venue. It was one of the places he'd taken Faith to during a weekend getaway to Melbourne, Florida, some ten years earlier.

While considering dining options, Jake's cellphone lit up. It was "Big John" Novak, Faith's father. Jake had gotten along very well over the years with Faith's father and her mother, Mary. Big John Novak was a retired Texas rancher who had struck oil on his property, almost going broke in the '80s, and then making it big time after that, turning ranching into more of a hobby.

As Texas ranchers go, the self-made oil and gas millionaire was cut from a Hollywood script. His nickname was originally John Wayne. But the humble John Novak chafed at it, always telling friends and family, in his smooth-as-whiskey and ever-so-slight Houstonian drawl, "There'll only ever be one John Wayne, and I ain't him!"

"Jake, this is John."

Jake sat bolt upright on his living room couch.

"Yes, sir," responded Jake.

"I don't know how to tell you this, Jake," said Big John, his voice barely squeaking out the words, "but Faith and those two little angels are gone. They're with the Lord now. They were in a terrible accident. Some young man in a big pickup broadsided 'em. You're the first person we called."

"What? *What*? That can't be. What *happened*?"

"All we know is that a big pickup truck ran a red light on a nearby county road tonight. It was dusk and raining hard. Faith was bringing Kimberly and Junior home from Junior's soccer match. They were only about three miles from the house when they got hit, Jake. Mary wasn't feeling well, so we didn't go to tonight's game. I feel god awful, son," said Big John, now sobbing. "Two state troopers just came to the house. Faith and Kimberly were pronounced dead at the scene. Junior was alive when they left the crash site, but he didn't make it to the hospital."

A deep, lonely, and terrible silence transcended Jake's soul.

"When did it happen?"

"A little over two hours ago," said Big John.

"Dad," said Jake, barely able to speak. "This can't be true. They are the most beautiful people God ever put on this planet. I don't know why God would let this happen."

"We don't either," answered Big John. "We don't either."

"I'm coming home, Dad. I will get there as soon as I can. Give Mom a big hug for me."

John had Jake on speakerphone, and he could hear Mary weeping in the background.

"Bye, I love you both," said Jake.

Time stood still as Jake fell forward from his couch into a kneeling and sobbing heap. Years of training and combat taught him to keep his emotions in check. As a leader, he had to. Not this time. Tears—and utterances to Jesus from the depths of his soul—flowed with no attempt to control them.

16.
GILANI DEPARTS

ON HIS THIRD VISIT to the internet café, Arman Darbandi received a coded email directing the implementation of a contingency plan. His partner, Farhad Gilani, was to return to Holland with Ruth Ackerman's femur bone, cross the English Channel, get to London, and catch a flight to Istanbul where he would meet with an Iranian contact. The contact would then take receipt of the bone and fly with it to Tehran.

Darbandi, on the other hand, would get his directives from his Athens-stationed handler soon. But for now, Gilani needed to be on his way.

Gilani had a simple, black backpack for this contingency. It included three days of the most essential items and clothing. The nondescript bag was never to be let out of his possession. Checking and sending a suitcase—one that contained Ruth Ackerman's femur bone—at the airport would present too many risks. However, not all international airports had good luggage security once a bag was checked. If he was ever required to open the carryon bag, Gilani would have a good alibi for the human bone inside of it.

"Go with Allah," said Darbandi to Gilani as he was about to drive away to his Dutch destination.

"I shall, my brother Arman," responded Farhad. "My destination is not such a long drive, so the time will pass easily."

Darbandi was relieved that his Lebanon-born Hezbollah partner was on his way with Ruth Ackerman's femur bone. This ensured a redundant means for getting at least one of Ruth Ackerman bones safely to Tehran. Darbandi now felt the full weight of his mission to get Ruth Ackerman's hip bone, now in his sole possession, back to Iran and the rogue Iranian authorities who awaited it.

The five-hour drive from Paris to Holland's seaside village of Westkappelle was uneventful. Since France and Holland were both part of the European Union, there was no border check. To cross from France into the Netherlands was as easy as driving from Michigan to Indiana or from California to Nevada. Surrounded on three sides by the sea, Westkappelle was easily accessible by land or by sea.

Being late spring, even Westkappelle's hardy Dutch natives thought it too early, save for a couple of exceptionally warm days, to go to its beaches or to venture into its frigid English Channel waters. With much of Westkappelle surrounded by a huge dike, any morning boats approaching its shoreline would be seen only by the occasional passersby, who would not give it a second thought. Given the busy sea passage and many boats nearby, barely an eyebrow would be lifted for a Dutch-flagged boat.

Although the UK government had decided to withdraw from the European Union, there was a transition period, rendering the Channel easy to cross with minimal customs or coast guard scrutiny, at least for the next few months.

After Gilani checked into the Hotel Conroy, conveniently close to Westkappelle's shoreline, he was happy his two fellow Hezbollah operatives were already in the suite. Having traveled to Westkappelle from Amsterdam, one operative would drive Farhad's rental car back to the original rental location near Gilani's neighborhood of Schilderswijk, a suburb of the Hague. The other Hezbollah member would follow him and pick him up after a late-night drop-off of the key and car.

"My brothers," said Gilani as Hashem opened the door. "It's good to see you in our lovely little vacation spot."

"It is good to see you, Farhad," answered Hashem and Mahmoud, almost simultaneously.

"Tomorrow will be a beautiful day," stated Hashem. "Your rendezvous is set."

17.
HOUSTON, TEXAS:
SEVEN YEARS BEFORE PARIS

JAKE FORTINA FELT two strong hands clutch his shoulders from behind. Sitting in the north Houston chapel's front row with Big John and Mary, he turned around and looked up. He saw his old friend's eyes welling up. Jake stood and turned towards the church's center aisle and his friend. Chet Parker, his old buddy from Fort Benning, managed to say, "I'm so sorry, brother."

Chet's wife, Cindy, standing next to Chet and fighting back tears, was not quite sure what to say. She managed to offer a hug to Jake. "My deepest condolences to you. I know Faith and the kids loved you very much and we do, too." Almost two hundred friends and family of Jake, Big John, and Mary were seated quietly behind them, observing the moment.

It was Cindy who had introduced Jake to Faith just before the Alabama game at Auburn University. The last time the two men saw each other was when they graduated from the US Army Infantry Officers Basic Course at Fort Benning. Chet had gone off to complete the US Army Ranger School in a winter environment, and then to upstate New York to serve with the Army's 10th Mountain Division. In a subsequent assignment in Afghanistan, Chet had been awarded the Bronze Star Medal with *V* for valor device for running through enemy fire to rescue one of his wounded and exposed soldiers.

Jake and Faith had moved on from Fort Benning to Italy. While they had subsequently served in different locations around the world, Jake, Chet, Cindy, and Faith had managed to stay connected and remain friends. When Chet and Cindy learned about the tragedy, they did not hesitate to travel to Houston from Fort Bliss, Texas, where Chet was now serving as the battalion operations officer in a mechanized infantry battalion of the 1st Armored Division.

Jake sat back down in the pew and looked at Big John, who was staring at the big wooden cross behind the chapel's altar. Jake thought that his father-in-law had aged seven years in seven days. As for himself, Jake wasn't sure how he would, or if he even could, get through this nightmare. It wasn't fair. Losing one of his soldiers in Afghanistan had caused emotional pain, but in that case, he had his nuclear family to come back to. They helped him deal with the loss. But now he was alone to face the world.

A man of increasing faith, Jake had spent the week since their death struggling to understand why a supposedly loving God would let something so terrible happen. Sleep came hard, and when he did doze off, he soon awakened hoping it was all just a bad dream. His feelings had gyrated between anger, sadness, and guilt. But it was anger, with a degree of guilt, that he felt most. *Why did God let this happen?* Jake sensed that it would take much of the rest of his life—or perhaps his next life—to answer that question, if it was answerable at all.

The thought of his early desires to serve his country and to have to leave his family for extended periods of time racked him with guilt. Would this indescribable tragedy have happened if he had taken a different path? Had he spent enough time with Jake, Jr., and Kimberly? Had he been selfish in following his desire to serve something bigger than himself, rather than leave the Army to choose a job that would have assured more time with his family?

Some ten years prior, Faith had positively rocked his world. She had introduced him to feelings deep inside that Jake had never known before. Although she was starting to build her own career accomplishments, Faith had deferred just about everything for Jake and the kids. She had been a wonderful mother.

Kimberly and Jake, Jr., had been great kids, too. While they were never happy about leaving a location, they had always adjusted well to every new home the Army had sent them to. The images of Jake and Jake, Jr. kicking a soccer ball together, and Jake and Kimberly skiing together down a mountain swirled in Jake's mind. But now, through absolutely no fault of their own, they were gone, instantly taken on a Texas country road. In their place was a gaping, dark, and indescribably painful void. It was incomprehensible to Jake why he, a soldier who had faced mortal danger, was still here, but the three people he loved most were gone.

Would hope and joy ever return to Jake Fortina's life?

18.
SECOND LOOK

CAPTAIN JEAN-LUC PERRIER did not expect to return so quickly to the Suresnes cemetery. But it just didn't make sense.

Has anti-Semitism become so extreme in France that these anti-Semites have resorted to desecrating and robbing the graves of Jews? he wondered.

This time, he brought a handwriting expert with him, as well as someone to inspect the first grave.

A second desecrated grave had been found by cemetery workers. This one said, *Death to the Americans.* From the cemetery's entrance, the second grave was in the far back and right corner. Perrier understood why it had been initially missed, especially given the steady rain and closure of the cemetery after the discovery of the first grave.

"Gentlemen, here is the first grave," he told his colleagues. "I'm going to have a look at the second location. Do your best to find out what you can."

As the two inspectors entered the newly boarded off area of the first grave, Perrier headed over to the second grave. Cemetery superintendent George Roberts intercepted him along the way.

"Captain Perrier, you were right," said Roberts. "We checked out the entire cemetery and found this second grave. It also has a Star of David headstone, and the gravesite looks exactly like the first one.

The ground has obviously been disturbed, and there is red writing on the headstone. It says, *Death to the Americans.*"

"That is terrible, Mr. Roberts," replied Perrier.

As Perrier and Roberts approached the headstone, Perrier saw red writing on the headstone, most likely done by the same person, with the grass and dirt showing subtle signs of alteration of Ruth Ackerman's grave.

"Other than the words on the headstone, there's no difference in the outside appearance of the two graves," said Perrier.

"The workers said the same thing," replied Roberts.

Perrier walked back towards the original grave of Daniel Gelb, located nearest the entrance and memorial sanctuary. Along the way, he informed Roberts to take the same action as was taken for the first grave.

"Board it up or put a tent over it as soon as possible, and only allow access to our investigators," said Perrier. "And please continue to keep this confidential. I don't want passersby to see the desecrated graves from the street."

"Understood," replied Roberts.

Arriving back at the first grave, Perrier spoke to the investigators accompanying him—both now on their knees observing the soil and the headstone.

"Gentlemen, when you are finished here—surprise—a second grave looks much like this one," said Perrier, now pointing to the back of the cemetery. "Be sure to thoroughly check it out as well."

"Will do, Captain," replied the handwriting expert as the other investigator nodded affirmatively.

After Perrier departed the cemetery, Jean-Paul Rafael, the second investigator who stayed behind, focused on the task at hand.

"What am I looking at?" he asked himself as he looked at the lumpy grass and soil area, which was slightly larger than the casket buried below. "More importantly, what am I looking *for*?"

He closely followed what appeared to be lines in the grass and topsoil.

The sod has obviously been tampered with, he thought.

Using his bare hands, Rafael tried to get a firm grip on what appeared to be a piece of sod, a rather heavy one at that. Sure enough, he was able to lift a piece about two feet by one foot in size. Trying to keep pieces of it from crumbling off, he carefully set the sod to the side of the grave.

Eventually, he carefully lifted all the pieces of sod to the side.

What the hell is going on here? he wondered.

Examining the soil beneath, it looked to be completely undisturbed.

Debating with himself whether to dig below, he finally decided he had to.

Perhaps the soil was somehow neatly replaced, and the remains below have indeed been disturbed? Investigator Rafael asked himself.

Taking the harder right instead of the easier wrong, which would be to forego confirming his suspicions and to just go home, he decided to dig.

"This is honest work," he muttered after about forty minutes of steady digging.

Over two hours later, he'd reached the top of the casket.

As he removed the final covering of dirt and inspected the casket's hinges, confirming that they were fully intact and that the casket was still sealed. Soaked in sweat but now relieved that the casket had not been molested, he used his portable ladder to exit the grave.

Rafael joked to himself as headed over to the second grave. *I should have become a graphic analyst,* referring to his handwriting expert partner who had departed the cemetery some two hours earlier. *Those people have it easy.*

As he examined the Ruth Ackerman grave, Rafael observed the same features in the grass and soil that he had examined at the Daniel Gelb plat. The sod had been neatly cut out in the same dimensions and patterns as those of the Gelb grave.

Staring at the grave, Rafael decided there would be no internal mental debate about further digging now. It was getting far too late in the afternoon, and it was thirty minutes past his official duty hours.

I'm not going to dig for hours through a bunch of wet, hard-packed soil again, only to discover that nothing has been disturbed, the exhausted investigator thought. *I'll come back and take a closer look at the Ackerman grave tomorrow, or perhaps the next day.*

19.
HEATHROW AIRPORT

THE LATE 1980S vintage Beechcraft 1050 yacht, with its thirty-five-foot length, had plenty of range and power to take Farhad Gilani and his two fellow Hezbollah members from the Dutch seaside village of Westkappelle to the English seaside village of Margate. Registered and flagged in Holland, the vessel made crossing the English Channel in mild weather no more treacherous than crossing Lake Michigan on a calm summer's day.

Gilani's handoff to two new Hezbollah operatives, an overnight stay in a London suburb hotel, and the trip to Heathrow Airport went as planned.

Awaiting his turn to go through the airport security scanner, he was anxious about his carry-on bag and whether it would get through the adjacent scanning belt without getting flagged.

"Okay, step through," said the British security agent, looking directly at Gilani.

He complied.

After stepping through the scanner, Gilani was relieved. No alarms.

Standing behind the British security agent was a British border police officer. Gilani noticed the officer whisper something in the security agent's ear. The agent then looked at Gilani.

"Sir, please step over here," said the security agent. "My colleague will do a follow-up check."

Another agent told Gilani to raise his arms and "stand fast" as he scanned Gilani's entire body with a handheld scanner.

Again, relieved the scanner made no alarming beeps or sounds, Gilani was told to proceed as the agent nodded to the conveyor belt where his black bag should soon appear.

Within minutes, another security guard, this one standing behind the conveyor belt, had placed his hands upon Gilani's black backpack.

Looking at Gilani, he asked, "Is this your backpack?"

"Yes, it is," replied Gilani, trying to appear calm.

Opening the bag in front of him, the security agent quickly checked the back compartment. He then went into the large inside pocket. The security agent acted as if that was where he intended to look all along.

Feeling the object, the security agent slowly removed it. Unwrapping an outer white plastic bag, he delicately exposed clear plastic around what appeared to be a bone of about fifteen inches in length.

"What is *this*?" he asked.

"It's a bone," responded Gilani.

"What *kind* of bone?" asked the agent.

"A human bone," responded Gilani.

"A human bone? Why do you have it?" asked the agent.

"I bought it at a flea market in Paris," responded Gilani.

"You bought a *human bone* at a flea market in Paris?"

"Yes, I did, in Paris," confirmed Gilani.

"Please step over here," the agent directed, pointing to a small area near the end of the conveyor belt.

Putting on his shoes and belt, Gilani observed the security agent speaking to another individual. Within minutes, a British Border Force officer, now accompanied by a second officer who seemed to come out of nowhere, approached Gilani.

"Please come with us," said the officer.

As his heart raced, Gilani was led by the two customs officials to a separate room. It was sparsely furnished with a large rectangular table in the center and four chairs, two on each side.

Gilani was seated in the room for about five minutes when the two British officers came back in. He was getting anxious about where their discussion might lead.

"So, you say this is a human bone that you purchased in a flea market in Paris?" asked the British Border Force customs officer.

"Yes, it is," replied Gilani.

"Do you have a receipt for the purchase?"

"No, I do not. Receipts are not exactly in great abundance at a Paris flea market," answered Gilani.

"What is the origin of this . . . bone?" asked the officer.

"The seller promised me that it was from World War I, from the Verdun battlefield," said Gilani. "As you might know, the French have a massive building at Verdun that is full of human bones, tens of thousands of them, from the gruesome battle there. People still find human bones in the area, all the time."

"Oh, do they now? And what exactly is your interest in this bone?" asked the customs officer.

"It's to make a lamp," replied Gilani.

"A lamp? Are you *serious*? Like a desk lamp?" The officer and his partner had puzzled looks. "You are going to make a *lamp* from this bone?"

"Yes, I am serious," said Farhad. "It's *really* to make a lamp. There is an entire market for lamps crafted from human bones. You might think I have a curious, maybe even sick, sense of humor, but c'mon, sir, the British do as well, don't they?"

"You are bloody serious, aren't you?" the agent asked. "People actually like to make lamps from human bones, do they?"

"Yes, they do," answered Gilani. "Even chandeliers."

"Well, why Verdun? Why France?" asked the officer.

"I like military history, and I am especially interested in World War I history," he said. "Verdun was the most horrific battle of the war."

"If you like World War I military history, can you name a major battle that the British fought in?"

Gilani's face drew blank, as the officer waited for him to name perhaps the infamous Battle of the Somme, where the British had over fifty-seven thousand casualties in one day, including almost twenty thousand killed, or the First Battle of the Marne, or perhaps the Battle of Gallipoli.

"Well, no, I'm more of a German-French military historian," replied a now perspiring Gilani.

Hesitating for a moment, the officer then said, "We see you are flying to Istanbul. What is your business there, to buy more bones?"

"No," replied Farhad. "I'm going there to visit a couple of friends. Of course, Istanbul has the Grand Bazaar, so if I come across something interesting, I might buy it. But that is not my purpose."

"Okay," said the customs officer. "I'll be back."

As he left the room, the officer's colleague, still seated, asked the Hezbollah operative if he wanted a bottle of water. Gilani said no and the officer stepped out as well. Gilani was left alone but visible through the one-way viewing glass of the spartanly furnished room.

In his office cubicle down the hallway, the British border police customs officer pondered this Iranian with the human bone.

I've seen some weird rubbish in my time but never a human bone, he thought. *This making of lamps with human bones can't be a real thing.*

Consulting the Interpol or Europol police databases with no result, British border police officer Tom Shanahan decided to consult Google, which quickly filled his computer screen with countless photos of lamps and chandeliers and websites featuring human bones— "and even human skin for lampshades, for God's sake."

After a moment of stunned silence, Shanahan called to his colleague and friend, Glenn Christian, in an adjacent cubicle.

"Hey, Glenn, did you know there is an entire market for human bones—and even skin, for God's sake—to make lamps and chandeliers and such?"

"Tom, *what the hell* are you babbling about?" responded Christian.

"Bones, freaking human bones, as lamps!"

Christian walked over and looked at his friend's desktop computer screen.

"What pure bollocks," he responded.

Shanahan had seen many contraband items, including those from living or dead animals and reptiles, which someone had tried to either bring into or take out of England and the UK. These included elephant ivory, tiger's teeth or paws, endangered sea tortoise shells, and other such sundry illegal items from mammals and reptiles. They were highly sought by various illegal collectors from around the globe.

But a human bone? This was a first.

Shanahan again checked United Kingdom, Europol, and Interpol police databases concerning "Farhad Gilani" to see if anything came up. Nothing did. Gilani's Dutch passport had checked out to be legitimate, too. Directly inquiring Europol or Interpol about a stray human bone, without first running some tests on it and identifying the sex and age range of its perished owner, would be fruitless if not laughable by the exceptional law enforcement and intelligence professionals toiling away in those international police agencies.

After confirming with his supervisor that the British customs office would take possession of the bone, Shanahan's supervisor advised him that without higher judicial authority, the Iranian could not be held in custody much longer. The customs officers did not have sufficient cause to suspect—other than the questionable nature and transport of the bone itself—that a crime had been committed. They therefore had no justification to further retain Farhad Gilani.

Heading back to the interrogation room, Officer Tom Shanahan knew what to do.

"Mr. Gilani," he said, addressing Farhad, who sat stone-faced, "we are going to let you proceed to Istanbul. But this bone is not going with you."

"*What*? Why not?" asked Farhad.

"Because it's illegal to carry such items across our border," responded Shanahan.

"Really? I was aware that exotic animals or animal parts could not be transported, but I was not aware of a restriction on old human bones," replied Farhad.

"Well, you're not taking this bone with you, lamp or no lamp," said Shanahan. "If you want to seek redress through the British courts, have a big day. But this bone stays here. You are free to leave, Mr. Gilani. Your Istanbul flight starts boarding in twenty minutes. If you don't dilly-dally, you'll make it just fine."

As he left, Gilani did his best to conceal the anxiety and anger that wracked his being.

"*Maybe* the Iranian was telling the truth," Shanahan murmured to himself as he headed back to his cubicle. "But my gut tells me he wasn't."

Addressing the British customs subordinate who accompanied

him into the room for the interrogation, Shanahan directed him to act.

"Be sure today's meeting gets properly documented. Once you hand the bone over to Scotland Yard, request that they run tests on it to see if there might be a DNA match out there somewhere. And when Scotland Yard runs those tests, we also need to know the *age* of this bone. Mr. Gilani's story suggests this bone is about one hundred to one hundred twenty years old. We'll see. Also, once the reports are run, make sure all of the circumstances and results surrounding our work, and the results from Scotland Yard, get sent out to Europol and Interpol."

20.
GARMISCH-PARTENKIRCHEN, GERMANY: FIVE YEARS BEFORE PARIS

AS JAKE HEADED SOUTH from Munich through the rolling verdant countryside of Bavaria, he could see the Alpine mountains along the Germany-Austria border as they began to peek over the horizon. His mind drifted to his recent promotion. Having spent almost seven years as a captain, he was gratified that he had made the cut to the rank of major. But his small promotion ceremony was bittersweet, and it felt perfunctory. Sure, his mother had managed to make it down to Washington from Michigan, and that was wonderful. But his beautiful family, with the two children he and Faith had brought into the world, was not there. In his remarks, after a colonel and his mother pinned on his new gold leaves, Jake thanked his family anyway, hoping, praying, that they could hear him and fully sense the gratitude that he had for their love and support.

When he walked by a soccer field and saw young boys playing, or saw something as simple as falling snow, it reminded him of making snow angels with Kimberly. Or when he would see a mother out shopping with her children who were about the same age as Kimberly and Jake, Jr, every single time it made him ache inside. Jake knew at some point, he had to figure out how to live through or with the pain and loss. He hoped that his one year at the George C. Marshall Center, located in the beautiful alpine town of Garmisch-Partenkirchen,

Germany, would represent the turning of a page and the beginning of a new chapter in his life.

The Marshall Center was founded in 1994 by the US Department of Defense and German Ministry of Defense. Initially, its post-Cold War mission was to engage senior officers and civilian government officials from the recently dismantled Warsaw Pact countries of the former Soviet Union, with the primary goal of introducing them to the Western ideals of civilian control of the military, cooperative civil-military relations, public accountability, effective inter-governmental relations, and other good governance concepts. Later, the Center expanded its mission to include combatting terrorism, transnational organized crime and cyber threats, and other national security challenges.

Several years prior to Jake's arrival, the Marshall Center had begun to offer a master's degree in international security studies. While Jake had been accepted at Columbia University and Johns Hopkins University, he had opted for the Marshall Center, providing one year of study sponsored by a nearby university in Munich while also taking national security courses and professionally networking at the Center.

Seven months into his program, Jake was taking one of the Marshall Center's premier courses, the Program in Terrorism and Security Studies. There were seventy-five government civilian, military, diplomatic, law enforcement and intelligence officials from forty-nine countries in the course. To be admitted, every course member had to somehow be in the fight against terrorism. This ranged from being an expert on terrorist finances, being a counterterrorism cyber expert, serving in diplomacy, intelligence, or law enforcement positions, or to being an actual military trigger puller, and everything in between.

On the first day of the four-week course, after taking his assigned seat with about three minutes to go before the start of the morning's main lecture, something unanticipated happened to Jake.

Who is that woman? he wondered. *She looks like she could be part of my family,* now switching his thoughts to his parents.

Unable to divert his gaze, the woman made direct eye contact with him. The striking lady with thick brown and slightly auburn hair, and olive-toned skin, did not avert her gaze until, slightly blushing, she turned her eyes towards the podium as the morning's speaker greeted the class.

A little more than eighteen months after he had lost Faith and the children, Jake Fortina knew he was not ready to move forward with a new romance. But he also knew at the very least that he *had* to say hello to this woman who had surprisingly caught his eye. Her military uniform looked very familiar, but given the distance between them and the fact that about a third of the class was wearing military uniforms, he could not quite nail it down.

At the midmorning coffee break, Jake sought the woman out. Stepping into her field of view as she conversed with two other people, he introduced himself.

"Hi, I'm Jake Fortina."

"My name is Sara Simonetti. Pleased to meet you, Jake."

Jake could now clearly see the woman's beautiful light-green eyes. After having spent almost four years in Italy, Jake also thought he'd heard a familiar accent. The uniform was now looking more familiar, too.

Looking at her Marshall Center–provided nametag, he could make out the word *Captain* preceding her name, and then, there it was, the Italian flag. The Marshall Center provided all student and faculty with nametags. At the same instant he clearly recognized the uniform, that of a Carabinieri officer.

"*Lei viene dall'Italia, no?*" Jake asked, showing off some knowledge of Italian.

"Yes, I am from Italy," responded the Italian Carabinieri captain in Italian.

The Carabinieri, the renowned paramilitary and law enforcement police force that was originally founded in the Kingdom of Sardinia, had existed in Italy since the early1800s. Much like the Spain's Guardia di Civile and France's Gendarmerie, the Carabinieri fulfilled the dual roles of a domestic law enforcement agency as well as a military police force when deployed abroad to international war and peacekeeping zones. The Carabinieri regularly sent its officers to Marshall Center international security courses.

Switching back to English, Sara asked, "How did you guess?"

"By your nametag, maybe?" Jake quipped.

"I forgot that we have these things," Sara blushed.

"Ha-ha, I will probably forget a lot more than that before this course is over," responded Jake.

Later, seated in his twelve-person seminar room, Jake couldn't remember when he so wistfully and spontaneously said something to another human being since the loss of his family.

In the remaining weeks of the course, he took time to get to know the intriguing Italian woman, who said she had been born in Florence, not far from the Ponte Vecchio. He learned that Sara's father had been a Sicilian-born Carabinieri captain who was killed by the Italian Mafia in the mid-1980s. Sara was only four years old when it happened. But as an adult, she was extraordinarily proud that her father had given his life for a noble purpose. She decided to follow his path of service to country.

Jake grew to really like Sara but would not let his feelings or social interactions with her cross over to the romantic side. Sure, a coffee or a lunch together in the Marshall Center Cafe, or a dinner at a local German gasthaus with other friends present. But nothing more.

When Jake said, *"Arrivederci"* to Captain Sara Simonetti on the day of the course's graduation, he had no clue she had more than a casual interest in him.

21.
GARMISCH-PARTENKIRCHEN: STARTING TO HEAL

AS JAKE DEPARTED his newest course at the Marshall Center, Countering Transnational Organized Crime, a flyer posted outside the main Marshall Center plenary room caught his eye: *WOUNDED WARRIOR AMAZING RACE, Volunteers Needed. Sponsored by the Wound Warrior Project, the American Red Cross and the Warrior Transition Battalion. See the Morale, Welfare and Recreation Office if interested.*

Jake remembered that the Landstuhl Regional Medical Center, located about five hours by autobahn to the west, not far from the French border, was where many American combat-wounded servicemen and women had been treated from both the Iraq and Afghanistan wars.

The Warrior Transition Battalion was dedicated to getting soldiers as healthy as possible—psychologically, emotionally and physically—before either sending them back to their military service or out-processing them for home. After the Korengal Valley firefight, Sergeant Dennis M. King had been sent to Landstuhl for some very delicate micro-surgery that had quite miraculously restored the full use of his wrist and hand. Jake decided to volunteer.

"So, what's this Wounded Warrior Amazing Race thing all about?" he asked the lady behind the counter at the MWR (Morale,

Welfare and Recreation) office, located on the nearby Artillery Kaserne, a German word for *barracks* or *garrison.*

"It's a morale and team building event we are putting on for about fifty members of the Wounded Warrior Transition Battalion," replied Susan Davis, the brains behind the event. "The format is kinda based on the reality TV show *The Amazing Race.* But unlike the TV show, where teams of two race around the world to win one million dollars, it will *all* take place right here in Garmisch-Partenkirchen, on one day. Teams of about five soldiers each will be formed up and must work their way through a bunch of clues, challenges and stations while making their way through the city. In the meantime, they'll hopefully learn something about Garmisch-Partenkirchen—and themselves—as they do. The team that successfully goes through all the challenge stations and has the fastest time wins. We did this once before and it was great. The German townspeople loved it, too, with many of the businesses providing prizes as well as support for the various challenge stations."

"Will the contestants win a million dollars, like in the real *Amazing Race?*" joked Jake.

"Maybe a bratwurst?" shot back Davis.

"What kind of volunteers do you need?"

"What we really need are volunteers to accompany each team as they go through their challenge stations. For example, we have one station where a German bakery will show the teams how to make a pretzel from scratch, and then they'll have to replicate making a pretzel, for time. At another station, after going up a ski lift, they will have to eat sauerkraut at a mountaintop lodge," she laughed. "Included in the race is also a ropes course, suspended between trees. It's up near the ski lift area, and they'll have to traverse the course as a team. You don't need to *do* any of these challenges, just accompany the team throughout the race. It will take almost all day, next Saturday."

"Okay, I'm in!"

A week later, after some pre-event briefings, Jake showed up at the appointed time at Artillery Kaserne. He'd already decided that when he met his team of wounded warriors, there would be no mention of rank or even the fact that he was an Army officer.

Everybody would be on a first-name basis. This was going to a fun event, without any bullshit formalities.

On Saturday morning he met his team of five combat-wounded enlisted soldiers. Jake immediately felt like he'd come home to family comprised of a hodgepodge of gender, race, and rank. Two of the soldiers had suffered traumatic brain injuries that only specialized doctors and equipment could detect. Both had been wounded by the concussing blast from improvised explosive device (IED) attacks. Another soldier had a prosthetic device from the knee down, also the result of an IED attack. As Jake was to learn that day, that was approximately reflective of the types of casualties from Afghanistan, with roughly two-thirds of the casualties occurring from the roadside or road-buried bombs. Some of the hidden bombs had detonated through the pressure applied by the heavy vehicles passing over them, while others were remotely detonated by human hands. Of the remaining two soldiers, one had suffered shrapnel wounds from a rocket attack and the second from direct small arms fire. And those were the physical wounds. The emotional and psychological ones were far more difficult to assess and every bit as deadly if left untreated. Jake instantly felt a kinship—no, a *love*—for each one of them. It was the first feeling of the sort he'd felt in almost a year and half.

As Jake and his team left the Kaserne on foot and began the race, he witnessed activity that affirmed the main reason why he'd joined the Army and had come to love it— different Americans with different backgrounds from different corners of the country, who had come together risking it all "to defend the Constitution of the United States, against all enemies, foreign and domestic." The group was chatting, scheming, and ribbing each other as if they had known each other since childhood.

Throughout the day, he would witness teammates helping each other as they overcame new challenges. On the ropes course, the soldier with the prosthetic leg was the star of the team. Jake observed two of the soldier's teammates on the ground watching the amputee. He looked like Spider-man, easily moving across the ropes, roughly twenty feet above the ground. Jake heard one of the soldiers on the ground admit to his fellow earth-bound buddy that he had developed a deathly fear of heights since deploying. Then, after observing

Spider-man make it look easy, he said to his buddy, "Hell, if HE can do it, we can do it!"

When the team arrived at the sauerkraut-eating station, it was learned that one teammate hated sauerkraut. And because of the medications he was on, his stomach began flip-flopping at just the smell of it. And then, after one brave attempt at a small bite of the fermented cabbage, he gagged and almost vomited.

"No problem!" said a buddy. "I'll eat your portion, brother! I love sauerkraut. It's the greatest natural colon cleanser on the planet!"

With every challenge presented to the team, whether it was figuring out clues for the next leg of the race or navigating Garmisch-Partenkirchen without a map, Jake swelled with pride knowing these incredibly resilient humans were part of his indomitable tribe. As the team finished the day in third place, Jake felt that he had gotten a front-row seat view of the incremental emotional and psychological healing that was taking place among the combat-wounded soldiers. And truth be told, for the first time since his terrible family tragedy, Jake felt some healing for himself, too.

22.
THE PRESIDENT'S DAILY BRIEFING

"JAY, I STRONGLY BELIEVE the report from Paris should be included in the president's briefing tomorrow," said the FBI's senior representative to the US government interagency intelligence team responsible for putting together the president's daily briefing. "It's a first."

"I'm gonna have to call bullshit on this one, Steve," responded the CIA agent.

The agent was responsible for the final draft version of the report before getting it approved by the director of national intelligence (DNI). Once approved, the report would be briefed to, or at least forwarded daily to the president. Some presidents were diligent in their daily reading of the report, others not so much.

"Just because some headstone in one of our overseas American cemeteries says *Death to the Americans*, and another says *Death to the Jews*, doesn't mean this rises to the level of the president. Right now, we have what *appears* to be a hate crime committed in one of our US cemeteries in France. Sure, it's despicable as it is, but it's too early to flag this incident to the president," said the CIA agent. "We have absolutely no idea who did this, or why."

"Jay, I hear ya. But again, it's a *first*. And at the very least, it could represent a real threat to us, and to Israel. And you know bad news does not get better with age, Jay," replied the FBI agent.

"I understand that, Steve, but I'm voting a solid *no* on this. We do *not* need to brief this to the president right now. He's got bigger stuff to worry about. If the DNI overrides me, so be it."

Within an hour, US director of national intelligence Herman Bulls sided with his senior CIA agent on the briefing team. This report from the US embassy in France about some anti-American writing on a US headstone would be excluded from the president's daily briefing.

But it had the DNI's attention, that much was for sure.

23.
ANXIOUS IN ISTANBUL

LANDING SAFELY IN ISTANBUL, Farhad Gilani flagged a taxi and headed to the modest apartment where he was to stay while supposedly delivering the bone to his Hezbollah contact. Reaching for his burner cellphone, Gilani felt anxious.

"Did you bring the cake, Uncle Farhad? My daughter is really looking forward to it," the Istanbul-based Hezbollah contact asked, having immediately recognized the caller ID.

"I had the cake with me, but a very unsympathetic British customs official would not let me bring it out of the country," said Gilani.

"*What*? How rude of him! Do not worry, I will pick one up before I meet you."

"Okay, I will see you soon," replied Gilani.

Panicked, Gilani was not sure what to do.

Should I go into hiding? If I do, they will pursue me to the ends of the earth. Or should I proceed, trusting that my years of life-risking service to Hezbollah in the Israeli war, in Central America, and in Lebanon will save me?

Perspiring as he thought about it, *I will go to the apartment*, he decided.

As he arrived and got settled into his Istanbul apartment, Gilani was thankful that it had been stocked with some chai.

Obviously, my contact does not plan for me to stay here long. He's planning to put me on a flight to Tehran, or elsewhere, tomorrow or very soon thereafter, Gilani thought.

Then came the knock on the door. Opening the door, Gilani looked at one of the biggest Iranian men he had ever seen, estimating the Goliath to be about ten years younger than him.

"Greetings in the name of Allah," said Gilani as he beheld his Istanbul contact for the first time.

"Greetings to you in the name of Allah and his prophet Muhammad," replied his contact. "I am Marduk."

"May I offer you a tea, Marduk?" asked Gilani.

"Yes, thank you," said Marduk.

As water was heating for the chai, Marduk addressed Gilani.

"Now, please tell me *exactly* what happened in London," he asked.

24.
A MISSING BONE

FRENCH DGSI INSPECTOR Jean-Paul Rafael returned to the American cemetery in Suresnes. He did not know what to expect as he approached the grave of the World War I US Army nurse Ruth Ackerman.

He'd left the Gelb grave thirty-six hours earlier, when, after exhausting digging, he'd found the casket perfectly intact. Other than confirming that the Gelb casket had been undisturbed, the blister-inducing digging felt like a complete waste of time. This time, however, he brought a colleague to help him.

"Henri, as a hate crime, this one is pretty odd," Rafael said to his colleague. "We have cleanly written messages on two Jewish-American headstones. We also have some sod that has been removed, and put back, from the top of the first grave."

"I really don't expect a different result here than from the Daniel Gelb grave," he continued. "But after that serious tongue-lashing I received from CPT Perrier for not completely digging out the Ackerman grave, we have no choice but to dig down all the way to the casket. I really appreciate you being here to lend me a hand."

"No problem," replied Henri. "This will only cost you two bottles of Châteauneuf-du-Pape," he added, referring to his favorite red French wine that was produced near his home in southeastern France.

"When was the last time you had to dig out a grave? After you finish, you might wish you had asked for two *cases* of that average red wine from Vaucluse!" Rafael chuckled, preferring a red Bordeaux.

As the two men removed the sod chunks and began digging, Rafael noticed that the soil was less hard-packed than that of the Gelb grave.

"It seems some digging has occurred here, Henri," he said.

"Henri, you need to get out of the office more," Rafael said to his DGSI colleague. "You are digging faster than a marmot!"

"We have hit the top of the casket," Henri confirmed.

Working to clean off the last few inches of dirt from the casket's cover, Rafael could see that the edge of this metal casket looked different than the one in the Gelb grave.

"These hinges have been broken," said Rafael.

Making additional space off to the side of the casket to be able to open it up, the men continued to dig, removing additional dirt from the side walls of the grave. Finally, using latex gloves to avoid leaving fingerprints and thereby potentially tainting what might end up being a bigger crime scene than first thought, the two men managed to open the casket.

Peering at the remains, Rafael announced, "We will need to get a specialist in here to confirm it, but my eyes tell me the hip bone and a femur bone are missing from Ms. Ackerman's remains."

25.
VIDEO TAPES

"SIR, WE NEED TO PETITION the prefect for authorization to review the closed-circuit television surveillance tapes in the area of the US cemetery in Suresnes," said French DGSI captain Perrier to his supervisor.

"We now know that in the context of this anti-Semitic and anti-American hate crime at the cemetery, the grave and remains of Ruth Ackerman were violated," continued Perrier. "Given when the crime was discovered, reviewing a twelve-hour period of the tapes from the area might provide us with some solid leads as to who perpetrated these crimes."

Not long after the 9/11 attacks on the Twin Towers and the Pentagon, and more relevantly, the London bombings of July 7, 2005, the French government decided to install video surveillance cameras throughout the city of Paris.

In 2012, the mayor of Paris announced a plan to add eleven hundred CCTV cameras to aid with traffic enforcement on the streets of Paris. However, there was significant pushback on this initiative by Parisian and French citizens. They were worried that their beloved city would turn into another London, where, in 2012, there was one camera for every eleven citizens. London had become the most video-surveilled city on the planet, and its cameras had proven essential to stopping at least one potential terrorist attack in November 2014.

Only a couple of months after the thwarting of the planned terrorist attack in London, Paris saw a different result. On January 7, 2015, Islamist extremists murdered ten journalists from the periodical *Charlie Hebdo*. The French satire-based publication had dared to make the prophet Muhammad the butt of its humor. Two Paris police officers were also killed in the attack. The attack fueled the fire of those French government officials and Parisian citizens who thought that more is better regarding Paris video surveillance.

While they were habitually used to enforce traffic laws, reviewing video surveillance tapes for criminal cases in France required judicial approval.

"Jean-Luc," responded Captain Perrier's police judiciary supervisor, "what do you propose that we ask for?"

"Sir, I recommend that we ask for video surveillance tapes of a six-square-block area, with the Suresnes cemetery at the center," he said, drawing out his concept on a notepad and showing it to his supervisor. "And I recommend they cover a ten-hour period, beginning from eight the night before the markings were discovered, to six the following morning. By six, it's fully daylight and the perpetrators would have been gone by then. The markings were discovered by the cemetery worker around eight-thirty or so."

"I concur, Jean-Luc," replied his supervisor. "This will require some thorough and mundane, but necessary, police work. Please write up the request for the prefect, and I will endorse it."

"Consider it done," replied Perrier.

26.
MAKE HIM DISAPPEAR

MARDUK DID HIS BEST to explain to his Iranian contact, located in Ankara, what had happened to Farhad Gilani in London.

"The British authorities seized our merchandise from Gilani, but let they let him travel on to Istanbul," he stated.

The Iranian contact in Ankara immediately notified Iran's intelligence minister. Marduk was surprised how quickly the intelligence minister responded.

"He failed his mission. Make him disappear," read the coded and cold message.

Given the prompt response, Marduk realized how important this clandestine operation was to his higher-level rogue contacts in the Iranian government. It clearly communicated the result that would befall any Hezbollah operative who did not accomplish his assigned mission.

Pulling up to Gilani's ground-floor apartment at three in the morning with two fellow Hezbollah operatives, Marduk reconsidered his unmistakable marching orders: *"Make him disappear."*

Back in Tehran, Marduk's Iranian government handlers knew Marduk was the right Hezbollah operative to run Iranian clandestine operations in Istanbul. He was ruthless, and executed orders perfectly. He would do anything for his Persian homeland and the Hezbollah, the self-proclaimed "Party of God."

"Entry into the apartment should be easy," said Marduk to his colleagues. "If Farhad reacts, in the name of Allah, my brothers, we must act decisively," Marduk said as he parked the white Range Rover outside Gilan's apartment building.

Marduk had one of two keys to the apartment. Gilani, slumbering inside, had the other.

Marduk signaled to one of his fellow operatives to go around the back of the building to block any escape attempt out the first-floor apartment's back window, and then waited three minutes to make sure his fellow Iranian was in position. In the event Gilani happened to make the six-foot jump out the window to the ground, the Hezbollah operative waiting for him would employ immediate lethal—and silent—force, killing Gilani as he hit the ground.

At the front of the apartment, Marduk inserted the key into the front door lock and gently pushed the door open, the hinge made an ever so slight and unexpected squeak.

Was the squeak enough to wake Farhad? Marduk was not about to wait to find out. Signaling to his accompanying Hezbollah colleague, who held a bright flashlight, Marduk quickly headed across the living room and straight for the open bedroom door.

In the next instant, his colleague entered the room in front of and to the right of Marduk, shining the blinding light at Gilani's headboard. A startled Gilani bolted upright and quickly reached for an object on his nightstand.

Within an instant, Marduk fired three rounds from his Heckler & Koch VP9 pistol, with suppressor, into Gilani's torso and head. Slowly approaching Farhad, Marduk put the pistol squarely on Farhad's temple and fired a fourth round.

"What the hell was he reaching for?" asked Marduk of his colleague.

"A kitchen knife," came the response.

Marduk's Hezbollah accomplice shined his flashlight through the back window, signaling to his colleague below that Marduk's aim had done its job.

As the third operative came around from the back of the apartment building and entered the front door, Marduk announced, "We must finish the job."

Without a word, the Hezbollah operative reached into his

backpack and pulled out a small handsaw and two butcher knives. Like surgeons amputating limbs on a seventeenth-century battlefield, the three men went about their gruesome work.

Their butchery complete, Gilani's body parts were stuffed into two body bags, each reinforced and made doubly strong by an additional outside body bag.

The Hezbollah operatives took the bags to Marduk's Range Rover. Placing them in the back of the vehicle, they added two thirty-five-pound cinder blocks to each body bag.

From the apartment, they drove to the Martyr's Bridge in Istanbul. The famous bridge connected the European and Asian continents. The deep water below was the perfect hiding place for their former Hezbollah colleague's remains. It was about two hundred feet to the bottom. The heavily trafficked Bosporus Straits divided the European and Asian continents while also connecting the Black Sea with the Sea of Marmara, and, by extension, the Dardanelles, the Aegean and Mediterranean Seas.

"He will *never* float to the surface, certainly not in our lifetimes." Marduk chuckled. "And *if* he does, the Turks, Asians, and Europeans can debate about which of the hundreds of international ships a day that come through these straits might have been responsible for his disposal."

27.
LYING LOW

DEPARTING HIS SAINT-DENIS APARTMENT for the Paris internet café, Arman Darbandi knew it was unwise to become habitual in his movements. Consistent patterns for anyone who is watching, leads to predictability. Predictability reduces personal security. As he had learned in his training as a Hezbollah operative, one never knows who is watching. Today, he would take an alternate route to the café.

Thinking about his upcoming email exchange with his Athens handler, Arman was wondering about his colleague Farhad Gilani. A few days since Farhad had departed, the period in which Arman and Farhad could safely talk had well passed.

By now, Farhad must be with his contact in Istanbul, or maybe even in Tehran, Arman thought as he approached the cafe.

At a computer terminal, Arman read a coded message that gave him pause. It was so alarming that he had to read it two additional times. He stared at it, his heart pounding.

The message said that Arman was "lying low" until further notice. The message implied that Farhad had either been compromised or had somehow not completed the handoff of Ruth Ackerman's femur bone to his Istanbul contact. *I know we are at war,* Arman thought. *But I hope my friend is safe and that our mission has only been temporarily disrupted.*

As Arman departed the internet café, he suddenly heard a very loud and annoying Arab man, about twenty yards away. As he spoke into his cellphone, the man slurred his words while apparently having an argument with his wife.

Briefly stopping and casting the drunk a disgusted glance, Arman continued on his way. His many years as a Hezbollah organized crime operative, however, made him cautious, so he subtly picked up his pace.

A third man posted in the back of a van about forty yards away took a half-dozen photos with his Nikon D500 DX camera.

One of these should provide us with a useful photo, the French DGSI photographer assured himself.

28.
WHAT'S MISSING?

CAPTAIN PERRIER READ the recently discovered information about Ruth Ackerman's missing femur and hip bones. His mind kept coming back to her grave and the cemetery. Very intelligent, but also intelligent enough to know that there is a time for humility, the perplexed French National Police captain thought he might be missing something obvious.

Why would someone want to write hate messages on two Jewish headstones and then take two bones from only one of the two graves, while leaving the other body unmolested? Perrier asked himself. *Why the Suresnes American cemetery in the first place? What am I missing?*

In the next instant, Perrier decided to call a colleague and police friend, Captain Laurent Lefevre. Now in their late thirties, they both had families and demanding law enforcement jobs and had not spoken in a couple of years.

"Laurent, how are you? This is a Jean-Luc. How is your family?"

"Jean-Luc . . . *Jean Luc Perrier?*" asked Lefevre.

"Yes, my friend, it's me. I know it's been a while. How are you? How is your family?"

"Jean-Luc, it is great to hear from you," replied Lefevre. "My family and I are great. And yours?"

"Yes, we are doing well, thank you. Listen, I should have called you earlier to check up on you personally, but I do have a professional question."

"Sure, what is it, my friend?"

"Why would anyone want to write hate messages on two Jewish headstones at the American cemetery in Suresnes, and take two bones from a grave there?" asked Perrier.

"Wait, *what*? *Two* headstones? Two bones from a grave? I thought there was only one grave?" asked Lefevre.

Since he had first visited the crime scene and had insisted that the investigation be handed over to DGSI investigators, Lefevre was not aware of a second grave.

"Yes, they were taken from a second grave. A hip bone and a femur bone from a female Jew's remains."

"I was not aware," said Lefevre.

"Tell me, Laurent. Why the Suresnes cemetery? It's one of the smallest American cemeteries in France. Why not the far more well-known Normandy American cemetery? Or the much, much larger and more notable St. Mihiel American cemetery near Verdun? Why *this* small one, in *Paris*? Is there anything exceptional about this cemetery?"

"There is one thing at the Suresnes cemetery that is different from all the other cemeteries in France. In that cemetery, most of the casualties were not a result of combat. Instead, they resulted from the Spanish flu of 1918 to 1919."

"Is that so? How did you know that?"

"I have been an official guest of the cemetery several times," replied Lefevre. "Towards the end of the war, the virus ravaged the soldiers in the trenches and at the field medical stations, and even at the large Red Cross hospital that eventually became the American Hospital in Paris. The war ended on November 11, 1918, as you might know, but the virus continued to rage among the troops who were either still being treated for wounds or who were waiting to get transported home. The initial round of the virus lasted well into early 1919, and then roared back later in the year."

"Perhaps the clue that would reveal the all-important motive, besides hate, of this crime's perpetrator is somewhere in this discussion," Perrier pondered.

Perrier hung up the phone, knowing he had potentially had a vital detail that needed to be shared with law enforcement analysts and top officials.

29.
CONNECTED

JAKE FORTINA STARED at the message on his LinkedIn page. Since he had lost Faith, Kimberly, and Jake, Jr., he had kept a very low profile on all social platforms. The LinkedIn message he was currently staring at was from Sara Simonetti.

Before Sara left Garmisch, they had connected through LinkedIn. Jake would occasionally visit the site for things that were of professional interest but not much more. This message from Sara, however, was a pleasant surprise. Their subsequent online conversation was in Italian.

"Ciao, my friend, how goes it in Paris?"

"Not bad," responded Jake. "How about you? How are things in Italy?"

"Good. But I have too much work. How is your favorite soccer team doing? It's Paris Saint Germain, isn't it?"

"Oh, so you remember?" replied Jake. "They're having a pretty good season. They should make a run at the next European Cup this summer. How about your team? Verona, correct?"

"Yes, you are right, Jake. The Italian *Serie A* league is really tough this year so Verona is doing okay, but not great. And hey, there is always next year!"

"You are so right!" Jake said.

"Okay, just checking in, my friend. Hope all is well. Take care!" said Sara.

"Likewise, my friend."

Well, that was odd, he thought. *But it was fun, even if we talked about pretty much nothing.*

Just as sometimes happens after hearing an old favorite song, for the next few hours Jake could not take his mind off his Italian friend.

It was nice that she reached out to me, though, he mused.

Living in Vicenza, about a forty-five-minute drive from the Romeo and Juliet city of Verona, Sara was very happy to have reached out to Jake. *Fortunately, he didn't take long to respond,* thought Sara.

Truth be told, she missed him. At the Marshall Center she'd met a lot of interesting and accomplished people, but Jake was special among them, *very* special. She had wanted to tell him that, but she didn't think the widower was ready to hear it. And she was right. Jake carefully kept a certain emotional distance while they were together in Germany. Sara rightly sensed that the young American army officer was not ready to leap into a new relationship. But try as she might, she couldn't forget Jake, either.

30.
THE ANALYST

THE FRENCH MOI intelligence analyst had been scratching her head for some time over the American cemetery hate crimes. It was a bit unusual for hate crimes to be brought to her attention. France was America's oldest ally, and this crime was a top priority.

Why were two bones taken from a single grave belonging to an American Jew? Michelle Marie wondered.

She had looked at the daily report provided by the Ministry of Interior's liaison officer to Europol.

As the European Union's collective law enforcement agency, Europol's straightforward goal was to achieve a safer Europe for the benefit of all the EU citizens. Headquartered at the Hague in the Netherlands, Europol supported twenty-seven European Union countries in their fight against terrorism, cybercrime, and other serious forms of organized crime.

Thankfully for Great Britain and her non-EU partners, when the UK initiated its exit from the European Union, the so-called "Brexit," Europol continued to work "with many non-EU partner states and international organizations, including the US."

The summary report from the MOI's liaison to Europol noted that a femur bone, most likely belonging to an adult female, due to its size, had been seized from an Iranian traveler at the London Heathrow Airport. The traveler was a middle-aged Iranian named

Farhad Gilani on his way to Istanbul. He claimed to have purchased the bone in a Paris flea market.

The report, classified at a low level, as no arrests were made nor was any criminal activity or intent verified that could be connected to the bone. According to the report, tests were being conducted by Scotland Yard to determine the bone's DNA, as well as the approximate age and year of death of its owner.

As the report was three days old, Michelle Marie wondered if perhaps another update on the bone might soon be forthcoming from Scotland Yard. Not about to wait to find out, she promptly called the French Ministry of Interior's liaison to Europol.

"I am working on a case in Paris that involves a missing femur bone. I request a DNA and carbon-dating update report on the mysterious bone that was taken from the Iranian traveler, Farhad Gilani, at Heathrow Airport in London. The bone is now in the possession of Scotland Yard. Please respond at your earliest convenience."

31.
THE DREAM
NINE MONTHS BEFORE PARIS

SARA SIMONETTI AWOKE staring at the slowly rotating ceiling fan in her bedroom. The late-September, early-morning Veneto sun was peaking in from her top-floor balcony of the late-nineteenth-century Venetian villa that served as her home. The villa had been divided into six apartments, three on each side of a center stairwell. Once owned by a Venetian duke, the villa stood adjacent to a wine-producing vineyard on the northeastern edge of Vicenza. Occasionally, Sara would go out and lay on the apartment's cement walled balcony naked, soaking in the enveloping Italian summer sun. On this morning, the only human in sight—or within earshot—was an Italian field worker, singing loudly among the vines below. Belting out a Giacomo Puccini aria, he was doing his best to sound like Luciano Pavarotti. In a nearby oak tree a songbird occasionally interjected with a tune of its own.

Sara's bedroom, with its cool, marble-covered floors and thick stucco walls, was normally cool enough on a late summer's night that the ceiling fan was not needed. But it had been an unusually warm, Indian summer's night, so Sara woke up surprisingly moist.

She wanted back in that dream. Sara wanted to *feel* it again. And she wanted to know more. That man with dark hair whose face she could not describe, or perhaps couldn't remember, had approached her as she stood in an undefined, misty dreamscape. Without a word, the man gently but passionately kissed Sara on the lips. There was no other physical contact—no embrace, no hug, just a kiss that conveyed a depth of love Sara had never felt before. Upon waking, she pondered if a love like that really existed on earth. The kiss left her with an elated, soul-satisfying feeling and a sense of heightened joy. Somewhat surprisingly, it also conveyed a touch of sensuality, borne of pure love and devoid of any of the guilt Catholic nuns had heaped on Sara when she was in middle school. *Who was that man?* Why now, approaching her mid-thirties, did she experience such a dream? What did it all mean?

The time leading up to the dreamy kiss had been very unsettling for Sara. For the previous seven months, she had not been with a man, nor did she desire to be with one. She had been briefly engaged to a Carabinieri officer. Wherever Sara went with him, the officer attracted eyes from both women and men. Occasionally, she thought she saw him making extended eye contact with another woman, but, at least the first few times, Sara gave it little thought.

He's gorgeous. Getting looks from other women is to be expected, she thought. She trusted him.

But then came the crushing revelations. First it was a close work colleague who broke the news, then a friend from a nearby town who revealed more troubling information. Sara's fiancé was cheating on her with one woman and perhaps with a second. The evidence on the first woman was irrefutable, while the evidence for the second highly suggestive. When she confronted her fiancé, he first denied it. Only later, with what Sara perceived to be feigned remorse, did he admit to both relationships.

Her trust shattered. *It's bound to happen again,* she thought.

The news about her fiancé was soul-crushing. But at the same time, Sara was thankful she knew the truth before mistakenly walking down the aisle with the man who she wrongly believed would be the lifetime lover and friend of her dreams.

32.
PROMOTION

"JAKE, THIS IS COLONEL UPSHAW," said the caller.

Colonel Andrew Upshaw had served as Major Jake Fortina's boss for over a year. Jake loved the "old man," now in his late forties. Jake considered himself blessed to have Upshaw as a mentor. Upshaw trusted Jake completely, and Jake was fully loyal to the US Army colonel and Virginia Military Institute graduate.

While attending the US Army Infantry School Officers Advanced Course as a captain, Fortina had befriended a Marine Captain Joe Russo. He was one of the many Marines the US Army and Marine Corps exchanged between their professional military education courses each year. Russo was one of eight Marines out of one hundred and sixty officers in the Infantry Advanced Course, which also included officers from allied military armies. What Russo told Jake over a beer one night fully resonated with him. "Leaders who are distrusting and micromanaging of their subordinates are not to be trusted. The exact opposite is also true. If you have a leader who fully trusts you, you can fully trust him in return."

The energetic and enthusiastic Upshaw had a reputation as a tough, but fair leader with a great sense of humor. Jake had told more than one US embassy colleague that he considered Upshaw to be part Ted Lasso—the ever-positive, unsophisticated but emotionally intelligent main character of the American comedy-drama television series of the same name—and part General George C. Marshall, the prominent American general and statesman of the 1940s and '50s, who was among the Virginia Military Institute's most famous graduates.

"Except Colonel Upshaw possesses a tad more sophistication than Lasso," Jake would joke with friends.

Gifted with a good ear for learning foreign languages, Upshaw spoke excellent French and Spanish, aided by a college semester abroad in Sevilla. In his duty position as the US defense attaché to France, he was charged with supervising or overseeing all US military personnel assigned to France. His duties also included serving as the senior US Department of Defense representative to the government of France.

"Congratulations, Jake, you've been selected for promotion to lieutenant colonel. You deserve it, buddy."

"Thank you, sir," replied Jake. "Glad to know the Army still has a sense of humor."

"Ha-ha," responded Upshaw. "You know the standard Army *blah-blah* that you always hear about being promoted mainly for your potential for future service?"

"Heck yes, sir, I've heard it once or twice," chuckled Jake. "Am not sure about that one."

"Well, in your case, Jake, it's not a bunch of bullshit. It will be about another year or so before you actually pin on those silver oak leaves and assume the rank of lieutenant colonel, so don't take your foot off the gas, *okay*?" added Upshaw.

"Got it, sir. And thanks again," responded Jake, who could sense his boss smiling over the phone. "I really appreciate it."

It was good news for Jake. He didn't start out in the Army thinking of himself as a career soldier. But now he was receiving an Army promotion to a fairly senior rank.

As a second lieutenant, I used to think lieutenant colonel was a rank for old guys who were about as powerful as the pope, thought the Catholic-raised major as he hung up the phone.

Like his promotion to major, the news was bittersweet. Jake thought about Faith, Kimberly, and Jake, Jr. In his first ten critical years of service, they had been with him every step of the way during his Army journey. A senior Army major with only four years to go before reaching his twentieth year of active service, Jake pondered whether he should retire.

Without Faith's loving support and Kim and Jake's resilience through several moves, I would not have made it to major, he now thought.

At US Embassy Paris, while serving as assistant Army attaché, Jake was expected to be an expert in US Army doctrine, equipment, operations, planning and training. He had impressed many senior officers and officials. Fluent in French and an excellent Spanish speaker who also knew Farsi quite well, he was mission focused and appeared to most to be a man whose competence was at the level of someone five, maybe even ten years his senior. He was highly thought of as a future choice for defense attaché at a major US embassy, or perhaps duty on the National Security Council, or perhaps even more, much more.

In his medal-bedecked Army blues uniform, Major Fortina had frequently caught the admiring eyes of international ladies—a good number who were married—on the diplomatic social circuit. That, however, was a moral line that Jake never thought of crossing.

He wasn't dating anyone, either. Sure, an occasional lunch or drink with an embassy civilian employee was okay. Single since his soul-wrenching loss of his family some five years earlier, his humble preference for most evenings—when he was not out on the hyper-busy Paris diplomatic circuit—was a generous but single glass of red wine. His Catholic father with Italian roots had assured him that the red vino, "consumed in moderation, of course," would sustain a long and healthy life.

"And, of course, what was Jesus' *first* miracle?" his father would always half-jokingly say, reminding Jake of the biblical account of Jesus of Nazareth's turning water into wine at the wedding of Cana.

Jake had come to prefer a French Saint Emillion, or occasionally a more robust Italian Amarone, the philosopher's wine, as Jake jokingly referred to it, because of how "smart" it made him. He consumed it with his evening meal and his reading companions—the *Economist*, *Wall Street Journal*, and *Le Monde* periodicals, along with the latest non-fiction military book or book on US or European politics. Early each morning, he would also spend a few quiet minutes with *Jesus Calling* and the Holy Bible.

Fortina's Christian faith had grown and become more personal, but he believed more in *living* his faith rather than talking about it.

While he still struggled with the tragic loss of the three people he held most dear in the world, it was his faith that carried him through that terrible ordeal. He deeply believed his family was in a far better place and often felt an eternal spiritual connection to them.

Before heading out the door each day to take varying transportation means—a military attaché could never become complacent and predictable in a big, international city like Paris—Jake would say a prayer, down a black double espresso, and head for the US embassy.

Located adjacent to the five-star Hotel Crillon and just off the Place de la Concorde, where many of France's royal elite met their demise to the guillotine during the French revolution of the late 1700s, the commute to the embassy by bus, subway, or on foot was easy. When he was not out on an official lunch, his lunch hour was normally spent in the embassy workout room.

During his commutes and workouts, when his mind had time to wonder, there was *one* lady Jake could not seem to get his mind off—the Florentine beauty, Sara Simonetti.

For goodness' sake, she's a Carabinieri officer. She has a busy career. Besides, she'll probably be married soon. She's too special not to be. What the hell am I thinking?

33.
A MOTIVE

IT WAS A DAY French DGSI captain Jean-Luc Perrier would never forget. It included one of those *aha* moments, in which the French DGSI's analytical work—along with information from international law enforcement colleagues in Great Britain and at Interpol—came together to paint a near complete picture. He was now ready to brief his boss who would pass the intel to, the French DGSI.

"Sir, I have some good news and I have some bad news concerning the American cemetery hate crime case," he began.

"Let's start with the bad," said Police Commandant Martin Vozzo.

"This case appears to be a lot more than a hate crime," said the captain. "We haven't pieced together every shred of evidence that we have, but we have enough to paint a, well, pretty bleak picture," said Perrier.

"Go on," replied Vozzo.

"So far, from intelligence developed by our DGSI investigators and intelligence analysts, along with information from the Brits, Europol, and the Americans at the embassy, we have determined five things.

"Number one," said Perrier, referring to his notepad, "the crime at the cemetery was conducted by at least two people, both of whom we expect are of Iranian origin and are likely to be working with or for Hezbollah in Lebanon."

"Go on," responded Vozzo.

"Number two, the analysis of the handwriting samples on the headstones implies someone who normally writes in Arabic script, and a Europol tip that originated from our British friends points to a female femur bone being confiscated by British border police from an Iranian traveler. The Iranian was flying from Heathrow to Istanbul when the bone was confiscated."

"Okay, got it," replied Vozzo.

"Number three, although two headstones were defaced in the American cemetery, only one casket was broken into. This was likely done to divert or slow down any investigation, which, unfortunately, it successfully did for almost forty-eight hours. The first grave was a ruse, a delaying tactic, to make us believe the second grave would also be unmolested. Except it wasn't.

"Number four, our internal Paris video surveillance shows a Peugeot 208, Dutch-plated rental car traveling in the area of the Suresnes cemetery at approximately 0410 hours in the morning when the defaced headstones were discovered."

"It's good to know that our video surveillance efforts are working beyond the occasional traffic violation," said Vozzo.

"Indeed," replied Perrier. "Number five, DGSI surveillance and intelligence people have been watching a man in the Saint-Denis area who looks to be Iranian. The Peugeot 208 was seen in the area of his neighborhood, but then we completely lost video surveillance of it a few days ago. Turns out it had been rented from an independent rental agency in a predominantly Arab neighborhood in Rotterdam. Some effective link analysis traced the car to the same Iranian who had been stopped at Heathrow."

"That's good work by our intelligence folks," said Vozzo.

"Not just our folks," replied Perrier. "The Brits have been pretty helpful with this, too."

"And most importantly," continued Perrier, "there were two bones missing from the second grave at the American cemetery. One was a femur bone and the other a hip bone. The DNA analysis conducted by Scotland Yard and our folks here perfectly linked the DNA of the femur bone to the DNA of the remains of Miss Ruth Ackerman, buried in that second grave."

"Okay, wow. So, it appears the Iranians may have acquired a bone from an American female Jew buried in an American cemetery.

Whatever for? What the hell does all of this *add up to*?" asked the police commandant.

"Sir," Captain Perrier corrected the police commandant as he took a deep breath, "not bone but *bones*. We think the Iranians wanted the bones—with the hip bone still out there somewhere—for the purposes of understanding why Ms. Ackerman, a Jew, was virtually immune to the Spanish flu of 1918 to 1919."

"That seems quite a stretch," replied the police commandant.

"Perhaps," said Perrier, "but we do know that Ruth Ackerman caught and then very quickly recovered from the Spanish flu, which had an extremely high death rate. Some camps experienced losing one out of four or five of their sick soldiers. That exceeds by far the mortality rate from COVID."

"Tell me more," replied Vozzo.

"Ms. Ackerman was exposed to the flu by a sick American soldier who later died. She had all the common symptoms. However, records from October 1918 indicate she recovered in less than a day and was no more affected than if she had a slight cold. She remained completely immune to the Spanish flu until her untimely death. Ackerman recovered faster than anybody had ever seen at that American field hospital. She became a legend among her peers and the hospital."

"Well, explain to me how she ended up in that grave, then," replied the commandant.

"She was killed in February 1919 by a Red Cross truck, a truck she, probably delirious from exhaustion, had stepped in front of late one night after another long day's work, caring for the sick and comforting the dying.

"In the fall of 1918 and into the spring of 1919 it was common for US Army nurses to work fourteen-hour days or longer as they tried to save young American and Allied soldiers' lives. They were the human angels of the Great War. Some of their patients were in the field hospital from lingering combat wounds. But the vast majority were there from that take-no-prisoners Spanish flu."

"Wow, that's a helluva thing." Vozzo paused for a moment before adding, "Do you think this leads us to Iran's direct involvement, or is it Hezbollah operating on its own?"

"We do not know the extent of Iranian government involvement yet," answered Perrier. "However, it is unlikely that this is a solo Hezbollah operation. We know that Tehran is always lurking on the margins—if not in full control—when it comes to Hezbollah. One theory is that Hezbollah will get a huge monetary reward if they pull this off, and another has it that Iran will further reduce its support to Hezbollah if they don't get it done, and a third simply proposes that Hezbollah has been directed to do this, with no quid pro quo. It fits into the standard model of Iranian influence over the Party of God."

"What about the Iranian who was stopped at Heathrow? What's his status? Can we pick up a trace on him?" asked Martin.

"We are trying to work with Turkish authorities on that Iranian's whereabouts. He apparently got off his flight in Istanbul, but that is the last data point we have on his location. We will continue to work with the Turks on this. Fortunately for us, the Turks and Iranians are not exactly kissing cousins, so we believe that if the Turks have anything on the missing Iranian, they'll give it to us."

"And the second Iranian?" asked the commandant.

"We last had him in the Saint-Denis area. We can't yet confirm his base of operations. However, we do have a fairly good, if a bit grainy, shot of him."

"How much do our American colleagues at the US embassy know?" asked Vozzo.

"They know some of what I just told you, but they will know almost everything once Minister Laplace has been fully briefed. Afterwards, with her green light, we'll fully bring in the US legal attaché at the embassy. I expect Minister Laplace will also give the American ambassador a briefing regarding what we know at this point."

"Good work, Jean-Luc. Keep me posted on this daily. Given the serious nature of what the Iranians might be seeking, this will be brought to the attention of the prime minister and president within the next twenty-four hours."

34.
A SPY IN OUR MIDST?

IT HAD ALREADY BEEN a long day for Special Agent Michael Beans of the FBI, who had gotten a heads-up that that the FBI's counterterrorism agents and analysts suspected a possible national security threat developing in Europe. It involved Iran and its development of a virus far more lethal than COVID-19 or its Delta variant. The reports from the FBI's legal attaché in Paris were getting a lot of eyeballs on them, not only within the agency but within the US intelligence community writ large.

Fortunately, Beans had a history of serving with the FBI caller on the other end. That took some gravity out of the call. Their service together in New York City was the first tour for both of them. They thrived in the tough NYC law enforcement environment, and now, having earned their spurs over the intervening years, they were high-level executives in the FBI.

Beans, a Black American Harvard graduate, shocked his family when he said he wanted to join the FBI. His family thought Beans would head off with his Ivy League diploma to the far more lucrative field of commercial real estate. His father had broken through the white-male-dominated commercial real estate business on the Eastern Seaboard, and made serious money developing, buying, and selling properties from New York to Philadelphia. As a result, the Beans family was very comfortable.

But money was not what got Michael Beans out of bed in the morning. Instead, it was public service.

Now, as the relatively new special agent in charge of Boston's FBI Field Office, the forty-five-year-old Beans was responsible for FBI operations in Maine, New Hampshire, Rhode Island, and all of Massachusetts. Since the horrific bombing of the Boston marathon and the nefarious use of Boston's Logan Airport by some of the 9/11 hijackers, the resilient city remained on edge.

Besides terrorist activity, Beans knew he had another major challenge on his hands: that of countering foreign intelligence operations, particularly in a place like Boston. As a huge innovation and technology hub, with its world-renowned research and development companies, not to mention universities, the greater Boston area was an incredibly "target-rich" environment for foreign spies. Boston's world-leading research technology centers held many valuable secrets sought by foreign governments.

"Michael, this is Darcy, from the National Security Branch," said Darcy Anderson, calling from the FBI's national headquarters on an encrypted phone network.

"Darcy, what good news do you have for me tonight?"

"Ha-ha, I wish I was calling to say you got a promotion, but you just took over in Boston, so forget about that," Anderson chuckled.

"Michael," continued Anderson, "a senior executive from Parker Pharmaceuticals walked into our headquarters here in DC. He reported that the Parker executive leadership thinks there is a spy in one of their Boston research departments. As you probably know, the Parker company has been heavily involved in developing a vaccine as well as treatments for the COVID-19 virus."

"Yep, I'm well aware of that," replied Beans.

"Well, what we know so far is that the suspect is a forty-something female doctor of Iranian heritage who has been a US citizen for a few years now," continued Anderson.

The word *Iranian* prompted Beans's full attention.

"Thus far, this appears to be a classic case of someone consistently staying behind after work and on weekends for no apparent reason, and research colleagues finding things out of place from the day prior, along with just general odd behavior and inappropriate questions being asked by the suspect."

"Any idea how long this has been going on, Darcy?" asked Beans.

"It's been her pattern for several weeks, maybe longer. I'll shoot further details to you on the classified email net. I just wanted to give you a personal heads-up. While I know these are only initial reports from the Parker executive, this has FBI headquarters front-office interest. I don't think I need to explain the national security implications, Mike."

"Roger, Darcy. I appreciate the heads-up," said Beans. "I'll get a team on this ASAP. I presume you'll shoot me the name of the Parker executive in the classified email?"

"Absolutely," responded Anderson. "The message will include everything the Parker exec told us. But there is one thing you need to know up front."

"What's that?" Beans asked.

"The French think she's trying to get secrets on developing vaccines for the Iranian government to inoculate its own people. Our analysts say this French analysis has legs."

"Sounds . . . damn serious," replied Beans.

"We at the headquarters agree. We'll get the classified details to you right away"

"Thank you, Darcy. And go Red Sox," said Beans.

"Screw the freakin' Red Sox. Go Yanks," said Anderson. "And PS, have a nice weekend, Michael."

"You too, buddy," replied Beans.

Beans knew his day was about to get much longer. Matters of national security had a way of ruining date nights, children's Little League baseball games, and sometimes even birthday celebrations. But Beans understood that from the day he had proudly graduated from the FBI Academy in Quantico, Virginia. It was part of being a G-Man.

35.
PHONE CALL

THREE NIGHTS AFTER RECEIVING THE NEWS of his impending promotion, which typically would occur within about a year after notification of selection, Major Fortina decided to make a phone call to an old friend from the 173d Airborne Brigade, Lieutenant Colonel John Knightstep. He was a former enlisted soldier in whom his officers had seen great potential for leadership, recommending Knightstep for the Army's Officer Candidate School (OCS). Graduating as a second lieutenant at the head of his class, Knightstep soon realized he loved the camaraderie and challenge of leading American soldiers as a junior officer. Recently promoted ahead of his peers to lieutenant colonel, he was now serving in the Pentagon as a personnel assignments officer.

It was a phone call most of Jake's peers had already made once or maybe twice, but—until now—one Jake had never thought about making in his sixteen years since graduating from West Point.

"John, give it to me straight," began Jake. "What is my next assignment looking like? I'm thinking seriously about retiring at the twenty-year mark. But, if possible, I'd like to do another tour overseas. As you know, I'm about four years away from my first possibility of retirement."

"Buddy, we will probably keep you overseas for your next assignment, although the Washington area remains a possibility. If it's DC, that probably means the Pentagon."

Jake shivered at the thought of working in the military brass–filled Pentagon, where a good field-grade officer (for the Army, the ranks of major through colonel) could end up becoming a clerk for a general, spending most of his time making fancy PowerPoint slides. It had always been Jake's intent to stay as far away from Washington as possible.

"Well, I'd prefer overseas, but shit, John, I'll take DC if I have to," Jake said.

"I know you will, buddy," chuckled Knightstep. "Your lieutenant colonel's promotion board was very competitive, so it's good you made that promotion."

"Was there a doubt?"

"Jake, you know I can't give you any specific details on that," replied Knightstep. "You should be pretty fired up about the promotion in any case."

"I *am* grateful, John," Jake responded. Sensing that there might be more to the story, he decided to press his friend for amplification. "But seriously, I'd like to know roughly, John—don't pull any punches, brother—was there *any* doubt?"

Knightstep hesitated before responding to his friend and fellow Army officer. He knew he was edging towards if not crossing a red line. In the Army, the internal deliberations of promotion boards were confidential. But the two officers were close.

"Okay, Jake, listen," said Knightstep. "You didn't hear this from me. But you remember the incident in the Korangal Valley, when that artillery unit did not provide your special forces team the fires you requested, and you later punched out that captain who had been on duty in the artillery battalion operations cell at the time of the incident, and put him in the field hospital for a night?"

"Yeah, of course I remember," Jake answered. "I can't say that I regret it. What happened to Sergeant Johnson was far, far worse."

"I hear you, Jake. While you have an otherwise brilliant record, there was the investigation about that incident, as I'm sure you also remember. That incident is now reflected in your official records with a Letter of Counseling. Now, that letter was supposed to stay in your *restricted* personnel file and *never* be considered by a promotion board. As a Letter of Counseling, instead of the more severe Letter of Reprimand, it should have just been a small, almost meaningless ding. But unfortunately, the Army changed the rules for your promotion board."

"Meaning?" asked Jake.

"Meaning that letter was read by all of the board members on the promotion board, all sixteen or seventeen of them. I know you're a better officer than that, and you should have been promoted early— earlier than me, for Pete's sake. But the bottom line is that you got selected for promotion . . . but just *barely*."

"Well, punching out that incompetent dirtbag was well worth it."

Knightstep again chuckled. "I have no doubt about that, my brother."

"Thanks much, buddy. I appreciate the straight talk. Give those fine folks in the Pentagon a good kick in the shins for me, will ya?"

"You got it, Jake," replied Knightstep, now laughing out loud. "And keep kickin' ass in Paris."

Jake deeply appreciated his old friend's candor.

I'm going to finish strong, no matter what, he told himself. *But when I hit twenty years of service, I think it will be time to move on.*

36.
A TOUGH SELL

LAURA SANDERS, the US legal attaché and the FBI's senior representative to France, Monaco and more than twenty countries in Francophone Africa, was pensive as she looked out her US Embassy Paris window. Sanders had cut her teeth in challenging anti-terrorism and international assignments, as well as significant leadership positions within the FBI, but she knew this would be a tough sell to the FBI headquarters. Loaning or exchanging personnel among major US government departments and agencies was not *that* rare, but then again, it was not very common, either.

Even this many years after the 9/11 Commission had seriously faulted almost all of the US government's intelligence and law enforcement agencies for not effectively working together to thwart the deadly attacks, she knew this would take come serious convincing of the FBI's senior leadership.

Yet somehow Sanders was confident that her boss, the FBI director of the Office of International Operations (OIO), would support her once he had all the facts.

He'll approve it because it will provide a positive example for how well the FBI is working with other departments and agencies in the US government, she told herself.

The approval for Major Fortina to join her US legal attaché team in Paris required the activation of a standing agreement between the

US Department of Defense and the FBI to exchange—or directly loan for duty purposes—personnel.

The arrangement was established so that the FBI and Department of Defense could exchange or loan law enforcement experts between the various Armed Forces law enforcement investigative services.

Other than in the combat zones of Afghanistan and Iraq, if Sanders was successful, this would be the first time the agreement would be applied outside of the United States.

As Sanders picked up the phone to call her boss, Don Britton, she knew it would remain a challenge to convince him that a US Army officer could help her team with a rapidly evolving national security threat. While unorthodox, her gut told her this out-of-the-box approach was the best means to understand and defeat this ominous threat developing from Iran.

In a phone call, Sanders's boss got down to business.

"What the heck is an Army *foreign area officer*?" Britton began. "I thought *all* US Army officers were supposed to be able to work in foreign areas." He chuckled at himself.

"Well, yes, but these officers—these foreign area officers—are *different*," she replied. "They are specifically selected and trained to serve in the ranks of major or Navy lieutenant commander, and higher ranks for international and political-military duties. They serve in US embassies and on major international military staffs. This includes with NATO allies, or United Nations peacekeeping forces, or at one of our combatant commands, like the United States European Command, US Central Command or US Indo-Pacific Command. They all have advanced university degrees in international relations or diplomacy, and all of them speak at least one foreign language. My military counterpart here, the US defense attaché at the US Embassy Paris, is a senior US Army foreign area officer."

"Tell me more. Why do you need *this* guy?" asked Britton.

"As you know, we are currently down to two team members here. Major Fortina, however, effectively worked with us previously on cyber threat issues. My deputy, Tom O'Conner, speaks very highly of him. Tom and Fortina attended a cybersecurity course together at the Marshall Center, in Germany. Fortina has also voluntarily worked with us on cyber threat issues in France, and he is working with our French colleagues as well."

"I'm familiar with the Marshall Center," said Britton. "The FBI Academy has had a long-standing faculty exchange agreement with them, and we, of course, continue to send our agents there for various courses on national security threats."

"Well, in addition to that, Fortina is fluent in French and Italian, and his Farsi is also very good," said Sanders. "He's also a former Army Green Beret with combat and anti-terrorism experience. He's recently been selected for promotion to lieutenant colonel, so he's not exactly a junior officer."

"Okay, Laura, it sounds like he's been involved in some national security business, but how do you plan on *employing* him to *help* with this rapidly emerging threat?" asked Britton.

"What I need most on my team right now is another set of competent and experienced eyes and ears. I also need someone who can work well with the French," said Sanders. "Of course, France has primary jurisdiction for this case, which has rapidly moved well beyond a hate crime to a *tier-one* national security threat. We strongly suspect that the Iranians are trying to develop a vicious virus and the vaccine to go with it. Our intelligence suggests that they plan to deploy the virus against the United States and Israel, while protecting Iranian citizens with a vaccine.

"I plan on linking Major Fortina up with Tom O'Conner, and I will make sure they are joined at the hip in posturing us and the French to deal with this threat," continued Sanders. "O'Conner has a lot of anti-terrorism experience, including tours in Afghanistan, Iraq, and even Kenya, just like Fortina. Neither individual, of course, will be able to make any arrests or apprehensions, but they will be able to rapidly inform French law enforcement and anti-terrorist authorities of the whereabouts of the one—and there might be more—Hezbollah member we believe to still be in the Paris area."

"And you're sure the French are okay with this?" asked Britton.

"I'm positive. It's a bit of a gray area, but as a member of the US Armed Forces, Major Fortina is covered by the Status of Forces Agreement with France and other European countries. That means he can move around most of Europe rather freely if needed. Again, his role will only be for surveillance and reporting purposes. In this case, he will *not* be—as you know, in France he *cannot* be—a trigger puller, unless defending himself.

"And there is one other thing," added Sanders.

"And what's *that*?" asked Britton.

"You know how our stateside undercover agents *must* look like or roughly imitate the groups they're trying to infiltrate or be around? Well, Jake Fortina looks like he could have grown up in Lebanon or Italy or Malta or Morocco or . . . maybe even Persia," she said, adding, "I know we have people like that in the Bureau, but they don't know France, and they may not speak Farsi, and they are not here *now*. Fortina *is* here now, and his boss is ready to release him to us for three months, and more if needed."

"Well, this actually sounds pretty innovational," said Britton, "but sometimes when we innovate too much, we assume too much risk. But this evolving Iranian threat is becoming too big of a deal to not address with all of our resources. I can get you some Bureau folks if you need them, but it will take at least four to six weeks—and that's the best case—to find the right people and get them cleared so they can work in France."

"Sir, thank you. But we don't have that kind of time," replied Sanders. "Furthermore, this idea of major government departments exchanging or loaning personnel to each other has been successfully accomplished by other USG departments and agencies. While serving in Afghanistan, I worked with a former US Army colonel and DOD civilian who was detailed to the State Department for several months. What I saw was someone who broke down interagency barriers and stereotypes and built bridges to the benefit of the entire mission and team."

"Well, if the State Department and Defense can work and play well together, which has not always been the case, then US federal government interagency relations might actually be changing for the better," Britton acknowledged.

"Indeed, one would hope so, sir."

"Okay, this decision is at my level to make. I approve your recommendation. I will inform the deputy and the director," Britton said. "Don't screw it up."

"Thank you, sir," responded Sanders.

Within the hour Laura Sanders notified the US defense attaché to France, Colonel Upshaw, that the plan was a go.

Her next task would be to brief the US ambassador to France Deborah Hunter.

37.
AN IRANIAN CONTACT

"FARHAD GILANI HAS FAILED his mission," said Iranian Intelligence minister Daghestani to the Ministry of Defense deputy. "And Arman Darbandi is still in Europe with Ackerman's hip bone. If we don't get it, and get it soon, it will set our research back many months. We must accelerate our means for getting the virus research secrets we need. We're being pressured by the vice-prime minister to speed up our project against the Israelis and Americans."

"What do you have in mind?" asked Deputy Defense Minister Khorasani.

"About two years ago we developed an intelligence contact in the United States. She is an Iranian who became a US citizen. She works at a major multinational pharmaceutical company in the Boston area," said Daghestani. "This individual was directly involved in the development of the COVID-19 vaccine. Until now, we have not pressed her for much information. Instead, we have let her work at her own pace. But she has many family members still in Iran, including some sick relatives, so we have a lot of leverage on her," said Daghestani.

"My brother, do you think the information she has been privy to is *that* critical to our developing a lethal Spanish 2.0 virus, as well us unlocking the secrets for developing an effective vaccine?" asked Khorasani.

"The information she could provide us will be vital. It is more likely to help us deploy a vaccine against the virus we are developing, then enhancing the lethality of the virus itself. The information she has gained about vaccinating people against viruses is incalculable. The American government spent billions of dollars in developing a COVID-19 vaccine, as well as treatments for the virus itself. Entirely new virus research frontiers have opened because of the unprecedented research efforts by the Americans, British, and other Europeans."

"What do you propose our next actions should be?" asked Khorasani.

"It is time for our contact to report everything she knows. If she does not yet have sufficient information to help our cause, we must pressure her to work harder. We need to know everything the Americans and Brits have done in acquiring a COVID-19 vaccine and learn as much as we can from them for developing our own Spanish 2.0 flu vaccine, before we deploy the virus."

38.
DIPLOMATIC SUPPORT

THE FIRST AFRICAN AMERICAN ambassador to France was finishing up on a classified email to the State Department. She and her deputy chief of mission Richie Sheridan, a Bostonian, and the number two person in the embassy, awaited the arrival of two key members—the US legal attaché and US defense attaché to France—of her "country team."

Deborah Hunter had been on US president Thomas Perry's short list to be his vice-presidential running mate. But during Perry's final deliberations to select his VP, it was discovered Hunter had cancer, forcing her to decline consideration. Her cancer went into remission not long after Perry was sworn into office, so Hunter became his choice for one of the top US diplomatic posts on the planet.

Hunter was getting to know both Laura Sanders and Colonel Andrew Upshaw quite well, having had both on her diplomatic team since her arrival some eight months prior.

"Richie, both are very competent, dedicated, and trustworthy professionals," said the ambassador and former US congresswoman. "After many years of dedicated public service, they are not even remotely people I would consider to be part of the so-called *Deep State*, a term I abhor and never understood. We will need to do our absolute best in assisting the French and in making our own determination of what this Iranian virus threat is all about. These two individuals will play a major role in that."

"I agree, Madame Ambassador," said Sheridan. "They are both topflight public service professionals."

As the two concluded their exchange, the ambassador's secretary, Ms. Lisa Rund, could be heard just outside of the ambassador's spacious office. Rund was directing Sanders and Upshaw into the office. Rund had been with Hunter for many years, and they understood each other better than some married couples.

"Please go right in," said Rund.

"Madame Ambassador," began US legal attaché Laura Sanders as the two embassy leaders sat down. "Thank you for taking the time to meet with Colonel Upshaw and me."

"It's my pleasure," said Hunter. "This apparent attempt by Iran to develop a virus, and perhaps a vaccine, is a serious national security matter that you may know more about than I do, and it is rapidly evolving. While the threat appears to be directed against the United States and our good friends the Israelis, I understand the French have jurisdiction for whatever happens on French soil. Do I have that about right?" asked the ambassador.

"Yes, ma'am, that is correct," said Sanders.

"So, how do we help the French help us?" asked Hunter.

"Our FBI assets over here are limited," began Sanders. "They are even more limited now that I am down two agents here in Paris. However, Colonel Upshaw has agreed—and the Department of Defense supports him on this—to allow one of his attachés to join our team for a period of at least three months and longer if needed."

"How did this come about?" asked the ambassador.

"Both of us were able to convince our respective chains of command that this, while a bit unorthodox, was the best and most timely option."

"And what option would that be?" asked Hunter.

"Madame Ambassador, I believe you know Major Fortina," said Sanders. "He works in the defense attaché's office."

"I do. He seems a very astute and capable officer."

"He is, Madame Ambassador," said Sanders. "My deputy, Special Agent Tom O'Connor, has worked with him before and speaks highly of him. They met at the Marshall Center, in Germany. My proposal is that the two work together on this case."

"Okay, I like the sound of this interagency cooperation. But are you sure you two won't be banished to the hinterlands for trying to actually work with another US government department, albeit against a rapidly evolving threat to the United States?" Hunter chuckled.

"Well, I *might* be banished." Sanders laughed. "That remains to be seen. But it's the right thing to do. Not to oversimplify, but this is a good match. Fortina has exceptional international, personal security, reconnaissance and even close combat skills, the latter of which will hopefully not be needed," said Sanders.

"Four combat tours between Afghanistan, Iraq, and Africa will do that to you," she continued. "And the Army thinks enough of him to have selected him for promotion to lieutenant colonel."

"Indeed, I'd heard that," said Hunter, now looking at her deputy. "Richie, what are your thoughts?"

"Well, this much I know. I've seen Fortina in action while working with the French and some of our international counterparts here in the city. He's diplomatically competent and very respected by French Ministry of Defense and Armed Forces officials. I think they will welcome his support. His foreign language skills are also solid. And since the crimes that launched this whole thing were committed in an American *military* cemetery, I think the French military and law enforcement officials will understand how this US Army officer fits into the overall picture."

"Correct," Upshaw said. "I've done some confidential checking with senior French military officials, and they get it. Even for a major—albeit a senior one—Fortina is highly respected and widely known by the French military, and certainly the Gendarmes, as well. If you are looking for the best all-around athlete to join this all-star team, Fortina is your man."

"Great. Now, Laura, please tell the ambassador and me more specifically about how O'Connor and Fortina will work together on this," said Sheridan.

"Their primary role will be to assist the French government in finding and observing the second perpetrator of the crimes that were conducted at the American cemetery. While the crimes were committed on the grounds of an American cemetery, the original international agreement with the French states that their law enforcement agencies will conduct criminal investigations of any crimes that occur on any of the fourteen American cemeteries and fourteen memorials on French soil. However, as the Suresnes cemetery crimes are now pointing to a full-blown national security threat, we will be working in the field directly with our French counterparts."

"In the *field*?" asked Ambassador Hunter.

"Yes. Excuse me, ma'am. Let me be clearer. I meant throughout France, depending on where this trail leads. O'Connor and Jake will not be able to make an arrest. As it stands now, they will not be able to carry a weapon on French soil, although we heard the French might change that. Their expertise will be used to assist in tracking, investigating, and analyzing the Hezbollah operative's movements until the French can bring him in—with Ms. Ackerman's hip bone, hopefully—for arrest and questioning."

"Laura and Andrew, I appreciate your rundown on this arrangement. I know this will be new territory in terms of US interagency and Franco-American cooperation, but this is well worth supporting," said Ambassador Hunter. "I will inform the deputy secretary of state first thing tomorrow morning."

"Thank you, ma'am," Sanders said.

As Laura Sanders and Andrew Upshaw departed the ambassador's office, they were proud to have gotten their cooperative arrangement approved by everyone who mattered. It was not an easy task. But they also knew the hard work was just beginning.

39.
CHANGE OF MISSION

"SHUT THE DOOR AND SIT DOWN," Colonel Andrew Upshaw, the senior US Defense Department representative to France, said as Major Jake Fortina entered his doorway.

"I've got some good news, and I've got some bad news," Upshaw said.

"Hit me with the bad first, sir."

"Jake, for the next three months, I'm pulling you off of attaché duty."

"And the *good* news?"

"The good news is that I'm assigning you to a completely new mission. Like I said, it will initially be for three months, but it might get extended if needed. I presume you've heard about the hate crimes that occurred at our American cemetery in Suresnes?"

"Yes, sir, I have been following the internal embassy reports."

"Well, Jake, there's more to the story than what's out in the public, or even what's currently circulating here in the embassy. The public is only aware of the desecrated headstones, nothing more. Now, this is very late-breaking—and highly classified—but one of the caskets, the one from the second grave, was broken into. Two bones were taken from that casket. They were part of the remains of a Ruth Ackerman who was a US Army nurse in World War I. She was a legend because she spent several months treating our doughboys who had come down with the Spanish flu, and while over ninety percent of the nurses at the time got the virus, and all got very sick and many died, Ackerman very quickly recovered."

"Well, sir, how the hell did she end up in that grave, then?" asked Jake.

"She got hit by a truck near the field hospital where she was serving."

"Aw . . . that's terrible, sir," said Jake, thinking of his own tragic loss.

Upshaw suddenly realized he had inadvertently hit a painful recessive place.

"Jake, I'm sorry," said Upshaw.

"Sir, that's not on you. It's on me. I know I must move past it, but there are times—there are times. . . " replied Jake, looking for the right words.

"I can't imagine, Jake," replied Upshaw.

This is why I love this guy, thought Jake. *There is no question that he cares about me.*

Collecting his composure, Jake continued.

"So why the missing bones?" he asked.

"The bones were taken by two Hezbollah operatives. We know this because one of the bones, her left femur, ended up in the hands of Scotland Yard when one of the two operatives—a Farhad Gilani, an Iranian—tried to get through British customs with it while on his way to Istanbul," explained Upshaw.

"What happened to this Gilani guy?"

"We don't know. The last word was that the Brits allowed him to fly on to Istanbul. But once he left the airport there, the Turks had no idea where he ended up."

"Istanbul? Interesting. And the hip bone?" asked Jake.

"The French believe it's in the possession of Gilani's sidekick. They don't have a name for him yet, but they think he's in the Saint-Denis area," said Upshaw.

"Yeah, I'm familiar with that area. Not exactly friendly territory for French law enforcement. So, where are you going with this, sir?"

"It's not where I'm going but where *you'll* be going, Jake. The US legal attaché here specifically asked that you help her team and the French DGSI track that second Hezbollah operative and when the evidence is right, help bring him in, preferably with that bone. And by her team, I'm referring to Special Agent Tom O'Connor, whom I think you know personally and have already worked with, on some cyber threat issues here in France."

"O'Connor? Yep, I know him. He's a solid citizen, quite respected here at the embassy. Met him at a cybersecurity course at the Marshall Center in Garmisch-Partenkirchen, Germany. O'Connor kicked my ass once or twice on the ski slopes there. We later went our separate ways but somehow ended up together here, a couple of embassy floors apart. Pretty crazy."

"Well, what's going to be even crazier is that you two are going to be joined at the hip as long as this operation is in effect. The primary theory right now has it that the Iranians want that bone—and Ruth Ackerman's DNA—so they can develop a deadlier version of the Spanish flu of 1918. Our fellow American civilian citizens and our Israeli friends top the list for whom the Iranians want to deploy the virus against. There is also a corollary to that theory, and here is the part that is even scarier: the Iranian government intends to develop a vaccine for their own people before coming after us with the virus," said Upshaw.

"What the hell, that would be cataclysmic," said Jake. "Yet, it's not all *that* shocking. After we knocked off their American-killing general, which I was thrilled to see, I was wondering when the revengeful Iranian chickens were coming home to roost."

"Those chickens, and a lot of other chickens, including our support of the Shah of Iran in the 1950s, '60s, and '70s. We backed a ruthless horse, Jake, and some of the Iranians haven't forgotten."

"What are my rules of engagement?"

"That's just it," said Upshaw. "There will be no engagements, at least not the kind that you were used to in Afghanistan and Iraq. Your job, first and foremost, is to support Special Agent O'Connor within the borders of France. He's got the lead. Think of O'Connor as your battle buddy. Secondly, you are to help him help the French, who are glad to have you both supporting their efforts. Now, there is one exception to all this, Jake."

"What's that?"

"Since you might end up close to the action, the French have just made an extraordinary exception to their national policy of not allowing allies to be armed on French soil. When US President George W. Bush visited here in 2004 for the sixtieth anniversary of D-Day, the French raised holy hell about our US Secret Service members being armed. Yet, in your case, they're going to allow you to carry a concealed sidearm."

"I really did not expect to be given the authority to be armed, sir. But I do appreciate it."

"I guess allowing an ally to be killed on their turf would be a lot worse than allowing one to defend himself," said Upshaw. "Kudos to you for developing a solid reputation with the French."

"Look, this is an odd situation in a lot of ways," the colonel continued. "While the crimes happened in a US cemetery, the French have jurisdiction. Jake, your primary mission is reconnaissance, just like in your old Special Forces days. *Locate* the second Hezbollah operative, *observe* him, keep observational contact for as long as safely possible, and report quickly and accurately to your French DGSI contacts. Of course, keep the US legal attaché informed too, but I'm sure Special Agent O'Connor will handle most of that business. Do not even *think* about trying to personally apprehend this guy. That should be left to the French. But if you find yourself in a situation where you have to defend yourself, do what you have to do. Is that clear?" asked the colonel.

"Yes, sir, it's clear. When do I start?"

"You'll meet with Sanders and O'Connor tomorrow morning, in Sanders's office, and from that point forward, you're working for the US FBI in France," said Upshaw. "Of course, keep me informed, but I'm lower on the priority list than the FBI or the French. I don't want you to be distracted by having to think about constantly reporting back to me."

"I don't want you to be distracted," thought Jake. *More vintage Upshaw. He trusts me completely. An insecure, non-trusting guy would have had me calling him every day, if not every hour.*

"By the way, you remember when I called you to say you were getting promoted, and I joked about you not taking your foot off the gas pedal?"

"Yes, sir, I do remember that." Jake chuckled. "Is this what you meant? Did you already know about this mission then?"

"No, Jake, I did not have the first clue about this mission then," said the colonel. "If I could, I'd go with you on this mission. But now I'm going to tell you something else in stretching an overused metaphor. Be safe out there."

40.
AMBASSADOR TO AMBASSADOR

"THANK YOU FOR TAKING THE TIME to see me, Madame Ambassador," said US ambassador to France Deborah Hunter to her Israeli counterpart, Israeli ambassador to France Miriam Lieb.

"It's my pleasure, Madame Ambassador," responded Lieb.

"I'm sure you are aware of the crime that occurred at the US cemetery in Suresnes, and I know our staffs have been talking. But I have been meaning to speak personally with you about this, ambassador-to-ambassador," said Hunter. "A lot of water has flowed under the bridge over the past few days, so to speak."

"I was aware of the discovery of the second desecrated Jewish grave at your cemetery," replied Lieb. "If you know more, I'd certainly appreciate hearing about it."

"Miriam, this is late-breaking, but I wanted you to know that Israel will have the full support of the United States government in solving these crimes, and the evolving national security threats, as we go forward."

"National security threats?" asked Lieb.

"Yes. To your country and mine," responded Hunter. "It seems the Iranians desperately wanted those two bones from Ruth Ackerman's grave because Ackerman contracted the Spanish flu, but she quickly and in almost miraculous fashion recovered from it. She worked tirelessly, constantly exposing herself to the afflicted American soldiers who had the disease, a great number of whom died. So did the majority of American nurses who were unfortunate to contract the disease. Ackerman not only survived, but she barely had the sniffles and bounced back very quickly.

"There has been a great deal of work and advancement in the paleovirology field recently," continued Hunter. "A lot of progress has also been made due to COVID-19 vaccine research, and the Iranians appear to want to achieve a full understanding of Ackerman's DNA makeup and how that affected her near total immunity."

"I forgot to add that the great majority of the dead at the Suresnes cemetery did not die from World War I combat; rather, they succumbed to the Spanish flu."

"Well, that certainly does explain a lot about why two bones were taken from Ms. Ackerman's grave." Lieb leaned forward slightly. "How did Ackerman die, then? What *else* can you tell me?"

"I will tell you everything I know, Madame Ambassador," responded Hunter.

"I appreciate that."

"Ruth Ackerman died in an accident near the field hospital she was working in. One of her bones has already been recovered. Scotland Yard is holding it. They have confirmed a DNA match to Ackerman's remains."

"How are you responding to the French government over this?" asked Lieb.

"My US legal attaché is working very closely with the French DGSI. Since the crimes happened on the grounds of a US cemetery and were directed towards our countries, and to Jewish people everywhere, we are providing them with a two-man team dedicated to help with surveillance. The French have been very open, forthcoming, and cooperative with their investigation."

"I have found them to be that way too," said Lieb.

"Oh, really?"

In the back of her mind, given the *Death to the Jews* epithet, Hunter had wondered the degree to which the French had been keeping the Israelis informed.

"Yes, they have been good about that," responded the Israeli ambassador. "They let us know about the epithet soon after it happened. They haven't directly involved us in most hate crime cases in the past because the crimes were most often hate speech—

spraypainted on some building or monument or headstone—without much substance behind them. France, as you may know, Deborah, has had a history of anti-Semitism. This case, however, is different, much different. It has national security implications for both of us."

"I am not an expert on anti-Semitism in France, but my staff has made me aware of a number of instances in Paris and around France where anti-Semitic drivel has been discovered. It's mostly been written in cemeteries or on monuments," replied Hunter.

"Yes, exactly," said Lieb. "It's an unfortunate fact of life that we must continue to deal with. Where do we go from here?"

"I will be sure that my legal attaché, Ms. Laura Sanders, provides updates to whomever you designate within your embassy," responded Hunter.

"Thank you, Madame Ambassador, and we will do the same."

"I appreciate that."

As the Israeli ambassador departed, she recalled the killing of two Israeli athletes and one German police officer by Black September Palestinian terrorists at the 1972 Summer Olympic games in Munich, Germany. Israel's foreign intelligence agency, the Mossad, widely considered to be the best in the world, tracked down each—save one—of the Palestinian terrorists who were involved in massacring those athletes.

In the subsequent global manhunt for the Palestinian terrorists that followed, the Mossad's first Palestinian target was killed in Paris. If anything, the Mossad had a reputation for being patient and thorough, and highly creative in their means of dispatching terrorists and enemies.

When the Palestinian terrorist answered his home telephone in Paris, Mossad operatives remotely detonated a bomb that they had placed in the earpiece of the man's phone, blowing the side of his head off.

As Ambassador Lieb and her small entourage were driven out of the US embassy gates, she felt confident knowing the Mossad was already on the case to find Arman Darbandi.

There are some things I can share with our American friends, and there are some that I cannot, thought the heavily guarded Israeli ambassador. *And I know it's the same for them.*

41.
NEW MARCHING ORDERS

MAJOR FORTINA KNOCKED on the office door of the US legal attaché to France. He felt comfortable knowing that he was stepping into friendly territory. He'd already voluntarily worked with the FBI legal attaché's team in solving and reporting on some cyber security challenges facing the United States from French soil. He'd also attended the Marshall Center's Cyber Security Studies course in Garmisch-Partenkirchen, Germany for three weeks, where he got to know FBI special agent Tom O'Connor quite well. As fate would have it, they both ended up at US embassy in Paris.

"Good morning, ma'am, Tom." Jake nodded to each as he simultaneously knocked and entered Laura Sanders's open office door.

"Good morning, Jake," said Sanders.

O'Connor replied with a friendly, "Hey, Jake."

"Jake, Tom has already heard most of this, so my discussion will be principally directed at you, okay?" Sanders said.

"Understand, ma'am." Jake kept his attention on her, eager to learn more details of his new assignment.

"As Colonel Upshaw informed you, we asked him—and the US Department of Defense—if you could join our team in resolving a rapidly evolving national security threat, one that threatens not only the United States, but Israel as well."

"Colonel Upshaw has informed me," replied Jake.

"Well, we appreciate you coming over to the dark side with us." Sanders chuckled.

"It's my honor and pleasure, ma'am. One team, one fight."

"I think you know the gist of why you are here."

"I got the rough outline from Colonel Upshaw."

"Let me add some details and re-emphasize what Upshaw told you," said Sanders. "For one, if *anybody* were to ask you why you're working with the FBI, your *official reason* is that we haven't fully resolved the crimes that were carried out at the cemetery. We are concerned that the crimes might be part of a larger hate campaign against the United States, Israel, and perhaps even Jews everywhere. There are enough enemies of America and Israel out there to make this a very serious cause for concern, especially since the crimes conducted at the Suresnes were a first for an American cemetery overseas. Got that?" asked Sanders. "That's the public narrative you should be parroting."

"Yep, roger all," said Jake.

"Furthermore," continued Sanders, "I know you know this, but I have to emphasize it. There can be absolutely no mention of missing bones or the Iranians trying to develop a vaccine or a new Spanish Flu virus, etc. The circle of people who have a need to know this information is extremely tight. And the classification level is high, for obvious reasons. Let's keep it that way. Your work, and Tom's work, if anyone *asks*, is pursuant to getting to the bottom of those writings that were on those headstones, and nothing more."

"I'm trackin', ma'am," said Jake.

"Okay, good. Now, let's talk about what will define success for your mission. Success is—when the *French decide*—moving in and apprehending the second Hezbollah operative alive, with the Ackerman hip bone that is apparently in his possession. That's the *result* we're after here," said Sanders.

"Roger, understood."

"If the French don't take the Hezbollah operative alive but we get that bone, that will be a distant second in terms of success. But I'm not interested in second place here, Jake," she continued. "The French need to capture the Iranian alive for maximum intelligence value.

"As to the rules of the road," she continued, "you're being

hired to work with Tom because of your international acumen, reconnaissance and surveillance skills, anti-terrorist background, and the fact that you have gained the trust of the French—and us," said Sanders. "But just realize that success here also includes no shots fired. Other than in an act of self-defense, the French will go ballistic—no pun intended—if Americans were to needlessly fire live rounds on their soil," said Sanders.

"I completely understand." Jake was confident he knew the boundaries he would need to operate within.

"Okay, gentlemen, I think you know what has to be done," said Sanders. "Like Jake said, 'one team, one fight.'"

42.
WE ARE TRACKING THIS

ISRAEL'S AMBASSADOR TO FRANCE Miriam Lieb was thankful for the congenial and cooperative meeting with her US counterpart.

I don't know where we would be without the Americans, she thought as remembered her grandmother, who was rescued in World War II from the Dachau, Germany, concentration camp, by US Army forces on April 29, 1945.

Lieb's priority after the meeting with Ambassador Hunter was to debrief her Israeli foreign intelligence and counterterrorism chief, a key member of her Israeli embassy country team. It was the third meeting about the subject of the US cemetery hate crimes that she would have with Ari Dayan, the head of Mossad operations in France and the principality of Monte Carlo.

Ambassador Lieb knew enough about her own national foreign intelligence agency that the Mossad always preferred, whenever possible, to let other national intelligence services do their work for the Israelis. The Israeli government would much rather the other international intelligence services get the public credit for any successful counterintelligence or counter-terrorist operation, even if the Mossad had a major hand in them. It was better for the Mossad to remain in the shadows, if not invisible. When intelligence agencies friendly to Israel wouldn't or couldn't do the required work, the Mossad would step in. Since the end of World War II, it was part of the Mossad's low-profile, always-in-the-shadows, neither-confirm-nor-deny mantra since its beginnings, and that of the Jewish state of Israel.

"Ari, where are we on the American cemetery case?" asked the Israeli ambassador.

"We are closely tracking this," replied Dayan. "The French seem to have the second Hezbollah operative, Arman Darbandi, under observation. He's in an apartment in the Saint-Denis suburb. I believe the French are within days of making a move on him. They apparently need more evidence to confirm he's their guy and to ensure they have a solid legal basis to arrest him. If they don't move soon, we may have to give them a hand."

"Do you need any more resources?" asked the ambassador.

"At this time, we are in good shape. We have three of our people involved, and they have him pretty well covered, including with cellphone coverage," said Dayan.

"What about the other Hezbollah operative, Gilani?" asked Lieb.

"Gilani disappeared after he got to Istanbul," said Dayan. "What really matters, though, is that the Brits seized that bone from him in London. That was key information, linking Gilani to Ackerman. However, my guess is that Gilani did not meet a happy fate in Turkey. As far as Hezbollah or the Iranian government is concerned, Gilani was damaged goods after giving up that bone to the Brits."

"What about the American ambassador?" asked Dayan. "What did she share with you?"

"She gave me assurances that the Americans are working with the French DGSI on the case. Just like us, the Americans see this as a rapidly evolving threat to national security. Their legal attaché is working it for the US embassy. The ambassador asked us to provide her with a name that the Americans could share information with."

"The US legal attaché is Laura Sanders, correct?" asked Dayan. "I will have Misha call her."

"Great, I appreciate that, Ari. If you need something, of course, please let me know."

"Thank you, Madame Ambassador," replied Dayan.

43.
THE PRESIDENT'S DAILY BRIEFING

"JAY," BEGAN STEVE FISHER, the FBI's senior representative to the US interagency intelligence team responsible for putting together the president's daily intelligence briefing, "this time, the crime in Paris needs to make the cut. The president needs to be fully aware."

"How the heck do you figure?" responded Jay. "What's new?"

"*A lot* is new. In one of the graves desecrated with the words *Death to the Americans*, two bones were removed from the remains of one Ruth Ackerman, a Jew and US Army nurse who died in a truck accident in World War I."

"Go on."

"The bottom line is this: French intelligence strongly believes the bones were taken from Ackerman's grave by Iranian operatives, probably from Hezbollah, because the Iranian government needs Ackerman's DNA to complete the development of a virus, a virus potentially worse than the Spanish flu of 1918 to 1919. Ackerman got the virus but recovered from it in record time, making her a legend among her peers and even US soldiers at the time. The Iranians want to know, based on recent advances in paleovirology, what they'll need in their new version of Spanish flu so it can overcome the defenses put up by Ackerman's DNA type. The Iranians want to develop a Spanish flu 2.0 with the goal of decimating American and Jewish populations around the globe. In other words, Jay, what we now have is a tier-one national security threat."

"What are the French doing about this? Do our US intelligence contacts in France know what's going on?" asked Jay.

"They're all over it," replied Fisher. "From the ambassador on down, they're on this. The French have the lead, obviously, as this is on their national soil. But we are fully supporting French efforts out of the legal attaché's office in Paris."

"Okay," Jack said. "We'll make a reference to this for tomorrow's report. I'll make sure DNI Bulls approves it in the event he has any questions. You're right. The president needs to know. Done deal."

44.
SURVEILLANCE AUTHORITY

"JAKE, HERE IS A RATHER GRAINY PHOTO I was able to get from the DGSI concerning the second Hezbollah operative," said Special Agent O'Connor. "They've had this old internet café in the Saint-Denis area under surveillance for a while, and they're pretty sure this is the guy. He's obviously trained in losing surveillance because on about one out of three times he's departed that café, the local DGSI folks—as good as they are—managed to lose him. They think they've got him pegged to one of the huge high-rise buildings in the Saint-Denis area, but they literally have seen him come out of two different stairwell doors of the same building, which must contain more than a hundred or so one- or two-room apartments."

"Besides the fact that he's pretty good at losing surveillance, how do they figure this is their guy?" asked Jake.

"He looks Iranian, for starters, which is different enough from Yemini or Pakistani or Egyptian. The French DGSI actually have an anthropologist on staff to help sort this kind of stuff out." O'Connor shook his head. "Although it is rarely one hundred percent conclusive by a simple photo."

"So much for profiling being a bad thing," Jake chuckled.

"Secondly, through some effective intelligence fusion provided by Paris video cameras, a Dutch-plated car was observed around the time of the Suresnes cemetery crime, along with another not-so-clear video freeze frame showing the passenger. Combined with frequent trips to an internet café, that makes this dude at least a person of strong interest."

"Well, in my humble opinion, I'd put it at not much better than fifty-fifty that this is our guy," Jake said, giving his partner a serious look. "Given that we don't have much else to go on, it would be worth it to do some more homework."

"Jake, as to the homework you mentioned, we've been given authority by the French to do some surveillance in the Saint-Denis area. Now, as you probably know after two years in Paris, Saint-Denis is not exactly home to Paris's rich and famous. In 2017 it recorded eighteen percent of all drug offenses in France."

"Damn, Tom, that's a high percentage for an area of that size."

"Of course, phone surveillance or anything with fancy observation or listening equipment, that will be the DGSI's to do. But we have been given the green light to look around the area of his probable apartment building, as well as that internet café," said O'Connor. "The French are pretty sure he's still in that general area."

45.
NEXT OBJECTIVE

ARMAN DARBANDI WAS GROWING WEARY of having to lie low. He realized he did not have the big picture about what had happened after the two headstones were discovered by the American cemetery officials. But he fully expected that their discovery had provoked immediate French law enforcement involvement. Darbandi understood that he had to protect the security of Ruth Ackerman's hip bone until he could get it into the right Iranian hands for eventual delivery to the covert contacts within the Iranian government in Tehran. As he departed his apartment, he was anxious but remained confident about completing his mission.

Farhad and I were very careful, he told himself. *There is only a very small chance that anybody might be on to us. But watching French television all day long is growing old.*

As Arman walked into a café he'd regularly used, he paid the usual cash fee for thirty minutes of online internet access.

Opening his email website and logging in, he read a new message. It was just one line of the email message from his Athens contact that got his attention.

The weather will be beautiful in Marseilles in three days.

The message gave Darbandi pause.

It was now clear that his next travel objective was the French Mediterranean port city of Marseilles. He had three days to get there. This pleased Darbandi. He knew that a small group of Hezbollah operatives ran extensive contraband, drug, and money-laundering operations in the southern French port city of almost two million people, 25 percent of whom claimed Islam as their religion. He knew two Hezbollah contacts there. Both had served with him in the 2006 Lebanon War with Israel.

"I expect to meet my next contact and receive my follow-up orders in Marseille," Darbandi murmured. "And then I'll get on a ship and sail for Iran."

As Arman Darbandi walked out of the internet café, a large man asked him if he knew the way to the nearest drug store. Darbandi recognized it as code.

He immediately gave the appropriate response. "Yes, I do. There are three within one kilometer of here."

"Thank you," responded the Iranian. "I am Reza."

"And I am Arman," responded Darbandi, thinking, *Who the hell names himself Reza, after that sonofabitch Shah of Iran?*

Darbandi had an uneasy feeling.

With the two men now walking with nobody in sight, Reza broke the ice.

"I am here to protect you. Our intelligence people believe someone else wants that bone you have."

"That is not surprising, but why *exactly* do they believe this?" asked Darbandi, surprised that Reza knew about the bone.

"I am not completely sure, but things seem to have a way of leaking out. I understand that the dark web is a curious marketplace," responded Reza.

"I've heard that, too, but I've never been involved with it," Darbandi truthfully responded.

"Nor have I," said Reza, being less truthful.

As they walked, Arman had a burning question. From an operational perspective, though, Arman Darbandi did not know what Reza might know.

Does he actually know something significant, or is he just a muscle-bound security guy? Darbandi wondered. *And if he does know something, will he tell me what he knows? But since he mentioned the bone, this guy already knows more than a typical security guy should.*

Darbandi decided he had to ask.

"I have a question for you, Reza."

"Sure," Reza said calmly.

"Have you ever heard of Farhad Gilani?"

"Farhad Gilani, you say? Never heard of him."

Darbandi sensed Reza was lying.

As they approached the entrance to Darbandi's apartment building, Reza made a momentous declaration.

"There has been another change in the mission," he said. "I will tell you more once we are inside."

Entering Darbandi's small, third-floor apartment, the air was tense. Darbandi shut the sturdy entry door typical of even the cheaper apartments in Paris.

"Can I offer you something to drink? Some tea, perhaps?" asked Darbandi.

"That would be excellent, thank you."

As the two men stepped into the apartment's small kitchen, Reza put down a small piece of paper, about the size of a Post-It note, on the kitchen counter. One could never be too sure about police acoustic surveillance. Pointing to the paper, Reza knew this was the safest way to communicate.

Written on the paper were the words *Bayram Kebab, Strasbourg.* Those words were seared into the experienced Hezbollah operative's brain.

In the next moment, the two men could hear shuffling feet outside their door.

Immediately, Reza grabbed Darbandi by the arm, looked into Darbandi's eyes, pointed to the window, and mouthed the word "go."

Immediately darting over to the one-bedroom apartment's main living room window, Darbandi grabbed his backpack, with the Ackerman bone, a pistol, Swiss Army knife, flashlight, car keys, water bottle, and a few small additional items. The first solid kick to the steel door came with a loud bang, quickly followed by another.

This is unlikely the French police, Reza thought. *They would have at least first rung the doorbell or otherwise announced their presence.*

Reza nodded to Darbandi who stepped out on the fire ladder and scurried down to the grassy area below.

The apartment door burst open. Reza got off the first shot, but the two international professionals, one from Russia and the other from Italy, were too good. One came in firing low and was immediately followed by the other, firing high. Within seconds, it was over.

Reza had a cherry-sized bullet hole through the center of his bloodied forehead. The gunfight was over, but the hit men's main target, Darbandi, was nowhere to be seen.

46.
SURVEILLANCE

IT WAS THE THIRD NIGHT of observing the apartment building from their US embassy vehicle. Tonight, it was just the Americans. Their French colleagues had been pulled away for another more urgent mission.

Unlike the armored Mercedes used for the ambassador, their VW Jetta was one of the smaller, older and more modest vehicles in the US embassy fleet. That was just how Special Agent O'Connor and Major Fortina wanted it. A higher-class model might attract suspicious eyes in the economically depressed Saint-Denis area.

Like all vehicles in the embassy fleet, the Jetta had common license plates, with the first two numbers correlating to the city of Paris. However, official diplomatic plates issued by the French government for its fleet were kept *inside* these vehicles in case the occupants were pulled over by French police. Embassy issued plates, along with personal identification, would confirm the diplomatic immunity of the vehicle's owner and that of his or her family.

"This is a fact of life for an FBI agent," Tom said as he stared at the building's entrance and adjoining sidewalk. "Hours of complete freakin' boredom occasionally punctuated by something of interest and maybe even exciting."

"I get it," said Jake. "It's a lot like operating in a combat zone. There are times when you're counting blades of grass or observing a trail for hours on end . . . and *nothing* happens. Other times, all hell might break loose."

"But I'm sure both our services have some other things in common too," said O'Connor. "Like, if you are on a recon or surveillance mission and get observed by your target, get compromised. Not good."

"Bingo," said Jake.

"Ever happen to you?"

"It did," replied Jake. "Once."

Sensing that Fortina did not want to talk about the subject further, O'Connor dropped it.

Suddenly, the two men observed—O'Connor with a telephoto lens and Jake with the naked eye—a man who looked very familiar at the building entrance.

"That looks like him," said O'Connor. "And it looks like he has company."

"Yep, and that is one big dude," said Jake. "Looks Arab, maybe, from here."

"Roger, concur," said O'Connor.

O'Connor and Jake observed the men entering the building's stairwell, and about two minutes later a light on the third floor.

"You see that light?" asked O'Connor.

"Yep, got it," replied Jake.

Within five minutes, two more men were observed entering the building. One looked Mediterranean, perhaps Italian or Spanish, with the other white and tall.

"More friends joining the party?" asked Jake.

"I don't know, but we should try to at least determine what apartment *number* that is at some point," said O'Connor. "It shouldn't be hard to find it once we're in the building. Looks like it's the third apartment over from the stairwell, on the third floor."

Through the third-floor apartment the two men saw an image of a man in the main apartment window that looked like Darbandi. The man was making quick moves.

"What the hell? Did you just see him dart in front of the window?" asked O'Connor.

"Yep," Jake said as he sat straight up.

"Looks like Darbandi is taking door number two," said O'Connor, observing Darbandi scurrying down the metal fire escape ladder.

"Did you just see what I think were muzzle flashes?" asked Jake.
"Sure did," said O'Connor.

"And who is *that*?" asked Jake, now staring at the window.

"That's one of the two guys we just saw go into the building!"

As Darbandi reached the final rung of the ladder and dropped
to the wet ground, Jake said, "I'm following him!"

Slipping out of the car and instantly in a steady sprint, Jake stayed
well enough behind the running Iranian to make sure he would not
suspect he was being followed.

O'Connor, still behind the wheel in the Jetta, watched the two
men who had just entered the building a few minutes before now
exit. Looking around frantically, one man ran while another limped
behind him in exactly the opposite direction.

Seconds later, Jake returned to the VW Jetta, which O'Connor
had positioned to immediately depart its parking spot.

"I got a vehicle ID," said Jake. "Let's roll!"

As the Italian and Russian returned to the building on foot,
having lost Darbandi's trail, they got a glimpse of a speeding Renault
Megane driving by.

O'Connor drove steadily until the Renault was in his sights.
Backing off, he kept a safe distance to make sure Darbandi did
not know he was being tailed as he took a southeasterly direction
through Paris's busy streets.

"The second guy who was with Darbandi must have been
additional security, and he sacrificed himself to buy some time for
Darbandi to escape," said O'Connor.

"Roger," Jake said. "And it obviously worked. We now know that
somebody else wants Darbandi, or wants what he has, or possibly
both."

"Yep. And those other two cats are still out there somewhere."

"Did you get a photo or two of them?" asked Jake.

"Nope," said O'Connor. "The light was terrible."

"Do you think they saw us?"

"I think that's about a fifty-fifty possibility," said O'Connor.

As O'Connor and Jake trailed the bronze-colored Renault, they
considered their next moves, one of which was to check in with the
boss.

"Ma'am, we're on his tail," said Jake on the phone with Laura

Sanders. "Something went down at his apartment in Saint Denis, and Darbandi made a run for it."

"Went *down*?" replied Sanders.

"Yes. We saw Darbandi enter his apartment with a second individual. Moments later, two men went into the building, and the next thing we observed, Darbandi came flying down the fire escape ladder and made a run for it. Then we saw muzzle flashes come from his apartment, and the two guys who went in the building after him later came out, with one of them limping. If they were chasing Darbandi, they went the wrong way. Bottom line is this: we got Darbandi's license number and we're tailing him now."

"Does he know you are tailing him?" asked Sanders.

"Not by the way he's driving, no, we don't think so."

"What about the other two guys?" she asked.

"We don't know where they are or exactly who they were. But we're pretty sure they are not following us. One looked to be maybe a Spaniard or Italian—not sure—and the other was a burly white guy. My guess—based on those muzzle flashes—is that the second guy who entered the building with Darbandi is now lying dead in that apartment," said Jake. "He never came out. He was maybe there to pass some information to or provide some security for Darbandi. Or maybe he was just an unlucky tea-drinking partner who was in the wrong place at the wrong time."

"Continue to follow Darbandi, Jake, and keep me informed to the extent you can. I will let the French know. Until the French get to his apartment and discover a dead body, they may not yet have enough evidence to implicate Darbandi," she said. "The only information they have at this point is that he's most likely Iranian and is associated with the other guy with the bone who got stopped in London but was later released. That's not a ton of evidence at this point."

47.
PARTNERS

"WE'VE GOT TO GO BACK in there and make sure he is dead," Luigi Gianfranco said to his partner, Antonin Markov.

The seasoned international criminals had met in Badu'e Carros, a high-security jailhouse in the little town of Nuoro, on the island of Sardinia. The Italian national prison was home to terrorists and dangerous mobsters, including Cosa Nostra, Camorra, and 'Ndrangheta.

Gianfranco, born in Polistena, Italy, was a veteran 'Ndrangheta *mafioso*. Originating in and around Italy's southern Calabria region near the toe of the Italian boot, the 'Ndrangheta (meaning "manly goodness" or "virtue") organization had risen to be Italy's most powerful and dangerous mafia network. The crime group was made up of smaller networks of hundreds of smaller family gangs throughout Italy and beyond. It had managed to extend its influence to industries in Italy's richer northern region and across the world. It raked in billions of dollars from drug trafficking, extortion, and money laundering.

In 2013 a Swiss research group claimed that 'Ndrangheta made more money than Deutsche Bank and McDonald's put together, with an annual revenue of over sixty billion dollars.

But the 'Ndrangheta's bosses saw their international mafia dominance as fleeting. They wanted more, a lot more. If that meant doing business with some of the world's leading terrorist organizations, so be it.

As the two men returned to the apartment, Markov was limping heavily. His thigh had taken a nine-millimeter slug from the one shot the Iranian was able to get off before Gianfranco took him out with three clean shots to the torso and head. Adrenaline had kicked in enough to keep the forty-something Russian strong man on his feet.

As the Italian checked the Iranian—lying faceup on the living room floor—for a pulse, it was confirmed.

"He's dead."

Gianfranco ripped a strip of a bedsheet from Darbandi's bed and wrapped it around Markov's flesh wound. Fortunately for Markov, the bullet had passed through his thigh, missing bones and major arteries.

Quickly surveying the apartment before departing, Gianfranco noticed a small piece of paper on the kitchen floor. On it were written three words: *Bayram Kebab, Strasbourg.*

With Markov still in the living room, Gianfranco quickly stuffed the paper in his pants pocket.

"We need to get you to our safe house, to see a doctor," said Gianfranco.

"It's not that bad." Markov grunted.

"The *hell* it isn't," replied Gianfranco.

Markov had earned his organized crime spurs with the Russian Tambovskaya gang. Now operating in many places throughout Europe, they had originated in St. Petersburg, Vladimir Putin's former KGB stomping grounds. From its roots in the early 1990s, the Tambovskava international criminal network had established an empire stretching beyond traditional rackets into legitimate industries like real estate, banking, and energy.

When the Spanish government started making inroads into the Tambovskaya organization, which had grown far too big even for the vast Iberian Peninsula, mid-level criminal Markov decided to make a break for it. That is, until the Italian authorities rolled Markov up in Rome for money laundering.

I'm glad I finally repaid my debt, Gianfranco thought as the two men reached their new Alfa Romeo Quadrifoglio SUV. *Markov saved my life in that prison.*

"Maybe you are right, Gianfranco," said Markov, now slumped in the passenger seat of the SUV. "I might be gettin' too old for this shit."

Before Gianfranco turned the ignition of the SUV, he called the 'Ndrangheta's on-call doctor in Paris.

"Doctor Phillippe, I'm with a man who was just shot in the upper leg. The bullet appears to have passed through. The man is conscious. I expect to be at our clinic in twenty-five minutes. See you there."

Doctor Phillippe, sixty-eight years old and retired for two years from a modest family medical practice, had been gently squeezed by three 'Ndrangheta mobsters to serve as an on-call physician twenty-four hours per day, seven days per week for their mob members in the greater Paris area.

While he knew better, Doctor Phillippe was told he would be treating downtrodden local immigrants who were financially supported by a generous Omani sheik. The one-hundred-thousand-dollar annual retainer—"for perhaps a few days' work per year," he was told with a wink—served nicely along with his savings to keep him and his wife plenty comfortable, even in spendy Paris. It was a deal he literally could not refuse. It also came with a small apartment that he would keep outfitted for medical emergencies, including basic surgery.

As the two hit men entered the eastern Paris suburb of Bobigny, it was not long before they reached their safe house. Which was not a house at all. It was a one-bedroom apartment in one of the several nondescript, off-white, fifteen- to twenty-story apartment buildings in the area, not far from the Hotel de Ville, which was not a hotel at all. It was Bobigny's city hall.

When Gianfranco and Markov entered the elevator, it was evident that Markov, now barely able to support himself, was growing weaker by the minute.

"I have to admit, this goddamn thing is beginning to really hurt," he said as they stepped out of the elevator.

Shuffling down the thirty feet of hallway felt more like a mile.

As they rang the apartment bell, the waiting Doctor Phillippe quickly opened the door. His trip to the medical safe house, up the elevator from his personal apartment six floors below, had required only about three minutes to accomplish.

Helping Markov get to the gurney in the bedroom, Phillippe quickly examined the operative who was sweating profusely.

"What do you think, Doc?" asked Gianfranco.

"I have good and bad news," said Phillippe. "The good news is that I can put him to sleep for about a couple of hours and clean and patch him up pretty well. But then he'll need antibiotics and forced hydration, which I have here, as well as rest. That *rest* part is up to him . . . and you, I suppose."

"And the bad?" asked Gianfranco.

"He's not going to be mobile for *at least* a couple of days, maybe longer, and then only with crutches and some strong pain medicine. The bullet did damage to some muscle mass. To heal up properly, he'll need bed rest for a few days and then crutches for at least a couple more weeks."

"Okay, Doc," Gianfranco said.

Looking around the apartment when he first entered, Gianfranco was pleased to see Phillippe had done a good job in stocking emergency medical supplies. Gianfranco smiled when he saw that the good French doctor also had wine and hard liquor generously stocked in the apartment.

"Well, my friend," said Gianfranco to his Russian partner, "it looks like our adventure ends here for you."

"*Da.* And *grazie*, Gianni," said Markov, referring to Gianfranco by his nickname. "I'm glad you're still a good shot."

"And I'm glad you're still a tough, vodka-swilling sonofabitch," said Gianfranco. He turned to Phillippe. "Doc, take care of this guy. Now it's getting late, and I've still got a lot of work to do. So, get started."

Gianfranco waited until the doc's syringe-delivered anesthesia put Markov fast asleep, and then announced to Dr. Phillippe, "You know who to call if you need anything. *Ciao, dottore.*"

Gianfranco left the high-rise apartment. The only words in his mind were *Bayram Kebab, Strasbourg.*

48.
MERCI, MONSIEUR!

ROUGHLY HALFWAY TO STRASBOURG, between Reims and Metz on French highway A4, Agent O'Connor and Major Fortina continued to follow the Iranian in the bronze Renault. They saw something they were not expecting—Darbandi's right turn signal was on.

"Is he taking the exit ramp to the Shell station?" asked Jake.

"Sure does look that way," O'Connor said, keeping his eye firmly on Darbandi's vehicle.

O'Connor instantly checked his rearview mirror and then reduced his speed. He did not want to run up on the rear of a suspicious Darbandi. Within seconds he had put about one hundred fifty yards between the embassy VW Jetta and Darbandi's Renault. Just prior to entering the exit ramp, he quickly pulled off to the road's shoulder and shut off his lights. After waiting about fifteen seconds, he turned the car lights back on and entered the exit ramp, proceeding cautiously into the large gas station parking area.

Hopefully, he had not allowed too much space to build between him and Darbandi, thereby allowing Darbandi to sneak out the opposite side of the gas station. But O'Connor knew that the risk of Darbandi running out the back door was worth not getting compromised.

"There he is," declared Jake.

With the bronze Renault now pulling into a parking spot in their sights, they parked their car about forty yards away. Jake was thankful this was one of those big European highway gas stations, providing parking space for about thirty or forty cars near the coffee shop and gas pumps, and about twice as many parking spaces farther on for eighteen-wheeler semitrucks. Even at a few minutes after midnight, this Shell station was busy.

O'Connor and Jake watched as an unsuspecting Darbandi calmly got out of his car and walked into the gas station's bathrooms, marked with a big blue and white *WC* sign. As he did, Fortina waited about thirty seconds, and then took the initiative.

"I'm going in to get coffee," he said, smiling. "The usual? Double espresso?"

"Sure."

Fortina entered the fully glass-paned coffee shop and walked up to the self-serve, bright red coffee machines present throughout many highway gas stations in Europe.

Well, it won't be as good as the coffee at the Italian espresso bars on the Italian autostrada, with the proud Italian baristas and their little bow ties, he thought, *but this commercial stuff will do in a pinch.*

The coffee machine provided black coffee, cappuccino, and espresso, with or without sugar and crème, including double-shots, green tea, black teak, and mint tea.

Fortina inserted the requisite euro coins for two double-shot black espressos. As he selected his choices and waited for the two cups to be filled, he furtively observed a figure peering through the storefront's ceiling-to-floor window. The figure, now clearer, was headed for the double entrance doors of the very coffee shop Jake was standing in. It was Arman Darbandi.

With a cup of espresso in each hand, there was only one move Jake headed for the very same double-glass doors Darbandi was about to walk through. As he approached the doors, Darbandi unsuspectingly held open the doors for the undercover Army major.

Not missing a beat, Jake walked through, avoiding eye contact while looking down at his two coffee cups while acting concerned about spilling them.

"*Merci, monsieur!*" Jake said.

Darbandi held the door open for this Mediterranean-looking French guy, one of millions in France. Darbandi did not respond and continued into the shop.

Arriving back at the car, Jake saw that O'Conner's eyes were as big as golf balls.

"Holy shit," he said. "I saw that, all of it. Did you get a good look at him?"

"Are you *shittin' me*? Uh . . . no!" responded Jake. "Eye contact would have been bad juju. I did everything *not* to make eye contact with that guy."

"Well, it must have worked," said O'Connor. "He never looked back and continued straight to the coffee machine.

"Did you see what was on his back?"

"No, I didn't, Tom. I was looking down, trying to make sure he couldn't see my handsome face. But let me guess—"

"Yep. I must have missed it when he first went to the bathroom. He was not about to leave that backpack in his car, even while taking a piss and grabbing a cup of coffee. I think we can be fairly certain he does not keep gym clothes in that thing."

As the two men sat in the shadows and focused on the entry doors to the coffee shop, they finally saw Darbandi walk out of the shop with a cup in his hand.

"Wanna bet it's chai?" asked O'Connor.

"Sure, I'll take that bet," replied the smirking Fortina. "Because there's not a chance in hell that it was chai. They had every other frickin' hot drink available in there, but chai was *not* one of the choices. Congratulations, partner," Jake said as he started to laugh, "you get to buy the next round."

The two men continued peering through several parked cars, using the intermittent cars to mask their observing eyes on Darbandi's next move. Three minutes later, the Hezbollah operative pulled out of his parking space. He continued slowly through the car parking lot and into the adjacent lot, full of parked eighteen-wheelers and then headed for the A4 on-ramp, passing a big blue European highway sign indicating directions to Metz and Strasbourg.

Allowing as much time as possible to keep a safe distance but not so much space that it raised the risk of losing sight of the bronze Renault, the two men pulled out of their parking place. They followed Darbandi in an easterly direction, on the French A4 autoroute.

49.
A MOMENTOUS NIGHT

IT WAS ALMOST 11:30 P.M., which was normally too late for a phone call, even to a high-level international diplomatic contact in Paris. But Laura Sanders knew she had to get the information to her French DGSI colleague as soon as possible.

As she dialed the cellphone number to the director of international relations at the DGSI, she also thought about contacting the US ambassador.

It's too late to bother her, she decided. *I'll get to the ambassador first thing tomorrow. For now, the DGSI needs to know. If Steinberg doesn't pick up, I'll leave a message for him to call me early tomorrow morning.*

"Hallo," Jean Steinberg said on the other end of the line. His last name conveyed his origins from eastern France's German-influenced border region of Alsace.

"Jean, this is Laura." Sanders had cultivated a strong professional, as well as trusting personal, relationship with her French law enforcement counterpart. They had shared three or four friendly business lunches over the preceding year, while also sharing French and US international law enforcement concerns and observations.

"It turns out it was a momentous night for your part of the Saint-Denis surveillance team to get pulled for another mission," said Sanders.

"Oh? How so?" answered the Frenchmen.

"Not more than an hour ago, Agent O'Connor and Major Fortina witnessed a second man return to the building with the Iranian. Shortly thereafter, two other men went to his apartment. Shots were fired, and the Iranian, our primary suspect, scurried down the fire escape and drove away. O'Connor and Fortina are on the Iranian's tail now. They surmised there is a dead body in that apartment because only the two men who later entered the apartment emerged. Neighbors might have already called the local police or 1-1-2. I will send more written details shortly."

"*Merci*, Laura," the senior French government official said. "We will check out the apartment right away. I have questions, but I will await your written report. Please let me know as soon as you have more operational details. I will do the same."

"*D'accord*," responded Sanders.

"I presume O'Connor and Fortina are okay?"

"They are fine, Jean."

What a helluva thing that our two guys were on surveillance duty tonight, she thought.

Sanders was particularly gratified by the personal bond of trust she had developed with Jean Steinberg. It actually made a difference when the heat was on.

50.
ANXIOUS IN BOSTON

FEELING VERY ANXIOUS, Avalie Zirani pulled into the Parker Pharmaceuticals parking lot. She had just received a message, dropped the previous night under a bush adjacent to the playground near her house. The message had placed terrible expectations on her. Until now, what her Iranian handler had asked of her was hard to achieve but doable, not leaving traces of Zirani's spying on Parker's methodologies for developing a COVID-19 vaccine. It had mainly been general information that she had provided to her US-based handler. But now, she was being required to provide answers to very specific questions about Parker's COVID-19 vaccine development.

Coming to America on an education visa, Zirani had excelled at the Massachusetts Institute of Technology, eventually finding her way to virology research and a doctorate degree. Staying in the US on a work visa, she was later hired by Parker Pharmaceutical after becoming a US citizen. Now, back in Iran, her widowed mother *and* her brother had cancer. The Iranian government plotters knew this, promising Zirani that "if you will provide us with the right information, in a timely manner, we will fly your mother and father to Germany for medical treatment."

Tens of thousands of wealthy Arabs and many Persians had traveled to Germany for first class healthcare treatment over the previous decades. Zirani had heard stories of entire floors of German hospital heart surgery wards, such as the one in Augsburg, being occupied by

Arabs. For those who sought the best orthopedic surgery, many traveled to Bavaria and Murnau's *unfall klinikum* (accident clinic), where some of the top Olympic athletes and skiers in Europe had their pictures plastered on the walls of the clinic's emergency ward. The United Arab Emirates even kept a consular office in the hospital. Helicopters delivered patients to the hospital almost daily from the horrific, highspeed accidents on Germany's autobahn and secondary roads.

To prevent them from fleeing Iran, Zirani's mother and brother were being kept on house arrest. Years of sanctions had put Iran in a terrible place in terms of sufficient and effective medical care for the Iranian people. Only the top 1 or 2 percent of Iranians could get high quality professional care, and then only if they were connected to the Iranian regime.

When Zirani reread the demands of the "right information and in accordance with our deadlines," she felt as if her mother and brother were already dead. But she knew she had to try, she had to try her very best, to help them.

I would never have made it to America without their help, she thought.

Zirani did not know about Iran's vicious plan to develop a deadly virus. However, she did expect that the Iranians were intent on developing a vaccine of their own. Zirani also did not know that the questions were coming directly from a small group of Iranian scientists and doctors operating in a clandestine research facility about thirty miles northeast of Tehran. All she knew was that she had a list of seemingly innocuous questions—some clearly posed by people who knew something about vaccines and virology—that she had to find the answers to. She rationalized that the information she was seeking through illegal means was entirely for the benefit of the Iranian people.

Worst case, this will make an Iranian pharmaceutical company rich, while hopefully saving thousands of Iranian lives, she rationalized. *I could answer about a quarter of these questions now, but the others will require more data and evidence.*

As Zirani walked through the scanners and bag checks by security agents just inside the Parker research facility entrance doors, her gut was churning. But she knew she had to act soon. It was the only chance her mother and brother had.

51.
BAYRAM KEBAB

"GOOGLE MAPS is a beautiful thing, isn't it?" Jake cracked a smile.

"Sure is," Agent O'Connor agreed with a smirk.

"Our friend is snoozing in his car less than one block from here, and it just so happens that the largest mosque in France is only about three blocks away."

"The largest in *France*?" asked O'Connor. "In Strasbourg? I thought the biggest one would have been in Paris or Lyons or Marseilles?"

"Nope, *this* is the biggest. Strasbourg has a fairly large Islamic population. Although, I presume this mosque is Sunni-based. But then again, it's France, which emphasizes secularism, so maybe the mosque—if it's publicly funded—is for both Sunni and Shia worshipers."

"No idea on that one," replied O'Connor.

"If Darbandi goes into that mosque, we're gonna have a hell of a time just strolling in there to see what he's up to. Unless I do it by myself."

"Yep, you could get away with it," said O'Connor. "Me? Blue eyes and blond hair? If I was really a tourist, I'd maybe have a prayer—pun intended—to get in without bringing attention to myself, so to speak. But people on the run like Darbandi normally have huge antennas up and can spot guys like me a mile away."

"Yep, no doubt. By the way, ever eaten a *doner kebab*, Special

Agent O'Connor?" asked Jake, trying to lighten the conversation while they observed Darbandi's vehicle.

"No, actually, I haven't. I've seen signs for them in Paris, though. What the hell is it?"

"All these years in Europe and you've never had a doner kebab? They're killer. They're roughly a Turkish version of a Greek gyros, but most places in Europe actually use turkey meat instead of lamb."

"Is that so?" replied O'Connor.

"And they're not kebabs—like shish kebabs—as we know kebabs in the US, with a bunch of meat and veggies on a stick. Doners are served with thin slices of meat in a large, open bun, about the size of a Whopper bun. Sometimes, they use pita bread. But the key is the yogurt-based sauce. Some places add raw cabbage or tomatoes, others add a few other veggies or goat cheese. A bit of cayenne pepper tossed in and they're awesome. They're even *better* with a cold beer. Back in Germany, we had a competition among friends to find the best one in town."

Parked across the street and about thirty yards from the Bayram Kebab shop, with its *Doner* and *Durum* neon lights flashing in the window, the two men observed that the English-language sign inside the door had just been flipped to *OPEN*.

"Well, I don't think I'll be trying one from this place," said O'Connor.

"Ha-ha, who knows. If our boy Darbandi sleeps long enough, you might get that chance. Oh, by the way, it's my turn to buy. Speaking of the devil," said Jake, nodding towards Darbandi as he headed in the direction of the very Bayram Kebab shop they were talking about.

"The question is," Jake said with a chuckle, "is he craving a doner, which I would completely understand, or is he meeting someone in there?"

"How do we find out without setting off fireworks?" pondered O'Connor.

"Like I said, you might yet get a chance to taste a doner after all," said Jake. "I'll give it a few more minutes and then go in and order a couple. Do you want yours spicy or mild?"

"*What?*"

"You heard me. Spicy or mild?" repeated Jake.

"Plain Jane is just fine for me."

After another minute of bantering, both men sat straight up in their car seats.

"*Who* the hell . . . isn't that the Italian-looking guy from Darbandi's apartment?" Fortina leaned forward slightly.

"I'll bet a half month's wages that's him," said O'Connor, observing the Italian man as he casually walked up to the Bayram Kebab shop.

"I gotta go in there," said Jake.

As the major started to open the car door, O'Conner grabbed him by the arm.

"Wait. Are you sure that back in Saint-Denis you were not seen by either one of those guys?"

"Not one hundred percent sure, no, but I seriously doubt they saw me."

"Jake, serious doubt is not good enough," said O'Connor. "I should be the one going in."

"Bullshit, Tom. When you get in there, what are you goin' to do? Place the first doner kebab order of your life with your perfectly English-accented French? And when he asks you in French what kind of sauce you prefer, or if you want it spicy or mild, will you know how to answer him? Hell no, that's not gonna happen. This one's on me. But you still owe me from that chai tea bet."

About to exit the vehicle, Jake realized the Italian hitman, rather than entering through the shop's small door, had stopped at the shop's takeout window.

Standing at the takeout window and looking inside, Gianfranco observed two men talking. One man was standing behind the counter, and the other was on the customer side. The two men were in casual conversation, as if they knew each other.

Farouk, the owner of the kebab shop, turned and saw a customer at the takeout window. Farouk eyed him with suspicion. Farouk's *OPEN* sign had just been placed on the door, ninety minutes before his regular opening time. The sign's only purpose was to signal to Darbandi that he was ready to meet him, not to invite customers in. Yet, he had a curious customer now standing at the takeout window, midmorning.

"Who the hell wants a doner kebab at nine thirty in the morning?" he mumbled to Darbandi.

Farouk reached for his Beretta nine-millimeter pistol, safely obscured behind the counter under a bag of tomatoes. Darbandi bolted for the back door, knocking over a couple of chairs behind him.

Gianfranco made his move, bursting through the front door.

Observing that the man who just bolted through his door had a pistol, Farouk fired twice.

Anticipating the shots, the Italian quickly got low. Farouk's two shots barely missed the Italian's head.

Getting off two shots of his own, Gianfranco dropped Farouk behind the counter.

Quickly checking to make sure Farouk was dead, Gianfranco worked his way past the strewn shop chairs and tables to the back of the shop, through the back door and behind the building. He was too late. The Hezbollah operative was nowhere to be seen.

As Jake peered through the Donor Kebab takeout window, fairly certain he had not been seen by the people in the melee, he knew he had to move quickly to avoid observation by the Italian. He stepped into the receded entryway of a nearby shoe shop.

Back in the car, Agent O'Connor made sure his car door was unlocked and placed his hand on his Sig Sauer P226 pistol. If he needed to, he would compromise his presence, especially if it meant saving his partner's life.

Gianfranco exited the front door of the shop, but not before flipping the OPEN sign to CLOSED. He walked quickly to his car.

Jake observed Gianfranco calmly drive away. He then walked to the car and rejoined the wide-eyed and waiting O'Connor.

As he did, O'Connor observed Darbandi, almost a block away, entering his car. Darbandi had apparently watched the Italian drive away. Darbandi waited for about ten minutes before driving off for the German border.

"Well, it looks like we get to do this again," said O'Connor. "*Sprechen Sie Deutsch?*"

52.
GERMANY

HEADING NORTHEAST out of Strasbourg on French secondary road A35, heading to Germany was a contingency O'Connor and Jake knew they had to prepare for in pursuing the Hezbollah operative. Switzerland was out, because it was not part of the European Union and was therefore far more challenging to enter. A southern route to Italy was always possible but heading for Germany, with its open borders and much closer access, was far more likely.

"Ma'am, we are northeast of Strasbourg, and we think Darbandi is headed for Germany. We are about six miles from the border. It is completely open and unguarded, as you know. I need to be able to go into Germany with Jake," O'Connor reported to the US attaché.

As a result of the so-called Schengen Agreement in the early 1990s, twenty-seven countries within the European Union had completely open borders between them, making much of Europe just like the open borders between US states. Border checks were only temporarily established for major events or exceptional circumstances, like a G-7 Summit or at times during the COVID-19 pandemic.

Much like among the fifty states, the Schengen Agreement was principally established to enhance the free flow of commerce and goods, with rare exception (for example, with Norway or the United Kingdom), throughout Europe. However, with those goods it also allowed for the free flow of criminals and illegal immigrants. In practice, this meant that unless an illegal traveler or terrorist was randomly checked, he could travel freely from country to country once inside the Schengen zone.

"Not a chance, Tom" came the firm reply from the US legal attaché to France. "We've been trying to keep this situation from kicking up public and diplomatic dust. You crossing that border as a US law enforcement officer, one who is accredited only to France for official duties, would cause all kinds of *Scheiße* to roll downhill from the German government. Not only would the director be on my case, but the ambassador and secretary of state would be too.

"While it's a gray area since he's temporarily working for us, Major Fortina *is* a US soldier, and as such is sanctioned by the Germans, as part of the US Status of Forces Agreement with the German government," she continued. "Tom, needless to say, different kettle of fish. Berlin will balk, and I completely understand that. They might *also* balk at Fortina being in his current non-military capacity, but I'm willing to take that risk."

"Ma'am, Jake and I work better as a team," O'Connor pressed. "We need to stay together."

"I get that, Tom, but this is not going to work. Imagine a Mexican law enforcement officer crossing our southern border into California or Texas, or a Canadian Mountie coming south into the US on his own accord. Tom, *do not* cross that border into Germany with Fortina. In the meantime, I will contact the US legal attaché at the US embassy in Berlin. The bureaucratic wheels on this will turn slowly, which is why Fortina has got to do his best to keep Darbandi in his sights, until the Germans figure out how they want to handle this."

"Roger all," Tom relented.

"And Tom, if Jake still has that French-government-provided pistol, he's got to give it up before he crosses into Germany. It was only intended for use inside France's borders. The Germans will rightfully go batshit crazy if they stop an American officer with a French-provided firearm inside their borders, and we'll play hell trying to explain why we violated their national sovereignty. You copy?"

"Roger," replied O'Connor.

Looking at his teammate as they trailed Darbandi, O'Connor knew there was only one choice. He would need to be dropped off while still in France and allow his partner to continue on to Germany.

"This *sucks*, Jake. I'm abandoning my wingman. But you heard Sanders. We knew this was the likely bargain going in. It's France *only*, at least for me," said O'Connor. "And I need your sidearm."

"I get it," replied Jake. "But I don't have to like it. This sucks for me too. Both of us could stay on this guy's ass forever, even if he went all the way to Tehran," groused Jake as he placed his pistol under the seat.

"Let's prepare for a quick stop near Roppenheim," said O'Connor, referring to the Alsace-Lorraine town with the typical German name just on the French side of the border. "I've got a cellphone and a credit card, and now not one but *two* lovely pistols," chided O'Connor. "That's all I need to get back to Paris. So, no sweat for me, Jake."

"Got it. Don't worry about me, either."

As Darbandi drove on the D4 two-lane road headed for the Rhine River bridge marking the border between Germany and France, O'Connor pulled over, quickly set the handbrake, and leaped out of the vehicle. Jake wedged himself into the driver's seat and took off, leaving O'Connor standing on the side of the road.

They had lost about twenty seconds in the maneuver, and Darbandi was now out of sight.

I've got to find him before he hits the German A5 autobahn, thought Jake. *If I don't catch up to him and I guess that he went north but instead he went south on that autobahn, it's pretty much game over.*

As he picked up speed, Jake was nervous. *Germans have those damn blitzers everywhere,* he remembered. The speed-trap cameras posted throughout Germany were something the Army major was all too familiar with. Americans *and* Germans called them blitzers because of the blitz—the lightning-like flash—the cameras gave off when you drove by, exceeding the programmed speed limit.

I practically have PTSD from the ones they had in and around Garmisch-Partenkirchen and Munich, Jake chuckled. *What a cash cow. But I gotta admit, they're pretty effective.*

Jake knew his only choice was to break the speed limit so he could get Darbandi back in his sights. And then, he saw it, a stoplight with several cars in front of him. With any luck, Darbandi's bronze Renault would be in that mix of cars stopped at the light.

"Thank God," he said aloud as the light turned green and cars in front of him took a slight curve to the left, bringing a bronze Renault clearly into his view.

That was too stinkin' close for comfort, he thought.

Backing off his speed, Jake had less than a mile to go before Darbandi turned on to the German A5 autobahn entry ramp and headed north for the city of Karlsruhe. Almost five hours later, he followed the Hezbollah terrorist into Bavaria's largest and Germany's third largest city, Munich.

53.
MUNICH TRAIN STATION

JAKE FOUND IT IRONIC to be standing in one of Europe's busiest train stations in one of his favorite cities in Europe. Home to the original Oktoberfest, a top-ranked opera house, a world-class soccer team, a beautiful Christmas market, and more urban bike trails than he'd seen anywhere except Copenhagen, he had spent a lot of his free time here during his one year at the Marshall Center. The Center was only about an hour's drive to the south, in the alpine town of Garmisch-Partenkirchen.

For now, Jake had to be as anonymous as possible to avoid the attention of the Hezbollah operative, the fourth person ahead of him in the train ticket line. As the Darbandi stepped up to the ticket counter, Jake listened. So did the fifty-something German train ticket salesman sitting behind the counter, patient as he eyed his next customer of the day.

"Do you speak English?" Darbandi asked the German in a raised voice.

"Yes, I do," was the German's reply.

"I need to buy a ticket to Verona, in Italy," said Darbandi.

"When would you like to depart?" asked the German, now typing into his desktop keyboard as he looked at his computer screen.

"On the next train possible," responded Darbandi.

"A train will depart in four minutes, which is not enough time for you to make it. The next train after that will depart at 1812 hours. Will that be okay for you?"

"Yes, that's fine," replied the Iranian.

"Do you want first or second class?" asked the German.

"Second class is good."

After the German typed something on his desktop computer, he turned the credit card price indicator screen towards the Iranian.

"I will pay in cash," said Darbandi.

Darbandi pulled a fifty euro bill out of his front pocket and placed it on the counter. The German took the bill, which barely covered the fare, and exchanged it for some small change and a standard second-class train ticket.

"The ticket is good for any seat in any car marked second class," said the German.

"Thank you," replied Darbandi.

Jake waited intently, watching to see if the Iranian would break to the left or right of the line. As Darbandi turned to the right, Jake looked down and turned slightly to the left while pretending to be engrossed in his cellphone.

The Iranian walked slowly by as Jake kept his head down, staring at his cellphone while keeping the Iranian in his peripheral vision. Jake waited for several seconds.

Suddenly, Jake could see that the Iranian, about forty feet away, had stopped and turned around. Jake wanted to see if the Iranian was looking at him but couldn't risk making eye contact. He could see enough to know that the Iranian was looking at his ticket; after a single but very long minute, the Iranian turned on his heels and continued on his way.

Relieved, Jake could see that the Iranian was walking towards a nearby coffee shop, with open seating, in the cavernous and bustling Munich train station. He had a critical decision to make. But his calculations quickly led him to what he thought was the only answer.

I cannot take this train with him, he thought. *If I do, between staying on top of Darbandi's movements and getting to my ground transportation in Verona, I will certainly lose Darbandi at the Verona train station. It will be physically impossible to do both.*

Jake knew that there were times in a mission, no matter how

critical, that you had to assume some risk. Knowing that he had three hours for the train to depart and another five-plus hours for Darbandi's train trip to be completed, Jake decided to drive to the Verona train station and be waiting for the Hezbollah operative when he got there. He hated the thought of letting the Iranian out of his sight, but he knew there was no other way. He knew the route in his sleep from his time spent at the Marshall Center.

It's about eighty to ninety minutes to the Austrian border from here and another three-plus hours, max, to get to Verona, Fortina thought. *That leaves me time for an espresso and panino along the way, and maybe even a shower before I have to be ready to meet Darbandi at the Verona train station.*

Jake stepped out of the ticket line. For several minutes he casually observed the Hezbollah operative drinking a coffee at a small round table in front of the cafe. What Jake did not know was that Luigi Gianfranco, feigning that he was reading the German periodical *Der Spiegel*, was standing at a large newspaper kiosk about sixty feet away. Gianfranco was observing the Hezbollah operative, too. In following Darbandi to the Munich train station, Jake had been careful, very careful. But this time the Italian had gotten the better of Jake, following Darbandi to the station without Jake's knowledge.

I'll find out where that Iranian sonofabitch is headed, thought Gianfranco.

Jake needed to check in with O'Connor. However, by reporting to a higher authority, he knew he could potentially expose himself to new directives, which could include being pulled off this mission. Yet, it would be irresponsible and possibly dangerous not to disclose his whereabouts.

At this point, I'm the only person who knows exactly where Darbandi is and where he's going. It would be a tragedy to let him ride off into the Italian sunset at this point, with millions of lives at risk, he thought.

Continuing to observe Darbandi, who was eating a sandwich a good distance from him in the crowded Munich train station, Jake called his FBI friend and colleague.

"Jake, how are you? *Where* the hell are you?" asked O'Connor.

"I'm in the Munich train station. I'm watching our Persian friend munch on a sandwich. He just bought a train ticket and will be headed for Italy in less than three hours. I can't stay with him on the train because I have to keep my vehicle for transportation once I get to Italy. I'm going to meet him at the Verona train station and see where our journey takes us."

"Roger, Jake. I will let Sanders know ASAP. There's been some chatter, some concern, about you being in a US Embassy Paris vehicle outside of France, working in what obviously is a gray area of international law enforcement. That's the bureaucratic side of the BS that's transpired over the past few hours. But you and I both know you have to birddog this guy. If you don't, we'll lose him for sure. By the time we get the Germans fully read in on this, it will be too late. Heck, it might be too late already."

"Roger that," the major replied. "I'll stay on him. I have some Italian contacts—including law enforcement. I will contact them as soon as I get on the road. But it's going to require a lot broader and more coordinated effort to catch this guy alive and, more importantly, to retrieve what is apparently in that backpack before it gets handed off to other Hezbollah members. And as you know, Tom, I'm now unarmed."

"We're on the same page," replied O'Connor. "Again, I will notify Sanders ASAP. Be safe, my friend."

"You too, Tom."

Grabbing a bratwurst and a coffee to go at a street-side bistro before heading out to his car, Jake was as certain as he could be that Arman Darbandi would get on his train.

Once in his car and in Munich traffic, he couldn't help reflecting on the irony of the situation he now found himself in.

When I was in the terrorism studies course at the Marshall Center, we came up to Munich to observe Bavaria's crack anti-terrorist response team in an operational demonstration. If the German and Bavarian governments had enough response time, along with probable cause, they'd easily be able to take care of business with Darbandi. But that's not going to happen today.

Departing the Munich train station parking lot, Jake headed due south out of Munich on the A95 autobahn, driving through the beautiful southern Bavaria countryside, eventually reaching the alpine town of Garmisch-Partenkirchen. He then crossed the Austria-Germany border at Scharnitz and, in twenty-five to thirty more minutes, drove through Austria to the Brenner Mountain pass connecting southern Austria with northern Italy. Then it would be on to Verona through south Tyrol, the German and Italian-speaking part of northern Italy.

54.
ITALIAN FRIENDS

AS FORTINA DROVE TOWARDS the German alpine town of Garmisch-Partenkirchen and the Austrian border just beyond it, he was overcome by a bit of nostalgia. He thought of the lovely law enforcement officer he had befriended at the George C. Marshall Center. For the previous four years, he'd kept in occasional touch with her through the Center's alumni network.

But she's an Italian Carabinieri officer, who has a career of her own, Jake reminded himself, pulling back from his thoughts and dreams about Sara Simonetti.

Now headed for Italy, he had a professional reason to reach out to her. Fortunately, he also had a very good Italian male friend and former Italian Army officer he knew in the Verona area. He would call both.

But first, he stopped on the Italian side of the Austrian border for one of Italy's best kept secrets—a perfect cappuccino made by a barista, dressed in his or her pretty little bowtie and hat—at a gas station.

"*Un cappuccino,*" he said as he walked up to the snack counter at the Trens Ovest gas station on the southbound lane of the A22 autostrada, near Campo di Trens-Freienfeld, Italy. Jake knew that in Italy it was mostly tourists who ordered a cappuccino after eleven in the morning. After that, most Italians—or at least that is what he was told by an American friend—preferred an expresso. But today he could care less about Italian cultural norms. Although it was after one, his first stop in Italy in a few years *demanded* a cappuccino, made at the hands of an Italian *barista*.

"*Tante grazie*," he said as his lips touched the creamy Italian coffee specialty.

Stepping outside the gas station snack shop, Jake walked over to a dog-walking area to put some distance between him and the other international road travelers. His phone on speaker mode, he called Carabinieri captain Sara Simonetti.

"*Pronto*," responded the familiar voice, using the standard Italian telephone greeting.

"Captain Simonetti? Sara?"

"Well, it's *Major* Simonetti now," she responded as her heart skipped a beat, recognizing the male voice at the other end. "Jake? Is that you?"

"Uh, yes, Sara, it's me. How are you?"

"I'm fine, Jake. To what do I owe the pleasure of this call?"

Jake was amazed at how well his Italian friend spoke English.

"Sara, I'm in northern Italy, headed for Verona. I will be there in three, maybe four hours max if the traffic is—

Sara interrupted. "Verona? *Why* are you coming to Verona? That's only about a forty-five-minute drive from where I live." She was stationed with the provincial Carabinieri headquarters in nearby Vicenza.

Having already known from the Marshall Center alumni network that Sara was in Vicenza, Fortina was delighted to hear her positive response.

"Yes, I admit it, I knew you were in Vicenza," chuckled Jake. "I'm actually coming to Verona for business. And I know it's very short notice. But I was wondering if you might join me for a coffee or a drink tonight? You know how they told us at the Marshall Center that we should stay in touch with each other for professional reasons, so that we could help each other with international security challenges?"

"Yes, I remember."

"Well, the US is facing a serious security challenge, but I'd rather not talk about it on the phone. I do believe Italy needs to know about it, though. I expect that our legal attaché in Paris is contacting your Italian embassy in Paris now, as well as with her US counterpart in Rome."

Sara was intrigued, though slightly disappointed. She was intrigued about what the international security challenge, but she was also disappointed that his call seemed to be for professional purposes only. The thirty-four-year-old Italian had been very disappointed that she and Jake had not kept in touch better after their friendly days at the Marshall Center.

"I'd be happy to meet you in Verona. I'm intrigued by what you might share with me, especially if Italy should know about it. Just let me know where and when."

"*Perfetto,* Sara. I have a place in mind and will text it to you shortly. Ciao, *ci vediamo a presto, amica mia.*"

"Ciao, *a presto*, Jake."

A few minutes later, Jake reached out to a close Italian friend he'd gotten to know during his Vicenza military service days, some fourteen years earlier. The two had stayed in close contact.

Davide Bovo was a former Italian Army officer who resided in the beautiful town of Peschiera-del-Garda, located on the southern shoreline of Italy's largest lake, Lake Garda. Bovo's home was about a thirty-minute drive from Verona. Jake, along with Faith and their then-infant daughter, Kimberly, had stayed at Bovo's home more than once. Jake thought that the amicable and highly boisterous Bovo was the best amateur Italian chef he'd ever known. His wife, Elisa, was very friendly as well. Bovo had a great sense of humor, often making Fortina belly laugh. Bovo's excellent Italian cooking was always abundant, and the top-shelf Italian wine always flowed freely.

Bovo's home would also be a great place to grab a shower—and if needed, stay the night—before Jake would drive off to see the female friend that he had very much missed.

55.
A TENSE RIDE

THIS IS THE SEAT, Arman Darbandi decided. Surveying the train car, he knew that for his southbound train ride from Munich, Germany, to Verona, Italy, the back corner aisle seat was optimal. It provided a complete view of not only the entire car, but into the next car as well.

Removing his backpack, he placed it in the window seat beside him. With any luck, no onboarding fellow passenger would take the vacant seat adjacent to his. Taking an eighteen-inch piece of quarter-inch, blade-resistant cord out of the cargo pocket of his backpack, he tied the cord onto the outside of backpack, and then onto to his right wrist. If he happened to fall asleep, God forbid, it would take some effort to steal the backpack, ensuring such efforts would wake him in the process. When the train stopped in Innsbruck to let off and take on new passengers, he would lean his body onto the backpack and feign sleep, hoping to dissuade anyone from requesting the unoccupied seat.

About fifteen minutes outside of Munich, Darbandi kept his antennas up for activity in his and the adjoining car. Allowing himself the occasional view outside of the train's windows, the Iranian was amazed at the rolling green landscape interspersed with the occasional picturesque lakes of the southern Bavaria countryside. Before long, the Germany-Austria Alps would come into view.

Suddenly, his personal warning antennas activated. Through the glass door of the adjacent train car, he saw two men, each with hair down to their shoulders, wearing jeans and leather jackets. They had abruptly stopped and were showing what looked to be police badges to three passengers. The passengers looked like they were from the Middle East. The two long-haired men were obviously undercover, either from Germany's border patrol or one of its security services.

Darbandi had to act fast. His sixth sense told him his forged French passport was not going to pass muster this time.

Casually getting up and grabbing his backpack, he moved naturally towards the single-stall bathroom, located between the train car he was seated in and the car behind him. As Darbandi left his seat, he avoided eye contact with the two men, who had yet to enter his train car. He could see they were preoccupied examining the travel documents of the three passengers they had obviously profiled.

Stepping into the cramped, single occupancy train bathroom, Darbandi immediately locked the door, put the lid down on the toilet, sat on it, and removed the dummy cord from his wrist.

If they saw me enter the bathroom and decide to wait me out, I don't want to have to explain this, he thought. *If they try to break this door down, I'll flush the pistol in the toilet.*

Fortuitously for the Hezbollah operative, it did not take long to hear the two German plainclothes officers shuffle past the bathroom door and pass through the next door leading to the adjacent train car.

"Thanks be to Allah," Darbandi murmured.

Darbandi waited another good ten minutes before exiting the bathroom.

As the train pulled to a stop in Murnau, about halfway between Munich and Garmisch-Partenkirchen, Darbandi watched as the two undercover Germans stepped off onto the station's platform, headed for either another train or perhaps home.

Seated nine rows away and posing as a married couple, two Israeli Mossad intelligence agents had observed the entire scene.

56.
BORDER INCIDENT

IT WAS A TRIP the mafia criminal Luigi Gianfranco had made numerous times. Driving through Austria's Inn Valley and bypassing the city of Innsbruck before heading up and out of the valley to the Brenner Pass and Italy's beautiful mountainside vineyards, the scenery always brought him back to thoughts of his Italian home at the southernmost end of the Italian boot. Although a hardened international criminal, Gianfranco's heart softened at the thoughts of Calabria.

But today he was on a mission for his 'Ndrangheta mafia bosses. He had to get his hands on Ruth Ackerman's hip bone, at all costs. The Iranian government desperately wanted it—and Gianfranco's 'Ndrangheta mafia dons planned to sell the bone to Iran, for millions of dollars.

Il signor Luigi Gianfranco took pride in knowing that he, along with his Russian partner, Antonin Markov, had been selected for this tough job. But now, with Markov unable to continue, the sole responsibility lay in Gianfranco's hands, at least until the 'Ndrangheta leaders provided him with another partner.

With a few miles to go to the Austria-Italy border, Gianfranco spotted the *Vipiteno-Sterzing* sign that told him he was about to cross over into Italy. Common to many cities, towns, and villages in the northern Italian region of Trentino-Alto Adige, which had been ceded to Italy after the breakup of the Austro-Hungarian Empire at the end of World War I, the road sign included both the Italian and German names for the town. Vitpiteno was its Italian name, and Sterzing was its German name.

As for almost all countries throughout the European Union, there was no permanent border check at the Austria-Italy border. But Gianfranco *would* have to stop and pull a toll ticket from one of the standard orange automatic ticket-dispensing machines before entering Italy's high-speed autostrada, the highway that traversed most of the Italian boot.

Much like the autoroute in France and the toll-free autobahn in German, the autostrada toll road existed to allow high-speed travel, normally up to eighty-five miles per hour, throughout much of the country. Gianfranco knew that this speed was frequently violated, and that violators were rarely caught or pulled over by Italian police.

When he'd eventually depart the A22 autostrada in Verona, Gianfranco knew he'd have to pay the appropriate fare for the roughly three-hour trip from the Austria-Italy border to the ancient Roman enclave of Romeo and Juliet fame.

Driving up to the toll booth to pull his ticket, Gianfranco could see two Italian law enforcement cars on the other side of the toll booths. One was marked *Carabinieri* and the other *Guardia di Finanza*. The Guardia di Finanza (Financial Guard) vehicle belonged to Italy's Ministry of Economy and Finance. It was essentially Italy's customs and tax law enforcement agency. The Guardia di Finanza was heavily involved in Italy's counter-trafficking operations, including human trafficking.

No big deal, Gianfranco initially thought. *They set these impromptu checks up all the time.*

That much was true. The Italians did often establish temporary and seemingly random border checks, mainly to screen for contraband or human trafficking entering Italy from eastern Europe. Increasingly, since the removal of the European Union's internal international borders with the Schengen Agreement in 1990, they did it to check for illegal immigrants and forcibly trafficked humans as well.

As he pulled away from the ticket-dispensing kiosk to be on his way, a gray-uniformed Guardia di Finanza officer step out of his car. The officer waved the dreaded and decades-old green-and-red "lollipop" at Gianfranco, signaling him to stop. In a split-second decision, he decided he had no choice, pulling his Alfa Romeo Quadrifoglio SUV, with its powerful 505 horsepower engine, to a stop.

Is it my French license plates that attracted the officer's attention? Or have the French police already connected Markov and me to the killing of the Iranian in Saint-Denis, and contacted the Italian authorities? Gianfranco pondered.

As the officer approached his vehicle, Gianfranco had an uneasy feeling, one he had felt before. It always forewarned trouble. He quickly assessed that there were two Carabinieri officers in a second vehicle and another from the Guardia Finanza remaining in the second vehicle.

Gianfranco was relieved to see that the two Carabinieri were sitting in a much slower Alfa Romeo Giulietta, one of several hundred Giuliettas in the Carabinieri inventory. He was thankful that they were not sitting in the much faster Alfa Romeo Giulia, which had the same powerful engine as his Quadrifoglio. There were few Giulia versions in the Carabinieri's vehicle arsenal.

Even worse would have been a Lamborghini Huracan, of which the Carabinieri had exactly three in service, for special operations. Gianfranco's Alfa Romeo Quadrifoglio would have been no match against the Lamborghini. There was no way that he was going back to some Italian jail. If not for Markov, he knew he would have died in that godforsaken Sardinian hellhole.

As a twenty-something officer stepped up to Gianfranco's vehicle, he knew he had to act.

"Your driver's license, registration, and proof of insurance," said the officer.

"Yes, sir," responded Gianfranco.

Turning his eyes to his glove box, he feigned a motion to open it with his right arm.

Instead, in one fluid motion, Gianfranco grabbed the Beretta nine-millimeter pistol from just under the passenger seat and turned it on the unsuspecting Guardia di Finanza officer, firing a single well-placed shot to the far left of the officer's upper thigh area. As the officer spun around and fell back, Gianfranco turned and quickly fired two shots at the nearby Carabinieri vehicle, breaking the window on the driver's side and cracking the windshield.

Gianfranco fired two more shots at the Guardia di Finanza vehicle. The officer on the passenger side had already taken cover on the opposite side of the affected vehicle.

Gianfranco then made a snap driving decision born of years of criminal experience. Instead of racing twenty miles down the autostrada to the next exit, which might give local police time to block the exit, he made a U-turn, crossed over into the northbound lane, passed through the far-right side, found an open toll booth, and then exited the autostrada, headed for the country roads of the nearby alpine Vipiteno-Sterzing area.

Checking his mirrors, Gianfranco was sweating profusely. But he was relieved that the Italian officers were not yet giving chase.

Pounding the steering wheel, Gianfranco was angry at his misfortune. But he knew it could have been worse.

Killing that kid would have been a mistake, he thought, wishing Markov had been able to finish their mission with him.

I wounded him, he thought, *so the other officers will have to stay and render aid. By the time the two Carbs figure out what just happened, I should have a good lead on them. But they will have a decision to make; either stay and render aid to the downed officer, or chase me.*

It was not long before Gianfranco was assured that they had chosen the former. Nobody was behind him as he guided the powerful Alfa-Romeo through the nearby alpine roads and villages. Still, he would be an easy mark in his car.

"Pietro, this is Luigi Gianfranco," the Italian mobster said, addressing his fellow 'Ndrangheta mafia member, who lived in the northern Italy mountain city of Bolzano. "I got into a bad scrape. I need a car and I need it fast. By tomorrow, half of northern Italy will be looking for my vehicle."

"Luigi," replied his mafia colleague. "Where the fuck are you? What happened?"

"I'm on a dirt road, about three hundred yards off of the SS44 country road, in the forest. My GPS indicates that I'm about twenty miles north of Merano. There does not appear to be a soul within at least a mile of me. I'm switching to Italian license plates now. But I got somethin' to tell ya, Pietro. I shot a Guardia Di Finanza officer just inside the border. I don't have time to explain, but I'm pretty sure I didn't kill him."

"I've had the TV on," replied Luigi, "and I've heard nothing. But it will likely be on the regional, if not national, news within an hour or so. Do you think you're being followed?"

"No, I don't think so. There was nobody on my rear or in the approaching lane when I pulled off. I've been here for about ten minutes. Pietro, I need a new vehicle as soon as possible."

"Luigi, listen," said Pietro, "we have a guesthouse nearby. It's located in a forested area near San Martino in Passeria. It's about a mile south of San Leonardo and it's only about nine miles south of where you are. It's called the Gasthaus Hochweg. Punch it into your GPS; you should see it come up."

"Okay, I got it," replied Gianfranco.

"As soon as it gets dark, go there. A man named Ugo will be waiting. He'll have another vehicle ready. If you need a place to stay, you can spend the night there, but I wouldn't stay beyond tomorrow," said Pietro.

"*Grazie*, my friend," replied Gianfranco. "I do *not* intend to spend the night. *Ci vediamo presto.*"

The Gasthaus Hochweg, its German name, typical for this part of northern Italy, was a modest, eight-room, Tyrolian-style bed-and-breakfast in the breathtaking Dolomite Mountain region of South Tyrol. While not a major money-making operation, the gasthaus was a profitable enough money-laundering operation for a couple of local 'Ndrangheta-associated families. It was also perfect for any 'Ndrangheta mob members and their families who wanted to leave sweltering Naples and Rome for the cooler summers of the high-altitude Dolomites. It was one of hundreds of such businesses, including several large hotels, the Italian mafia organization had around Italy, and even in some places in Europe outside of Italy.

Within the Italian 'Ndrangheta mafia organization, it was understood that these places could be used if a mob member got himself into trouble and needed a place to hide out. But woe be to any mobster who led, inadvertently or otherwise, the police to one of these places.

57.
ON HOLD

"JAKE, THIS IS TOM," said the caller. "Are you okay? What's your status?"

"I'm still tracking our friend, but I'm not with him at this moment. I'm headed south on the A22 autostrada, about to pass the exit for Bolzano. I'm set to meet our friend later tonight at a train station, somewhere in Italy, for a cup of real espresso." Jake chuckled. "Just the two of us, reminiscing about our fun trip through Europe."

O'Connor laughed, then asked Jake to hold on. Moments later O'Connor came back on the line.

"Stand by for the legal attaché, Jake."

"Roger."

"Major, this is Laura Sanders," said the familiar voice. "I understand you are in Italy. We *may* have to pull the plug on this mission. The ambassador is getting nervous about you being outside of France. If the shit hits the fan in Italy, we are going to have a lot of explaining to do about how a US Army officer assigned to Paris got tangled up trailing a Hezbollah operative through Germany and Austria, and into Italy. The French were okay with you operating here in France under our FBI top-cover, but I'm not sure how the Italians will respond. We have spoken with the Italian ambassador here in Paris, and he is contacting the key authorities in Italy now about this rapidly evolving situation."

"I hear you, ma'am. But knowing the Italians, they'll be receptive to me trailing this guy. Let's remember, I'm the only one in this part of Europe who really knows what this Iranian looks like or how he moves. Nobody down here in Italy does, that's for sure. If we lose Darbandi's trace, in a few months we'll both be watching CNN with the Iranians announcing that their homemade killer virus is about to kill, or worse yet, *has already killed*, millions of Americans and Israelis."

"I understand, Jake, but—"

"But an Iranian-made Spanish flu 2.0 will make COVID-19 seem like the common cold," interjected Jake. "I'm pleading with you to convince the ambassador, or whoever you have to, to keep me on this mission. Personally, ma'am, I'm no big deal. Tom O'Connor could do this job better than me. But nobody knows this guy Darbandi like I do now."

The phone went quiet for several seconds.

"Ma'am, are you still there?"

"Yes, I'm here. I hear you, Major. But do not get tangled up with Darbandi. Remember your original rules of engagement. For now, follow, observe, and report. We will try to get the Italian authorities read into this as soon as possible. If they say you can stay on the job, okay, I'll agree to it, and so will the ambassador. But if not, you're coming home to Paris ASAP. Is that clear?"

"Yes, ma'am, it's clear."

"Good. Now be safe."

58.
DINNER WITH A FRIEND

JAKE APPROACHED THE ITALIAN *TRATTORIA* six blocks from Verona's Porta Nuova train station. He realized he had less than two hours before Arman Darbandi's train arrived.

But first, he needed to see Sara Simonetti. Jake had intelligence that he needed to share with the Italian Carabinieri major. The US embassy in Paris was alerting the US embassy in Rome that an Iranian Hezbollah operative was entering—or was already in—their country. The US embassy in Rome was expected to pass this critical intelligence to the appropriate Italian law enforcement officials, providing all the details.

As he waited for Sara, Jake recalled a time he had gone to the base gym, adjacent to the Marshall Center, for his lunch period. As he was climbing the gym's stairs to the second-floor cardio equipment, he'd heard someone pounding a leather boxing speedbag. Jack was familiar with the sound. He had boxed on an intramural team and had done well at the West Point Open Championship, finishing third, but pounding the teardrop-shaped speedbag was not a training technique he had mastered. He couldn't quite get the timing down. By the sounds of the steady rhythm and force of the punches, Jake had been expecting to see a hulk of a man taking his frustrations out on the bag.

Instead, as he crested the steps, his eyes widened as they fell upon a very fit, soaked-in-sweat Sara Simonetti.

As the beauty came into his view, Jake had managed to eke out a manly "*Ciao*" to Sara, who had briefly stopped her flurry of punches and acknowledged with her own "*Ciao*" before continuing.

As Jake thought about that chance meeting some four years later, he realized their brief encounter in the gym was something that often reminded him of why he liked Sara. Yes, she was beautiful, but not in the runway model or Hollywood depictions of beautiful. Sara reminded him of some of the Midwest girls he'd had a crush on. They were equally beautiful, slamming a volleyball in the face of an opponent, wearing a prom dress, or shoveling snow on a cold Michigan night.

Gazing into his cellphone while keeping one eye on the trattoria's revolving glass door, Jake's heart fluttered with anticipation. The Italian beauty he had met in a counterterrorism course in Germany was entering the restaurant. She had let her flowing brownish auburn hair down and was wearing tight new blue jeans, a colorful long-sleeved top, and the most beautiful earrings. At this moment, Jake could not believe—or perhaps had been too depressed to see it back then—just how beautiful and athletic Sara Simonetti was.

Standing up and stepping forward to greet her, he extended both his arms from the waist. Sara mimicked Jake before realizing her purse was getting in the way. Somehow their hands and eyes met.

Giving each other light, European-style kisses on the cheek, Jake said an enthusiastic, "*Ciao, cara!*"

Sara responded with a warm, "*Ciao,* my friend."

"How are you, Sara?" asked Jake, getting a waft of Sara's subtle perfume.

"I'm great, Jake," she responded.

Jake pulled out Sara's chair from across the table, giving them both a good view of the front door. Rather than speaking business-like across the table, this also brought her a little closer to him, important for the sensitive nature of what he needed to tell her. It would not do well for the other couple in the trattoria, sitting several feet away, to hear any of the information he was about to discuss. But it also felt good just to have his Italian friend closer.

Sara placed her mid-sized purse on her chair between her thighs. She had seen far too many police reports where a tourist had hung a purse on the back or off the side of her chair, only to have it snatched away by a passing thief, never to be seen again.

As the waiter approached the table, Jake stopped him in his tracks. Originally just going to order coffee, he realized they had plenty of time to get a bite to eat. He first ordered a bottle of non-carbonated water and a carafe of Lugana white wine, from the nearby Le Morette winery. Just to be sure, he confirmed his choices with Sara.

"*Va bene cosi?*" he asked.

"Perfect," she responded.

"How is Vicenza, Sara?" he asked. "I spent some time there several years ago."

"I know. I remember you telling me that in Garmisch," she said. "You still have your cute Veneto accent."

"Well, I'll take that as a compliment."

"I meant it as one. Vicenza has been good to me, but I don't intend to be there forever. Germany was good to me, as well," continued Sara.

"Oh? How so?" asked Jake.

"I learned a lot from the counterterrorism course at the Marshall Center," she said. "And I met some really good people there, too."

"I know what you mean," Jake said, hoping he was firmly included among the "good people" she mentioned. "There *were* a lot of good people there. It was great to meet so many bright, dedicated, and competent people from around the world."

"Tell me," she asked, "how is Paris?"

"Paris has been interesting and quite different from what I'm used to. It's certainly different than my military attaché posting to Baku, right after I left the Marshall Center. Baku is a beautiful city, and there was sufficient work to do, but the diplomatic pace in Paris is almost frenetic compared to Baku. There is something going on in Paris all the time."

"I imagine you had a lot of official social engagements there, Jake."

"I *have* had a lot of official engagements in Paris. And I've consumed more than my fair share of champagne for my country while listening to the latest military and political concerns of Europeans and government officials from around the world." He chuckled.

"But *unofficial* engagements, not so much," he continued.

"Why is that?" Sara leaned forward.

"Believe it or not, I was not interested in a lot of dating," he said. "And what about you, Sara?"

"I'm afraid I can't tell you anything exciting about my life over the past four years either. I was engaged to another Carabinieri officer, but about a year ago some friends broke the news that he was cheating on me, so that was the end of *that* love story. Besides, police work makes for some pretty long days and weekends."

Afraid to ask anything further about her current social status, Jake changed the subject. The waiter brought their main meal of fresh mushroom tortellini in a wine and cream sauce.

"Well, I did ask you to come here for business, so I suppose I should get on with it," said Jake.

"If you insist."

"Unfortunately, I must." A quick look around revealed the nearby couple displayed no interest—if they could even hear them.

"About two weeks ago, there were these hate crimes in an American cemetery in Paris," Jake explained, going on to give Major Simonetti the full details of the Iranian plot.

"So, that's it," he concluded. "Italy will soon have a Hezbollah operative in its midst. I believe he poses little threat to the Italian people and government, but what he has in his possession could very well help the Iranians mount a major threat to my country and Israel."

Looking up from her wineglass, she responded.

"Who are you, Jake, some kind of Jack Ryan?"

"Far from it," he laughed. "It was kinda odd how I got involved in this in the first place. I guess you can blame part of this on the Marshall Center, where I met an FBI agent. We both ended up at the US embassy in Paris. But here I am now in Italy, *bell'Italia*. Where Arman Darbandi goes next is anybody's guess. Besides, my FBI buddy is stuck back in Paris, and I'm the only one who's really had a good look at this Hezbollah guy and who knows what he's up to, at least in this country, at this moment."

"Jake, I will report all of this to my chain of command as soon as we part ways this evening. It's my expectation that they will be very receptive to helping out any way they can. As I told you one day back at the Marshall Center, Italy is America's best friend in Europe," she said, smiling.

"I don't find that hard to believe."

Sara's cellphone buzzed, and as she glanced down at it, Jake could see a look of concern.

"Excuse me for a moment, Jake," she said.

The emergency message app on her phone was used by the Carabinieri to alert its officers in the event of a local emergency or warning. The messages typically addressed very recent or evolving events like missing children, escaped convicts, bank robberies, and major local crimes, like when a police officer was shot, or worse, killed.

"You know the Italian you just told me about? The one from the apartment shooting in Paris. Could you identify him?" asked Sara.

"I could," replied Jake. "Why?"

"I just read a message from the Caribinieri emergency network. A man driving an Alfa-Romeo Quadrifoglio shot a Guardia di Finanza officer at the Austria-Italy border, south of the Brenner Pass, earlier this afternoon. Fortunately, the officer is expected to live. The suspect spoke and looked Italian, but his vehicle had French license plates, with Paris numbers."

"The guy from the Suresnes apartment and Strasbourg," mumbled Jake.

"We can't be sure, but this seems to be more than coincidence. One of the officers nearby got a quick look at him. They are doing a composite sketch as we speak.

"Instead of you needing Italy's help, Major Fortina, Italy might need your help," she continued.

"Do you know anything about the suspect's status?"

"I only know from the message that he is at large and apparently pulled a pretty slick driving maneuver at the Vipiteno-Sterzing toll gate, crossing several lanes of oncoming traffic at the toll booths, reversing his direction, and exiting the autostrada for the nearby mountains," said Sara. "He could be back in Austria now, or he could be among us in Italy. We've apparently lost any trace of him."

"Well, my bet says he's in Italy," Jake said. "He's targeting Arman Darbandi for a reason. Darbandi is expected to pull into the local train station in about an hour and a half, and I would bet a half month's pay that the Italian will be—if he isn't already—in the neighborhood."

After almost an hour of conversation, good food and mostly untouched wine, Jake knew it was time to go.

"Jake," said Sara as they parted ways, "we'll be in touch. I will be in contact very soon. At the very least, the Carabinieri will need your help with the composite sketch currently being worked up on the Italian."

"I'm more than happy to help, Sara."

"I know you are . . . my friend."

As he departed the trattoria, Jake hoped that when this operation was over he'd get to see Sara again, very soon, and under different circumstances.

59.
YOU ARE CLEARED

IT WAS EXACTLY what Jake needed to hear as he awaited the late-night train from Munich.

"Jake, this is Tom. From the US side, you've been cleared to continue the surveillance mission. Our ambassador is working with the Italian ambassador here in Paris to make sure Italy understands what is happening in their country. We expect key Italian government officials to be on board shortly."

"Tom, thanks for this news. It eases my mind to know I'm not out on some shaky limb."

"Jake, this has now been declared an official tier-one US national security threat. It's gone all the way up to the FBI director, and the secretaries of state and defense. The president has also been made aware. US military commanders in Europe have been alerted of the threat, and the Iranian's presence on the Italian peninsula. The commander of the US Sixth Fleet and his staff in Naples have overall lead for any military support, if circumstances should require it. The Special Operations commander for Europe in Stuttgart is working directly with the Sixth Fleet headquarters. We'd like the Italians to roll the Iranian up—with that bone—but if that doesn't happen, the US will step in if we have to."

"Roger all, Tom. Do I have a point of contact at the Sixth Fleet headquarters, in case that military support is needed?"

"Roger, Jake. I will text you the number to the Fleet's operations cell. They're looped in with the Italian Carabinieri, US helicopter assets, and, of course, US Navy Special Ops. They can tap the entire range of military means available. But I re-emphasize, the Italians, at least for now, have jurisdiction. But I suspect it's going to take the Italians some time to catch up with events on the ground."

"Understood, Tom. *Viva Italia.*"

"And, oh, by the way Jake" chuckled O'Connor. "Don't let your culinary interests divert your ass from the mission."

"I'll try not to," laughed Jake, "unless I see a doner kebab shop. If that happens, I'm screwed."

60.
PORTA NUOVA TRAIN STATION, VERONA

JAKE POSITIONED his US embassy–issued VW Jetta in the optimal parking spot. He could easily see the main exit doors to Verona's Porta Nuova train station, a line of parked cars waiting for passenger pickup, much of the train station's adjacent overnight parking lot, and, in his rearview mirror, any approaching, drive-by vehicles for passenger pickup. The Verona station was busier than he had thought it would be at this hour, carrying passengers in night trains to distant places in Europe such as Nice, Berlin and Moscow.

It was almost 11:30, which allowed him to surveil the area in darkness, but it was so late in the evening that local police security minding the parking places would be gone. But the train station's outdoor lights were not very bright, forcing Jake to leave his vehicle to get a better view of the people flowing through the station's exit doors.

About five minutes before Darbandi's inbound train from Munich was expected to arrive, Jake stepped out of his vehicle and approached the station's main exit doors. Keeping a casually low profile, he broke out his cellphone while standing outside of the station doors, just off to the side of what would soon be exiting train passengers.

As the first passengers exited, he feigned a cellphone conversation while he observed the doors, trying to identify Darbandi. Unless a passenger looked sharply to his left upon exiting the station, he would have no idea Jake was standing there.

But then things got complicated.

Who the hell is that guy? Jake wondered almost out loud as an Arab—perhaps Iranian—man who had just parked his car in front of Jake, began slowly walking towards him.

Is he coming for me . . . or will he stop and just stand here, like me, waiting for a passenger?

Within seconds it was clear—the man was walking straight towards Jake.

In the adjacent overnight parking lot, Major Sara Simonetti, who had followed Jake to the train station and parked as close as she could to the station's main doors, knew she had to move very quickly.

"Excuse me, sir, do you know if the train from Munich is on time?" the Hezbollah operative, in almost perfect English, asked Jake.

"*Non capisco,*" replied Jake in perfect Italian. Jake knew that the likelihood of a forty-something male in Italy not understanding English was far higher in Italy than north of the Alps, where most people spoke English quite well. He calculated that this was something the Iranian probably understood too.

The Iranian gave Jake a puzzled look, as if things did not add up. In the next instant, Sara seemed to appear out of nowhere.

"*Ciao, carissimo!*" she shouted at Jake from about twenty steps away, as if she had known him all her life.

"*Ciao, Elisa!*" he called out, summoning the name of his Italian friend's wife, as to not reveal Sara's identify.

Sara walked briskly up to Jake and gave him a hug and a kiss right on his pleasantly surprised lips. He gladly played along, kissing and embracing her passionately, as if he'd been away from his lover for far too long.

Sara did not know that Fortina's heart was throbbing—and not because of the menacing Arab-looking stranger nearby.

The Hezbollah operative, observing the entire scene, realized he had made an error in judgment and walked quickly back to his car. He was wrong about the suspicious man standing by the train's exit doors. The man was clearly Italian, and these were two Italian lovers openly expressing their passions in public.

Still embracing Sara while looking over her shoulders and behind her, Jake watched the suspected Iranian man head back to his car.

"That must be Darbandi's ride," Jake whispered. "And he was checking me out."

Still facing Sara with his hands on her hips, Jake asked, "Sara, what are you *doing* here?"

"Didn't you forget to say, 'Thank you, my dearest friend'?" she replied.

"Si, *grazie*, many thanks, my *dearest friend*." Jake chuckled, his knees a bit shaky after the most wonderful kiss he'd shared in years.

"Now what?" he continued.

"What do you mean now what? It's pretty simple. I'm going with you."

"The *hell* you are." Realizing his response was a bit harsh, he apologized. "Are you sure, Sara? Don't you have somewhere to be tomorrow?"

"I did," she replied. "But I'm feeling a bit ill, *cough, cough*."

"That was the worst fake cough I've ever heard," he chuckled.

Jake needed to decide before Darbandi came through the station's main doors. But there was only one choice.

"Okay, you're coming with me, Sara. I should say I very much appreciate this. And I do, I really do. I know you can handle yourself— heck, you're a Carabinieri officer, so I expect you're the better part of our new two-person team. But I hope this is the right decision for you."

"Well, it wasn't only your decision to make, Jake. You're in *my* country now. And trust me, Mr. American Army Major, it will be the right decision, not for me or Italy, but for you."

"Okay then, get ready, because our man should be here any minute." Right on cue, the man walked out the Porta Nuova train station main doors and headed straight to the waiting curbside vehicle.

"That's the Iranian, Darbandi," Jake said.

Sara did not respond, instead doing her best to take a mental photograph of the dark-haired man carrying the black backpack. The dim train station lights were barely sufficient to get a decent look.

"What he supposedly has in that backpack is what I told you about before," said Jake.

"*Supposedly*?" asked Sara.

"Yes, supposedly. The French police are almost certain he's got the second bone from Ruth Ackerman's grave. The only problem is, nobody has actually seen it. And Darbandi has done his fair share of traveling since he left Paris. As far as we actually *know*, he might be carrying some old gym clothes."

"That's a rather unpleasant image, Mr. Fortina," Sara said, the corner of her lip curling up.

"It would be a helluva thing if it turns out that I—I mean *we*—have been chasing a bunch of old gym clothes, wouldn't it?" asked Jake.

Sara only smiled.

As the two Iranians pulled out of their parking place, Jake began a routine he was well familiar with—give Darbandi's vehicle plenty of room to get ahead but not so much as to completely lose sight of it. That was much harder to do in the evening, particularly without tipping off the two Iranians to the fact that they were being followed. The fact that there was still other traffic on the streets of Verona was helpful. But because they had both been seen by the Iranian driver, the duo had to be extra careful.

There were a lot of ways to detect a tail. Jake's gut churned, putting him back in Afghanistan's Korengal Valley for a moment.

No, no way, no compromise, he asserted to himself. *I will follow these sonsabitches back to France, or to Iran, or wherever, if I must.*

In a few minutes, Jake's gut spoke to him again. In his rearview mirror, another car appeared. It was lurking back, just as Fortina was with Darbandi. Taking immediate action, he pulled into a roadside gas station. The suspicious vehicle behind him passed by the gas station. Cautiously, Jake proceeded again.

"Well, at least we know he wasn't following *us*," he said.

Not responding, Sara was busy typing a message on her phone.

"You seem to be pretty preoccupied there, Major Simonetti."

"Jake, I've got to let my people know what's going on. If he learns after the fact that I'm doing this, my boss will be upset. But he'll understand, at some point. I had to jump the chain of command."

"How big of a jump was it?"

"I have a friend—an old mentor, really—who is the Carabinieri commander of the entire Veneto region, including Verona, Vicenza, Venice and beyond. His headquarters is in Venice. Brigadier General

Sebastiano Comitini will know what to do with the information I just sent him.

"As I said," she continued, "you know exactly what the Italian guy looks like. I have requested his composite sketch be sent to me to make sure we in the Carabinieri get it right. Who knows, Jake, you might someday even be a witness in an Italian court."

"Well, *that* would be an adventure. Will they have lots of good espresso available?"

"More than you can imagine."

"I guess it will be worth it, then."

"You never know. You and I might need help with these two Iranian characters before we know it," said Sara. "Once the upper levels of Italian law enforcement and government know what is at stake concerning the United States and Israel, I expect they'll get their heads in the game pretty quickly."

"I gotta ask, Sara, are you armed?"

"What do you think I have inside this fancy purse I'm keeping between my legs? Bonbons?"

Sara felt the purse on the seat between her thighs, assuring herself that her Beretta PX4 Storm Subcompact pistol was still there.

Jake smiled at the thought of her thighs, again checking the road ahead. It was now clear that the car he let pass by at the gas station was following the Iranians too.

"That could be our Italian friend from the border right there," said Jake. "Then again, just about thirty hours ago he was in a different car, so it could be *anybody*, really. But one thing is for sure: the driver is as interested in Darbandi as we are."

After about fifteen minutes of driving towards the outskirts of Verona, it was clear Darbandi was headed west, on Italy's E70 autostrada, destination unknown.

As he kept his distance, Jake mentally ticked off the possibilities of where the Iranian operatives could be headed.

Is it Milan, maybe? Will they turn north to Switzerland or keep a westerly bearing and head back to France, to the French Riviera? Marseilles? Or perhaps head south down the Italian peninsula? This could get tricky. And I've got to take care of my partner.

61.
BACK IN BUSINESS

LUIGI GIANFRANCO WAS ELATED. His connections had come through. Awaiting Arman Darbandi's arrival at the Verona train station, he knew he could not afford to make another mistake like he and Markov had made in the Paris apartment.

In Paris, I was within fifteen yards of the most valuable human bone in the world, Gianfranco reminded himself. *Next time, I have to be faster than the Iranian.*

Gianfranco had pulled his gray Fiat Tipo into the train station with plenty of time before the Iranian's expected arrival time. Twice changing parking places so he could get closest to the train station's exits, he finally settled within sixty yards of the station's main doors. With the aid of opera binoculars, he could easily spot his target.

"Got him," he whispered as he observed the Iranian exiting the station among a handful of giggling, young Italian women.

Darbandi entered the awaiting black Jeep Cherokee, parked curbside. It was a direct forty-yard walk from the station's front doors. Gianfranco had to immediately leave his parking place to be in position to follow the Iranian and his driver.

"Son of a bitch!" he yelled as he pulled his car out, realizing someone had just cut him off to pay their ticket before exiting the lot.

As the elderly Italian lady finally pulled her car through the exit gate, Gianfranco was relieved. But he was not in a position to observe the black Jeep Cherokee leaving the train station area.

Making some quick traffic maneuvers, he spotted Darbandi's vehicle and was quickly just two cars behind. That was okay for now, as long as he could keep the Cherokee in full view. One of the two cars soon pulled into a gas station.

"This is better," muttered Gianfranco.

As he followed Darbandi's vehicle out of Verona and towards Milan, he thought the darkness would be his friend, too.

62.
FATEFUL PIT STOP

"TERRORISTS MUST HAVE WEAK BLADDERS." Jake looked over at Sara. "Or they just drink too much tea."

"And you make that judgment after one stop?"

"Well, actually, no. I have some experience with this."

"I don't know what to think about that, Jake," giggled Sara.

The duo had followed the two Iranians in the black Cherokee as it pulled into a twenty-four-hour Agip gas station, on the Italian E70 autostrada. The station was located on the side of the southbound lanes between the Italian cities of Brescia and Cremona.

Jake observed a second car, realizing it was the same one that overtook them back in Verona. The car pulled into a parking spot only four spaces away from the Iranians.

"Did you see the second car, Sara? The one from Verona? It's pretty clear it's following our Iranian friends."

"*Si,*" she replied. "It appears there is only the driver. No passengers."

Jake entered a parking space with sufficient distance to safely remain unobserved by Darbandi and his driver, but not so far as to lose a clear picture of what was happening. Jake and Sara waited.

"Well, they must not realize they are being followed," said Sara. "Darbandi jumped out of the vehicle and headed to the bathroom almost immediately after the car was parked."

"Sara, do you think Darbandi is meeting someone in the station?"

"I'll go have a look." Sara reached for the door handle.

"Wait! I should go, Sara."

"No, actually, you shouldn't, Jake. Darbandi has seen you before, right?" She looked at him knowingly.

"Actually, I'm not sure. He *might* have seen me at a gas station in France, but still, it should be me who goes in there."

"Well, we are in Italy now, *my* Italy," said Sara, getting out of the car and heading for the gas station.

"Crap," Jake whispered.

In the next instant, as his heart pounded and his mind raced with all the things that could go wrong, Jake realized how much he cared for his new Italian police partner.

Nothing can happen to her, he proclaimed to himself.

Ten minutes passed and Jake grew restless. Finally, Darbandi emerged from the men's restroom, heading for his car. The Italian emerge from the other car and confronted the unsuspecting Iranian and pulled a gun on him, demanding the backpack. Darbandi slowly raised his hands.

"Where is the finesse in *that*?" Jake mumbled. "This will not end well, right here at zero dark thirty in a gas station parking lot."

Jake saw the second Iranian, who had quietly emerged from the car, approach to within ten yards behind Gianfranco. The second Iranian slowly raised his pistol, with its extended length suggesting a silencer on the barrel. Gianfranco's knees buckled and he collapsed right where he'd been standing. Darbandi's driver approached the Italian crumpled facedown in the parking lot.

The two Iranians quickly grabbed Gianfranco by the arms and dragged him across the tarmac between two parked cars and up to a weed-covered fence line that bordered the back of the gas station. As they did, Sara exited the bathroom door just in time to see the Iranians dragging Gianfranco's body. She quickly stepped back and out of the view. The two Hezbollah operatives dropped the body near the weeds and headed for their vehicle.

They scanned the area, convinced that the late-night attack happened so quickly that no one else saw it. The Iranians quickly pulled out of their parking space, and an instant later, Sara emerged from the bathroom building. As the Iranians drove off, she ran over to check Gianfranco's pulse. There was no sign of life.

Pulling out her cellphone, she quickly took a photo of the Italian.

"He's dead," she said as Jake pulled up the car and she jumped in. "But we have no choice. We must follow those two."

Heading down the E70 autostrada in a southerly direction, they caught up to the two Iranians in no time. As they did, Sara called her boss and left him a message.

"Sir, this is Major Simonetti. The American major and I just witnessed the shooting of a man who very closely resembles the composite of the suspect from the Austria-Italy border shooting. He's dead, lying near the rear fence line of an Agip gas station parking lot. I'm forwarding a photo. The station is located on the southbound side of highway E70, between the Brescia and Cremona exits.

"Our American friend confirms he's the man who was recently involved in the Paris and Strasbourg shootings. We are trailing the Iranian and his driver, who also looks to be Persian or Arab. We are headed southbound on E70. It was his driver who shot our suspect. Will report back when we have more information. No need to engage in support of us until we have a better idea of where they are headed and what they are up to."

━━━━━━

Four Italian carabinieri officers, followed by an Italian ambulance, arrived at the Agip station on the E70 autostrada within about fifteen minutes.

"Sir, it's Captain Gigi Francavilla speaking," said their leader as he called his boss. "The body is exactly where Major Simonetti said it would be. It was positioned next to the parking lot perimeter fence, in some high grass. He was easily missed by the few travelers through the gas station between midnight and now. He was shot from the back, cleanly through the heart. The shooter was either very lucky or a professional."

"Does he match the composite of the suspect from the border incident?" asked Lieutenant Colonel Michelangelo Risi, the commander of the nearby Brescia Carabinieri station.

"He does. He had personal ID on him, but I question its authenticity. We are running checks, which will include DNA samples. Who knows, maybe he's in our database."

"Good work, Captain," replied Risi. "Get him in the ambulance and out of there as soon as possible. Make sure to comb the area for any other clues, but before dawn arrives, be on your way."

"*Si, signore*," replied Francavilla.

Risi decided to await calling his boss in Venice, seeing no reason to wake him before six. He was thrilled. This was a great day for law enforcement in Italy. It was a day that would add to the Carabinieri's highly respected law enforcement legacy in Italy and Europe. It didn't matter that the Italian criminal was killed by an Iranian Hezbollah operative. What mattered was that within twenty-four hours of a rare violent incident at the Austria-Italy border crossing of Vipiteno-Sterzing, in which a young Italian Guardia di Finanza officer had been shot, the Carabinieri already had the assailant. The identification of the suspect by a Guardia di Finanza officer at that scene—and a search of the Carabinieri's DNA database—would soon provide confirmation that the now-dead shooter was an 'Ndrangheta mafia operative who had escaped from a Sardinian prison years before.

And to think we were tipped off by an "off duty" Carabinieri officer and a US Army major, Risi mused.

63.
PORTOFINO

THE EARLY-MORNING SUN would not make its appearance over Italy's western coastline for another two hours or so. For the pursuers of the two Iranian Hezbollah operatives, it was an odd but beautiful place that they had been led to. The colorful and iconic port village of Portofino was well known to many tourists from around the world. The popular Italian singer Andrea Bocelli wrote and sang songs about it. Located on Italy's Ligurian Coast, Portofino is about twenty-five miles south of its historically famous—thanks to Christopher Columbus—and much larger neighbor, Genoa.

"We have to be careful," Sara told Jake as they parked their vehicle as far from the two Iranians as possible to still permit surveillance.

"Portofino is a small village with a limited waterfront of perhaps four hundred meters or so," she continued. "There will be several hundred tourists here, and we might be able to use that to our advantage. But this village does not provide a lot of room to maneuver, if you know what I mean."

"I completely understand," said Jake. "I actually got to visit here during my Vicenza tour." He left out the fact that he had done so with Faith.

"It's a beautiful village but a curious place for a stop by two Hezbollah operatives on a mission," he continued, purposely shifting his mind away from wonderful memories of his deceased wife. And then, the thought cascaded over him as if from a gushing waterfall.

"Unless—"

"Unless *what*?" Sara asked.

"Unless they are going to make a break for it by the sea," said Jake. "I don't know, maybe they'll rent a boat and try to head out to international waters."

"That's plausible," responded Sara. "Portofino doesn't make a lot of sense, otherwise. It's a dead end. If they decide to *drive* elsewhere, they will have to go back out on the single road out that brought them in here. Not exactly the wisest thing to do. Or maybe they'll conduct a hand off here. In any case, we have no choice but to stay on top of them."

"I agree, Sara. It will take everything we have to make sure they don't slip away from us without us being compromised. I've been in this situation before, and we can't let that happen."

"Meanwhile," continued Jake, looking at his watch, "it's the middle of the night, but I think it's time we update our higher authorities and request some support. I'll call the Sixth Fleet Operations Center. They need to know about this development ASAP. If our two Iranian friends do try to make a break for it to international waters, the US Navy has got to be ready. They might be our only chance, and even then, it will be a stretch at best."

"And, Jake, you know whom I have to contact—ASAP, as you say, correct?" said Simonetti. "There may be another way."

"I *do* know that. I understand this is still mainly an Italian show."

"No, not mainly, my friend," responded Sara with a wink. "It *is* an Italian show. But we Italians appreciate the help from our American friends."

64.
WARNING ORDER

US NAVY CAPTAIN DIRK DEVERILL, located at US Sixth Fleet Headquarters in Naples, had informed his staff when he went off shift at midnight that if a call came into the Operations Branch from an American Army major tracking two Iranian operatives across Italy, to notify him immediately.

Within hours of Major Jake Fortina's situation report, the Sixth Fleet commander, Vice-Admiral Robert Huber, directed US naval assets be deployed in response to a variety of contingencies involving the Iranians. Fortunately, key elements of the fleet were in the last day of a local Mediterranean naval exercise, so the transition to a quick response footing off the Ligurian coast was straightforward. Families were unhappy because some of their sailors were not coming home from the exercise as scheduled, but that was the nature of maintaining twenty-four-hour readiness in a NATO environment. Admiral Huber knew that selected elements of the fleet had to be postured and ready if the two Iranians tried to make a run for it by sea.

Captain Deverill's planning team jumped into action. Contingencies were developed for various scenarios, including the use of coastal patrol ships and air assets, including helicopters. High altitude reconnaissance capabilities were also planned for, as were special operations forces, including a SEAL team.

It would not be the first time that a similar, and very unconventional, plan had been put into action by the Sixth Fleet.

On October 3, 1985, the *Achille Lauro* left Genoa to begin a cruise of the Mediterranean Sea. It was carrying over seven hundred international passengers and a crew of over two hundred. Days later the ship docked at Alexandria, Egypt, and hundreds of passengers left the ship for touring. After the passengers had left the ship, with about one hundred still onboard, four men with AK-47 assault rifles accosted the *Achille Lauro*'s crew. They then forced the captain to sail the ship out of port.

The men—who had been posing as passengers—were members of a Palestinian Liberation Front group led by Mohammed Zaidan, more commonly known as Abu Abbas. After taking over the ship, Abbas demanded that Israel release fifty Palestinian prisoners. Israel refused, and the ship headed to Tartus, Syria, where authorities, at the request of the US and Italian governments, did not allow the ship to dock.

On October 8, the terrorists mercilessly shot Leon Klinghoffer, an elderly, wheelchair-bound American Jewish man, and threw him overboard. The hijackers then forced the ship to sail to Cyprus, where they were again denied port.

The hijackers forced the *Achille Lauro* to sail back to Port Said. They then established radio contact with Egyptian government authorities. In exchange for releasing the hostages, the hijackers demanded safe passage through Egypt and immunity from prosecution. Egypt agreed, and the men were allowed to disappear into Port Said.

Though Egypt claimed that the hijackers had left the country, US intelligence reports indicated that they were still in Egypt. The plane on which they had planned to escape was located, and US President Ronald Reagan gave the order to intercept it. On the evening of October 10, US fighter jets intercepted the passenger aircraft and forced it to land at a NATO air base in Sigonella, Sicily. Italy had been informed only minutes before that the United States wanted custody of the hijackers. A standoff ensued between US and Italian forces. Eventually, Italy arrested the hijackers, but Italian authorities allowed their leader to escape for Yugoslavia.

The four hijackers were tried in 1986, in Italy. Three received sentences ranging from fifteen to thirty years in prison.

This time, given the guidance from the US Command Authority—

the US president and secretary of defense—there would be no repeat of the standoff between US and Italian authorities that occurred during the *Achille Lauro* affair. The Italians would have the lead for whatever operation developed. If, however, the operation was to evolve to international waters, then all bets were off. In Italian coast waters and on the Italian mainland, it would be an Italian show, unless the Italians specifically asked for intervention or support by the Americans.

65.
ITALY GETS IN THE GAME

MAJOR SARA SIMONETTI'S REPORT and the quick recovery of
Luigi Gianfranco's body by the Carabinieri caused a stir in the senior
ranks of Italian national law enforcement. The visual confirmation
of Luigi Gianfranco, backed by DNA evidence, proved that Italy had
gotten their man. It was a godsend for the Carabinieri to solve this
case less than twenty-four hours after the shooting at the Italian
border town of Vipiteno-Sterzing.

But now Italy had another major problem. Two Iranian Hezbollah
operatives, who might be holding the final keys to Iran's development
of a killer influenza were on the loose within Italy's borders, had now
been sighted in the Italian seaside village of Portofino.

"*Signor Generale*," began Sebastiano Comitini, commander of
all Carabinieri forces in Northern Italy, "I believe this situation calls
for the activation of the GIS." The GIS was the Gruppo Intervento
Speciale, or Special Intervention Group. "Our conventional
Carabinieri *could* take care of this business on their own. But given
the gravity and potential impact to America and Israel in light of this
Iranian threat, I believe we need to be on the conservative side. We
need to bring in our best."

"*Si*, Sebastiano, I agree," responded Lieutenant General Ennio
Chiavolini, commander of all Carabinieri Forces in Italy. "Our
conventional forces are entirely capable of moving in and capturing
these two Iranian *bastardi*. General Dalla Chiesa, who did a

magnificent job leading our conventional Carabinieri and supporting our Guardia di Finanza forces against the Red Brigades in the 1970s, would be rolling in his grave if he knew we were looking outside of our conventional Carabinieri forces to accomplish this mission. But times have changed, Sebastiano. Today, we have forces perfectly tailored for this operation."

"I concur, *signore*," replied Comitini.

"What is your recommendation on a timeline, Sebastiano?" asked Chiavolini.

"We must move as quickly as possible. We should plan on a raid in the early hours of tomorrow morning, under the cover of darkness. We have the advantage of a night-vision capability, which the Iranians have shown no sign of possessing. And we know the terrain too."

"I will issue the order immediately," responded Chiavolini.

66.
BOSTON STING

"SIR, THIS IS MICHAEL BEANS," began the caller. "We got her. We arrested Avalie Zirani early this morning. Her arrest was uneventful."

"What was the evidence that enabled us to bring her in?" asked the FBI's director of operations Rex Schuberg.

"She made a simple but crucial mistake. She left a thumb drive in the wrong place, which turned out to be the right place for us to find it," responded Beans.

"Is she being cooperative?" asked Schuberg.

"Yes, *very* cooperative. Still has family in Iran. Zirani is worried about their fate, as well as that of her immediate family here in Boston," said Beans.

"Do we know if she actually passed any research or antivirus secrets back to Iran?" asked the operations director.

"As best we can ascertain by what's on the thumb drive, some sensitive information has unfortunately been passed," responded Beans. "But we still have some more investigative analysis and questioning to go through to corroborate our initial assessment. We should have that complete within forty-eight hours."

"Obviously, if what you learn changes, let me know immediately. The intelligence community is going to be all over this, as will the president."

"Roger that," responded Beans.

"What about the press?" asked Schuberg.

"It was a quiet arrest," said Beans. "We have not released anything to the public—yet. But you know how this game goes. It will only be a few hours before the press is aware."

"Roger," responded Schuberg. "We'll need to craft the press release soon. The headquarters staff here can help with that. Given what is going on in Italy at the moment, this adds up to a broader international security threat. The Israelis will be clamoring for information, too. All major pharmaceutical companies that were involved in the COVID-19 vaccine development need to be notified and be on security alert, as well. There may be more than one Avalie Zirani out there. And, Michael?"

"Yes, sir?"

"Tell your team I'm extremely proud of them. Helluva job in getting this done."

67.
STAYING THE NIGHT?

SEARCHING FOR A SUITABLE ROOM for which they had no reservation, it was the third hotel that the two Hezbollah terrorists had walked into in Portofino. Only, this time, they did not emerge from the Albergo Genovese.

"It's probable that our two Hezbollah friends are spending the night there," said Sara.

"Well, it's either that or they're just looking for a place to take a short break. We need to keep our eyes on that place," said Jake.

"The good news is that besides the exit door out the kitchen, it only has one main public exit."

"Correct, Sara, and I think the chances of them traipsing out through the kitchen are pretty slim."

"Agreed. I propose we get a table in front of the Café Liguria. We can safely observe the hotel exit from there. I will show my Carabinieri badge to the owner. Unlike in Calabria, where I served for two long years, the locals here in Liguria are pretty good about respecting the Carabinieri. You and I can sit at a table and rotate the watch, if needed."

As the two approached the Café Liguria, Sara's eyes lit up at a sign that read *Camere Disponibile*—"rooms available."

As Sara walked into the café, Jake sat at one of the café's six outside, marble-topped round tables, about forty yards from the entrance of the Albergo Genovese. Within seven minutes, Sara returned.

"Okay, Major, I just got us the deal of the year. There are four rooms upstairs, above the café. I rented one of them for twenty-four hours, at the Carabinieri discount rate," she said. "I don't know about you, but I could use a shower. Would you like to go first, or may I?"

"Us Army guys only need a shower about every third day," said Jake. Realizing just how corny he just sounded in trying to be funny, the obviously fatigued Army major quickly added, "That's wonderful, Sara. Thank you for doing that. You go first. I'll enjoy a cappuccino and keep an eye on the hotel."

"I won't be long," she replied, clearly grateful for the chance to freshen up first.

Sara walked to the back of the café and ascended the stairs leading to the four modest rooms, and entered the room she had reserved. It had two separated single beds and a single nightstand between them. What she saw next made her even more delighted. The room's only window had a perfect view of the Albergo Genovese's main exit door. *If we need to, we could take turns getting a nap here too,* she thought.

Then she thought better of it. *Too risky to do and still be ready if our Iranian friends make a move.*

After showering, Sara contacted her Carabinieri headquarters from the room.

Downstairs at his table, soaking up the morning Mediterranean sun, Jake let his mind drift for a moment, thinking about Sara.

I could easily fall in love with you, Sara, Jake thought. Immediately annoyed at himself for allowing such a thought during a dangerous mission, Jake thought just how odd—*unbelievable, really*—that he had ended up in this idyllic seaside town the way he and Sara had.

Returning downstairs, Sara provided an update.

"Jake, I informed my higher-ups about the location of our two friends. If they are still in that hotel before dawn breaks tomorrow, the plan is to have one of our Carabinieri direct-action teams roll them up. Our Florence headquarters will send a two-man reconnaissance team in the late afternoon to check out the hotel and confirm the room number—*or numbers*—of the Iranians. The assault group will arrive at midnight and be in position by 0300 hours. Sometime after that, the Iranians will get their wake-up call. Our job is to just keep an eye on that hotel and report if anything changes."

"Understood, Sara," replied Jake. "I did the same thing. I fully appraised the US Sixth Fleet operations cell of our status and that of the Iranians as soon as you went upstairs. Key operational units of the fleet were already on standby, so I expect the required contingency assets will be deployed off the coast within hours, just in case Darbandi and friend try to make a break for it by sea."

"Okay, *my* friend," responded Sara.

Right on cue, the Café Liguria waiter did exactly as Major Fortina had instructed him to do, in perfect Italian. "Right after my friend shows up, please bring her a cappuccino and chocolate croissant."

"Well, thank you so much, Jake," Sara said, happily surprised, as the waiter placed the Italian breakfast delights on the table. "Besides the fact that I am Italian, how did you know I loved cappuccino and chocolate croissants in the morning?"

"I remember a certain conversation we had during our Germany days. You said it was hard to find a good cappuccino north of the Alps. I was actually paying attention."

Major Sara Simonetti beamed.

Mission accomplished, thought Jake.

68.
A MAJOR NATIONAL SECURITY THREAT

"AARON," BEGAN ISRAEL'S PRIME MINISTER Mira Abrams, "where are we on the Iranian Spanish flu case?"

Abrams, who had risen through Israel's political ranks after proving herself to be a highly competent, cool-under-fire, and resilient Israeli Defense Force officer, didn't like to beat around the bush. This was particularly true when a major national security threat was facing the state of Israel.

"Madame Minister, our two operatives are in place," responded Aaron Sharon, the retired Israeli three-star general and director of the Mossad, Israel's national intelligence agency. "They have been providing updates. The Italians and the Americans have the two Iranians in their sights."

"When would you expect the Iranians to be apprehended . . . or killed?" asked Abrams.

"I can't say with one hundred percent confidence, but I assess that will happen within the next twenty-four to forty-eight hours, at the most," replied Sharon.

"That is good to hear, Aaron. But on the off chance our Americans and Italian friends come up short, what's our plan?" asked the prime minister.

"Our operatives will engage directly, if required," replied the Mossad director. "But, per our rules of engagement, and per your guidance, this would have to be an absolute last resort."

"Correct, Aaron, only as a very last resort," said the prime minister. "And what about the location of the Iranian virus development facility in Iran? What is our latest intelligence telling us?"

"We are tightening the circle on that place. There are only two research facilities in Iran, either of which could be working on a virus or vaccine of this nature. One in particular, about thirty miles northeast of Tehran, has had some unusual activity over the past four weeks. Our intelligence contacts report that the Iranians are working feverishly to develop their own COVID-19-like flu vaccine there, but the evidence increasingly shows that it might be a lot more than that."

"Once we have confirmation, I know you will inform me, Aaron," said Abrams.

"Indeed, I will, ma'am," replied Sharon.

69.
ITALIAN VACATION

THE TWO ISRAELI MOSSAD AGENTS were as surprised as Majors Simonetti and Fortina were to find themselves in the beautiful Italian coastal town of Portofino. The agents posed as Mr. and Mrs. Eden Caplan, a married couple from Israel on vacation. Yet their real purpose was anything but relaxation. They were experts at tracking and countering major Hezbollah operations around the world, particularly when those operations targeted Israeli citizens. They wanted to be sure that the Italians or Americans would capture or kill the two Iranians, with Ruth Ackerman's hip bone salvaged.

While the military wing of Hezbollah of Lebanon preferred a low-low approach—*the less the world knows, the better*—to their terrorist, illicit, and criminal activities around the world, the Mossad had written the book on the low-profile approach decades before Hezbollah. In fact, the Mossad's striving to keep its international espionage and direct-action operations out of the public eye had been extremely successful. Their activities rarely, if ever, made the news, and then only on speculation and little or no evidence.

In this case, the Mossad leadership—with the knowledge of Israel prime minister Abrams—expected that the Americans and Italians would be able to handle business and recover Ruth Ackerman's bone, before it reached the Iranian government and the researchers who were trying to develop a killer vaccine. Mr. and Mrs. Caplan were given a complete hands-off order by the Mossad headquarters in

Israel. If the Americans and Italians failed, however, the two Mossad agents could step in, but only if absolutely necessary.

All were on standby, awaiting the Iranians' next move, which came as dusk verged on complete darkness.

The two Hezbollah operatives emerged from the Albergo Genovese at 9:45 p.m.

"By the way they are dressed," whispered Sara, "it doesn't look like they are headed out for a cup of tea."

"My bet says they're heading for their car," Jake said.

"You might be right." Sara kept her eyes firmly on the two suspects.

Within minutes, it was proven that Jake was dead wrong.

"They are taking the trail into the wooded area," said Sara, referring to the coastal forest, just behind the Italian port town, that hugged the Ligurian sea, north of Portofino.

Jake got on the phone to the Sixth Fleet's 190-feet Cyclone-class patrol ship, with its crew of twenty-eight officers and sailors, located off the Ligurian coast. In international waters, the ship sat barely beyond the twelve-mile limit of Italy's coastal waters.

"The two Iranians are on the move," reported Jake. "They are on foot, paralleling the coast, about one hundred yards inland from the water, and heading north from Portofino. We are trailing on foot. Will provide updates as the situation permits."

Immediately, the ship's commanding officer alerted the nearby SEALs, divided among two US Navy Mark V.1 patrol boats, each armed with 7.62 millimeter and fifty-caliber machine guns.

Fortunately for Jake and Sara, the trail they were on, about the width of a car, was made up of hard-packed dirt, which helped cushion their steps. There was absolutely no undergrowth on the trail, prompting Jake to whisper, "This trail must get used a lot."

The duo moved with stealth along the trail, deliberately picking up their feet with each step to avoid shuffling and possibly kicking a stone or tripping on a tree root. They could barely make out the two figures some forty to fifty yards in front of them aided only by some reflective star lights and a rising half-moon off the nearby sea.

Suddenly, the two Iranians stopped. The two majors couldn't be sure in the poor lighting, but it seemed the Iranians had not only stopped; they'd also turned around and were looking back.

Without saying a word to each other, Jake and Sara immediately stopped and got down, lying as flat as they could on the soft, dark earth.

About ten seconds went by as they barely made out the two standing silhouettes, still frozen on the trail in front of them.

Then, a breath of relief.

Apparently turning back around to restart their walk, one of the two Iranians turned on a flashlight. That was a sure sign that the two terrorists were unaware that someone was behind them. The two Hezbollah operatives continued walking, a bit more briskly than before. While the flashlight allowed the Iranians to move faster, it also helped Jake and Sara keep up.

After almost two and half miles and two hours on the wooded, rolling, twisting, and semi-darkened trail, Jake and Sara observed the distant outside security lights of a building nestled in a rocky cove. Walking another two hundred yards, the two Iranian operatives stopped, just off the trail, and overlooking the old abbey and the shoreline below. Their silhouettes were highlighted by the outside abbey lights behind them.

Grabbing Sara's arm, Jake signaled her to stop.

Taking off his jacket, Jake knelt and shrouded the light of his cellphone with his jacket. Google Maps would answer the obvious question.

"It's the Abbey of San Fruttuoso, built by Benedictine monks in the tenth century," said Jake, unable to suppress his love for Italian and Roman history. The ancient Roman cloister, now about seventy yards down the trail and nestled slightly above a small, rocky bay, was positioned slightly below the Iranians new lookout post just off the trail.

"One of two things are going to happen," whispered Sara. "Either they are going to meet someone in the abbey, or they are going to be picked up by sea. Your thoughts?"

"Your guess is good as mine," Jake whispered back. "I was already wrong once. But I give the sea pickup a slight edge. If they were going to meet someone here, they just as well could have come here in the daytime. But with the abbey there, meeting a boat here in full daylight would not be very discreet."

Jake promptly sent a text message to the Sixth Fleet coastal patrol boat commanding officer, describing their new location and that of the Iranians. Sara followed suit with her Carabinieri contacts.

The Carabinieri assault team had been getting positioned in and around the Hotel Genovese when they got the word that the Hezbollah terrorists had slipped out of Portofino by foot over two hours earlier.

More than an hour went by, with the Iranians still seated just off the trail, and the lights of the abbey shrouding their silhouettes just enough to make them visible. Jake and Sara remained secluded just off the trail, with some forest undergrowth adding additional cover to the darkness and their prone positions. They were not letting the two terrorists out of their sights.

And then, they heard the approaching boat.

"Guess you were right this time," Sara grinned.

70.
IN POSITION

HAVING JUST RECEIVED the location coordinates of the two Iranian Hezbollah operatives, Navy lieutenant Brad Murphy knew he needed to review the team's planned maneuvers before putting his SEAL team into action.

Lieutenant Murphy felt fortunate to have what every commissioned officer in command of soldiers, sailors, marines, airmen, or coastguardsmen hopes to have on his team—a highly experienced and trustworthy NCO. In this case, Murphy had one of the best NCOs—and SEALs—he could hope for in Chief Petty Officer Jack Stevens.

Stevens was highly experienced, competent, savvy, and always completely focused on the mission. He was also humble and always learning, which Murphy liked. He and Murphy had outlined an overall contingency plan before asking fellow SEAL team members for input, some of which was quite helpful in improving their original plan.

At Murphy and Stevens's disposal were two Mark VI Special Operations watercraft. Murphy would be in charge of one boat, while Stevens would be in command of the second. With a top speed of forty-five knots, the boats were sufficiently armored that they could withstand small arms fire, but agile and powerful enough that they were highly maneuverable. Yet, whether it included boarding a midsize ship, subduing a yacht, or capturing a rowboat, every mission was different. No matter how you trained, some degree of risk was inherent in every mission.

With four SEALs, including the team leaders, on each boat, they would be ready to intercept the Iranians if they tried to escape Italy by sea.

"Gentlemen," began Murphy, "tonight our mission has straightforward objectives. Our primary objective is to retrieve a human bone being carried by an Iranian Hezbollah operative named Arman Darbandi. That bone was stolen from the grave of a US Army World War I nurse in Paris. Iran wants that bone for its DNA value in developing a deadly virus to deploy against the United States and Israel. This is a tier-one national security threat we are dealing with.

"Our secondary objective is to take Darbandi alive. I don't have to explain to you the intelligence value this experienced Hezbollah operator will provide to our intelligence community," he continued.

"For tonight's operation, you've all seen the plan and we've rehearsed it, but I will now do a final review of the main actions. Boat One, with my team, will await Darbandi's boat in international waters, just as Darbandi's boat exits Italian coast waters. We—Boat One—will spotlight Darbandi's boat, signaling it to stop at about a hundred yards out. That should cause them to at least slow up, maybe even actually stop. Boat Two, commanded by Steve, will stand eighty to a hundred yards off the portside until Darbandi's boat passes, and then once it does, Boat Two will come in from the aft side to perform a boarding operation. The captain—or whoever is at the helm of Darbandi's boat—may have to be eliminated if that boat does anything but stop and surrender. If they try to run us, we will implement contingency two. Rules of engagement for MIO, including the use of deadly force, are in effect. Any questions?"

This would be a tricky nighttime maneuver. But after having gone over the team's plan and rehearsed it several times, including with map and sketch rehearsals, Lieutenant Murphy knew his special operators were ready. They would own this night.

71.
HEZBOLLAH RENDEZVOUS

AS THE FORTY-FOOT, Libyan-flagged fishing boat approached the abbey's small bay, Darbandi used his flashlight to signal his location, high above the water and the rocky banks adjacent to the abbey. He and his fellow Hezbollah operative still had to make their way about forty yards down the narrow trail to the abbey's dock.

As the boat approached the dock, a small light came on inside the sparsely inhabited abbey, which was now used for tourists who could only reach it by sea or a rather challenging two-to-three-hour hike through the adjacent forest.

The Hezbollah planners for this rendezvous did their homework, Jake thought, viewing the scene from above the small bay. He and Sara were about forty yards from Darbandi and his sidekick, who had started to descend the trail to the water.

Jake and Sara, crouched over, moved up the trail about fifteen yards. They then quickly reassessed the situation, almost simultaneously deciding to get on their hands and knees and crawl about another ten yards to get a better look from the bluff at the boat below.

"If anyone inside the abbey gets suspicious and alerts Italian law enforcement about an unscheduled fishing boat stop at the abbey, the abbey's remote location would require at least a two-hour response time," Jake whispered. He could barely hear the voices below.

"Greetings in the name of Allah," said Darbandi as he and his security guard approached the boat from the dock.

The outside security lights of the abbey partially illuminated the boat and dock, silhouetting the figures boarding, as well as those already on the boat.

"With the two that were on the boat, it looks like there are four of them, including Darbandi," whispered Sara.

"I will update the SEAL team now," said Jake.

As he firmly gripped his cellphone, it unexpectedly illuminated the surrounding forest, which did not go unnoticed by an Iranian on the boat.

Three pistol-fired shots rang out, causing Sara to shove the kneeling Jake on his side as she covered him with her body, and covered the cellphone with her hands.

Embarrassed, Jake knew one of the rounds fired from the boat had come dangerously close to them. For several seconds they both lay silent in the high wet grass above the cliff. Finally, Sara slowly and slightly lifted her head to get a look at the boat below. She could see one dark figure standing on the bow of the boat, now with a rifle. He was searching the dark cliffs in front of him.

A shot from that rifle could be lethal, thought Sara.

A second light, much brighter than the first one, came on inside the abbey. The three shots had awakened someone inside.

Sara slowly lowered her head back down within a half inch of Jake's, and he could feel her taking slow, measured breaths.

"We must go, now!" the boat's captain ordered his crew, throwing the boat's engine in reverse and backing out of the small inlet. Eventually, he turned the boat around 180 degrees, and headed out to sea.

"They're leaving," said Sara as she rolled off of Jake. "And, my friend, I think I was hit, maybe by a deflected rock?"

"What? Where?"

"My left arm, above the elbow," answered Sara.

With the boat now at least three hundred yards offshore, Jake shielded his cellphone light from the sea as he shined the phone closely to Sara's arm. There was a small pink furrow just above the elbow. It was slowly oozing blood, but thankfully, no artery had been struck.

"Thank God, you'll be alright, Sara. It is bleeding a bit, so I will need to stop that now. But it does not look serious."

"Oddly enough, other than feeling as hot as hell, it doesn't hurt that much," said Sara, adrenaline coursing through her veins.

Taking off his shirt, Jake quickly made a field bandage out of it. Wearing just a T-shirt under his light jacket now, he felt a chill in the air, but it was bearable. He had been *much* colder on Army missions, and for extended hours at a time.

"*Grazie, dottore,*" said Sara.

"*Grazie*? I should be thanking you, Sara!"

72.
TRIPOLI BOUND

SAFELY ABOARD THE TRAWLER, the Hezbollah terrorist felt the safest he had felt since his journey from Paris began.

"Where is our next stop?" asked Darbandi of the ship's captain.

"The port of Tarbulus, in Tripoli. It will take us three, maybe three and half days. From Tripoli, we fly you to Tehran."

Darbandi pictured a hero's welcome as he arrived in his home capital. But coming back to reality, he knew that would not be the case as this operation was known only to a very few people within the Iranian government.

Jake stood on the bank high above the bay and watched the trawler lights as they faded, headed for the Ligurian Sea's twilight horizon. He was embarrassed that he had put Sara and himself in danger, but could not afford to dwell on the mistake. His message to the SEAL team, floating twelve miles offshore and just beyond Italy's territorial waters, had been brief.

Situation Report: Libyan-flagged fishing trawler—approximately forty to forty-five feet in length—heading due west from the San Fruttuoso abbey, located approximately two to three miles north of Portofino. Estimate trawler's speed to be ten knots per hour. Four armed individuals on board, including high-value target, confirmed. Boat's running lights were on as it left port.

After Sara completed her own situation report to Italian law enforcement authorities, including the Carabinieri anti-terrorist assault team now in Portofino, Jake sheepishly addressed what had just happened.

"That was a bone-headed move on my part," he said. "I don't know how or why my cellphone lit up the way it did, but that doesn't really matter at this point. What mattered was your reaction."

"No problem, my friend," she responded. "It will only cost you another cappuccino and *two* chocolate croissants in the morning."

Jake smiled broadly in the semidarkness. Aided by the increasingly strong starlight, Simonetti could see his wide smile, and it stirred her own.

73.
ALL IN A NIGHT'S WORK

US NAVY LIEUTENANT Brad Murphy could hear the trawler. A moment later he saw it on the water's dark horizon, about two hundred yards straight off his bow. It was only somewhat surprising that it had its running lights on.

They could have just as well kept their lights off, but they obviously wanted to look like a legitimate fishing trawler, the SEAL team commander thought.

With the trawler about eighty yards out, directly off the bow of his Mark VI Special Operations boat, Murphy could see SEAL Team Boat Two creeping up behind the trawler, exactly as planned.

"Flash the trawler," said the lieutenant.

A SEAL teammate instantly flicked on a twelve-inch spotlight.

Seeing the bright, almost blinding light, the trawler's captain immediately throttled back, slowing the trawler to less than half its original speed. It then slowly sputtered forward, approaching SEAL Team Boat One. Suddenly, the trawler captain had a panicked change of heart and decided he was going to run the trawler past the spotlight—and what he perceived to be a small boat directing the light in front of him.

Observing the change in the trawler captain's behavior and the accelerated boat speed and changed direction, the SEAL team's best marksman, Petty Officer Second Class Bob Horan, firing from Boat

Two, squeezed off two rounds from his MK 14, 7.62 mm Enhanced Battle Rifle.

The trawler's captain, standing at the ship's wheel, dropped instantly.

With the trawler now lurching forward with nobody at the wheel, Murphy immediately directed that the boat-one spotlight be shut off. He did not want to wash out the nighttime advantage the SEALs on Boat Two had with their night-vision goggles.

Within seconds, SEAL Boat Two came aside the trawler from the rear.

Darbandi, seated just inside the cabin, scrambled for the pistol in his backpack and fumbled it, dropping it on the deck. He then wildly threw the backpack out the back of the trawler and into the dark waters of the Ligurian sea. After going from looking into the spotlight to near blackness, the darkness disoriented him, and the hastily thrown backpack almost landed in Boat Two behind the trawler. A SEAL quickly scooped it out of the water.

Darbandi's security guard tried to get off a shot from the trawler, but it became his last act on earth. The lead SEAL who boarded the boat dispensed the Hezbollah operative with two clean shots.

In less than two minutes, Boat Two had the Libyan-flagged trawler under control. Darbandi was taken alive, as was one of the boat's original crew members. Ruth Ackerman's bone was safely in the possession of Chief Petty Officer Jack Stevens. The SEALs thoroughly searched the dead Iranians and the boat, and seized the terrorist's weapons, all of which could provide crucial evidence as to who they were dealing with.

"All in a night's work," Lieutenant Murphy murmured in satisfaction.

74.
PRESIDENT TO PRIME MINISTER

IT HAD BEEN a momentous briefing to President Thomas Perry. The Iranian Hezbollah agent Armand Darbandi had been captured in international waters of the Mediterranean Sea. More importantly, Ruth Ackerman's hip bone, which had been desperately sought by the Iranians, had been recovered and was in the presence of the US Navy. The president made a couple of phone calls.

"Madame Minister, we have recovered Ruth Ackerman's bone, and we have Arman Darbandi in custody."

Feigning no knowledge of the events, Israeli prime minister Mira Abrams said, "That is wonderful news, Mr. President. Israel is extremely grateful for the effective American military and diplomatic intervention in this evolving, and ugly, threat to our nations. Please thank the courageous American men and women involved in recovering the bone."

"I will certainly do that, Madame Prime Minister," said the president.

"What are your next steps, Mr. President?" asked Abrams.

"Madame Prime Minister, we will immediately debrief and extradite Arman Darbandi to the United States for trial."

"Mr. President," replied Abrams, "concerning Darbandi—"

"Concerning Darbandi," replied Perry, "we will give your intelligence services a chance to question him as well, here in the US."

"I appreciate that, Tom," replied Abrams.

"I will have my ambassador in Tel Aviv work with your government to make sure that happens, sooner than later," replied Perry.

"Thank you. If there is anything Israel can do, please let me know."

"I will certainly do that, my friend," replied Perry. "But before I say goodbye, Mira, do you have any further intelligence on what is happening in Iran?"

"Our intelligence services are learning more each day," replied the prime minister. "We are getting very close to having some solid, actionable intelligence. When we do have more firm evidence, you and your government will be the first to know."

"Thank you, Mira."

75.
THREE DAYS LATER

AT ZERO DARK THIRTY, the four Israeli F-35I Adir stealth fighters taxied on the runway of Israel's Navatim Air Base, in the Negev desert.

A Ben-Gurion University graduate, Israeli Air Force captain Isaac Peretz had graduated from the IAF's arduous and highly respected flight school and training program, lasting three years. With two combat missions under his belt, the thirty-one-year-old senior captain was honored to be leading the three other pilots—two on their first combat missions—to their assigned target in Iran.

As the four F35I fighters roared into the early-morning darkness over Israel, Prime Minister Mira Abrams picked took the top-secret phone from her military aide-de-camp, who had patched the call through to the White House.

"Mr. President," said Abrams, "I want you to be the first allied head of state to know that Israel has confirmed the location where Iran is working on a deadly Spanish 2.0 flu virus. We just launched four F-35s to strike the Alavi Research Center, located some twenty miles northeast of Tehran. We will seek to minimize civilian casualties and collateral damage, but we are going to obliterate that facility in less than forty-five minutes."

"Thank you for the warning, Madame Prime Minister," responded President Perry. "I know your highly skilled pilots will be fully successful in their mission. I wish them Godspeed, as do the

American people. What they are about to do will put a decisive finish in stopping the Iranians in their tracks and save the lives of hundreds of thousands—if not millions—of American and Israeli citizens."

"Thank you, Mr. President," responded the Israeli prime minister.

"Will you announce this act of justice to the world, or keep it confidential?" asked President Perry.

"We will keep this one completely confidential, Mr. President, and I ask you to do the same," replied Abrams.

"You have my word," replied Perry. "No comment."

"Let's let the Iranians believe whatever they want to," added Abrams. "We will neither confirm nor deny anything."

"I understand completely," responded the president.

On a mid-June morning, thirty minutes before the sun began to rise over Tehran, Iran's efforts to develop a lethal virus intended to infect and kill millions of innocent Americans and Jews around the world were completely eradicated. Millions of potential American, Israeli, and Jewish victims around the world would never know the full story. It was the nature of high-stakes battles fought by quiet professionals.

76.
LOVE, ACTUALLY

THE COOL EVENING BREEZE coming off Italy's Lake Garda shoreline brought with it the summer floral scents of the garden below. It had been five days since the Hezbollah terrorists were killed or captured. For US Army major Jake Fortina and Italian Carabiniere major Sara Simonetti, two of those days were taken up fully debriefing US and Italian authorities in Italy on the dead Italian mobster Luigi Gianfranco, as well as their surveillance of the Hezbollah operative Arman Darbandi and his Hezbollah cronies. Within a week, Jake and FBI special agent Tom O'Connor would do the same with French and British law enforcement and intelligence authorities.

During the preceding days, Jake realized he had fallen hard for Sara Simonetti. In their daily interactions, there had been small gestures and signs that she felt the same way. More importantly, Jake heard a voice deep in his consciousness and soul that he had not heard—nor felt—in years. It was Faith's voice.

"It's okay, Jake, it's okay. I am in a beautiful place with the kids. But you are not, and you need to be, Jake. You need to fall in love again."

After almost six years of not fully opening his heart, Jake knew that it was time to again love another human being.

Sitting on the balcony of the separate upstairs apartment of his Italian friends, Davide and Elisa Bovo, it was the first real chance Jake and Sara had to talk about anything other than surveillance, law enforcement matters, or cappuccino.

"Tell me more about your time in Baku, after the Marshall Center," Simonetti said. "You didn't say much about it in Verona, before all of the fireworks."

"It was a very interesting tour at the embassy there," said Jake. "The people of Azerbaijan are very friendly. But it was not anywhere near as fast-paced as Paris has been. And certainly not as fun as our last five days together have been," he said with a wink.

"I heard the ladies in Azerbaijan are quite attractive," said Sara.

"Well, maybe, but I was pretty busy with work, so I really wouldn't know. Maybe next door in Armenia, it might have been a different story."

"What do you mean?"

"Ever heard of the Kardashians? Their biological father descended from there."

"You mean those people Americans used to obsess about?" asked Sara.

"Yes, those people," chuckled Jake. "And I'm kidding. It would have been no different in Armenia. In Baku, I was very focused on my work."

"Well, that makes you sound like a pretty boring guy, Mister Fortina."

"I can *be* quite boring, actually," he replied.

"So, Mister Boring, I have to ask," said Sara, her heart beating faster. "You remember how at the Marshall Center we were told we'd always have international friends and colleagues—just a phone call away—to help us out with our international security challenges? *You* know, to 'cut through the red tape,' as they said. Is that the reason you called me, Jake Fortina? For some professional assistance?"

Jake smiled. "Well, it was *a* reason," he responded. "But *maybe* it was more of an excuse to see an amazing—and amazingly beautiful—Italian *signorina.*"

Sara realized it was the first time Jake had referred to her as anything but a friend. She also felt—more like hoped—since first seeing Jake in the Verona taverna that he had feelings for her which he had simply not yet chosen to fully reveal. For sure, since the taverna dinner, there had been plenty of clues along the way. For her part, Simonetti knew that she had absolutely fallen in love with him.

"You are very special, Sara."

"*Grazie*, Jake. And so are you."

With a smile in his eyes, he leaned in closely as they sat on an outdoor wicker love seat. As the warm Italian summer breeze flickered the candle on the small table, the candle's soft light enveloped them both.

Jake took a long, loving look at Sara. She soaked it in without flinching. He leaned in really close and said, "Sara, I will tell you why I am really here. *Ti voglio molto bene.*"

"*Anche Io ti voglio molto bene,* Jake," she responded.

As their lips met, Jake Fortina and Sara Simonetti embraced. Their passionate kiss went on for several minutes. They had spent several continuous and full days together, three of which they had entrusted their lives to each other, more than four years after they first met in Germany. Their embraces and kissing grew ever more passionate, going for several more minutes and leaving them half laying on the cramped and increasingly uncomfortable love seat.

Standing, Jake took her by the hand and pulled her up to him and took her in a full embrace. Their bodies tightly pressed together, they felt every sensuous bump and curve of each other. She, only slightly shorter than Jake, pulled her head back and looked into his eyes.

"We need to loosen up this shirt," she whispered.

Looking deep into Jake's eyes, she began to slowly unbutton Jake's shirt, beginning near the top and slowly, deliberately working all the way down. Jake reached behind the small of Sara's back, grabbed her blouse with both hands, and slowly pulled it up as her tight jeans stubbornly resisted releasing the blouse. She grabbed Jake's now fully open shirt at Jake's upper arms, pulling the shirt down and with Jake's more than willing assistance, completely off. Still a bit sensitive with her bandaged arm, she slowly pulled her blouse over the top of her head. Despite his trembling hands, Jake managed to gently unsnap her laced bra, dropping it on the love seat below. She brought her hands, fingers facing up and palms against Jack's back, and simultaneously pulled Jake towards her, inhaling him in and firmly kissing a surprised Jake on a nipple. Jake reciprocated. She then reached down and playfully unbuckled Jake's belt.

With both naked from the waist up and barefooted on the cool marble balcony floor, Jake led her through the balcony door to the queen-sized featherbed in the semi-dark room. The room was sparsely lit by a rising half-moon and the diluted brightness of a nearby streetlight. She sat down on the end of the bed and Jake gently eased her back. As her back and then head touched the mattress, she reached down with both hands and removed her jeans. Jake thought he could see the naturally tanned tint of her shimmering skin, gifted by a magnificent Creator and over two millennia of Roman DNA intermixed with that of the Italian peninsula's Germanic, Greek, Norse, and Spanish invaders and occupiers. Still standing at the foot of the bed, Jake stepped out of his pants, leaving them on the floor where they dropped.

"I'll get the door," he said softly.

Jake stepped towards the balcony door, intent on closing it. Instead, he turned in the doorframe and cast a quick glance down the lake's moon and starlit coast. With her heart pounding while watching Jake's every move, Sara Simonetti knew that Jake was ready to take her to exquisite heights. As Jake closed the door and turned back towards the bed, she also knew she was more than ready to go there with him.

77.
ONE YEAR LATER:
SARDINIA, FINALLY

IT HAD BEEN more than a dozen years since Davide Bovo had first invited his American friend Jake Fortina, then a junior Army officer, to the beautiful sand Mediterranean beaches of Maddalena, on the Italian island of Sardinia. In the interim years, Jake's military assignments, many moves, and life in general had gotten in the way, precluding him from accepting his friend's invitation to visit the beautiful island. Jake was finally able to say *"si"* to his friend's invitation to come to Sardinia. Quite unexpectedly, he found himself on this Italian paradise with his new wife and his dear Italian friends from Peschiera-del-Garda.

"You need more vino!" said Bovo as he poured another generous class of the chilled Sardinian Vermentino wine in Mrs. Sara Simonetti-Fortina's empty glass. "The mussels and spaghetti call for much wine!"

"*Grazie*, my friend," said Sara, thoroughly bronzed after a beautiful week under the Sardinian sun. "Cheers to the chef!"

Their location on the western-facing terrace of Bovo's summer home was idyllic. The blazing orange ball off on the sea's horizon provided a glorious finish to an unforgettable day spent on Sardinia's glistening beaches and azure waters.

Jake and Sara's spring wedding in Vicenza's Santa Maria Annunciata cathedral had been one for the ages, complete with a spiritually moving choir and over 150 guests from ten countries in attendance, including friends and family from both sides of the wedding. Lieutenant Colonel Chet Parker, Jake's old friend from Fort Benning and the Auburn-Alabama game, served as Jake's best man. Colonel Andrew Upshaw and now Sergeant Major (Retired) John Heather, from Jake's Army Special Forces days, also attended with their wives. The nearby reception went on well past midnight and into the early morning hours.

Turning to her husband, she asked, "Where's our next vacation spot going to be, Mister Jake?"

"I can't think of one at this very moment, *cara*," he replied. "And I hate to talk about anything related to work, but I do have news about our next assignment."

"Oh?" replied Elisa Bovo, Davide's wife.

"Where might that be?" asked Sara.

"The US embassy . . . in Rome," replied Jake.

"*Viva Italia! Viva América!*" exclaimed Davide, raising his glass. Three toasted in unison.

"And let's not forget our French friends who broke the virus case open, and our other friends—whoever they are, ha ha—who slammed it shut!" added Jake.

"*Vive la France! Vive* whoever!" toasted Sara, chuckling at her oblique reference to the Israelis.

A year after the successful Israeli attack on the Iranian virus development plant northeast of Tehran, Western media outlets were reporting serious internal political strife in Iran. Rumors of who did the bombing of the plant northeast of Tehran and why they did it—to stop Iran from developing a virus more deadly than the Spanish Flu or even the Black Plague—had been leaked out to the public for several weeks. In Iran, a new generation of Western-leaning Iranians was clamoring to take over the leadership of the country.

As Jake looked off to the setting Mediterranean sun, he thought of the extensive international cooperation and kaleidoscope of US and international players it took to stop this tier-one threat to the US, Israel, and Jewish people everywhere. He was grateful that his fellow American, Israeli and Jewish friends were living their lives in peace and security, almost entirely oblivious to the evil, life-destroying menace which had been defeated—at least for now.

ACKNOWLEDGMENTS

THE AUTHOR ACKNOWLEDGES and is grateful for early draft manuscript reviews by Elisabetta Benadetti, PhD; Angela Owens; Dennis Mansfield; and Colonel (USAF, Ret) Mike Guillot. Melissa Gray also provided a keen eye for the copy editing of an early manuscript. A later manuscript review by Major General (US Army, Ret) Gordon "Skip" Davis was exceptionally insightful and appreciated.

The author also acknowledges and is grateful for the professional support of the Koehler Books design and editing team, to include Skyler Kratofil, Anna Torres and Joe Coccaro.

CPSIA information can be obtained
at www.ICGtesting.com
Printed in the USA
JSHW051952220722
28383JS00001B/65

9 781646 637331